It's very hard to write time travel and I keep a watchful eye on it when I know about it, but Theresa Sneed has accomplished time travel so well, I find myself in awe of how she did it. Twists and turns at every point in this tome. I love how she wove in the true history, which includes her own many greats-grandmother, Susannah Martin, who was one of the "witches" hanged for no more reason than the rants of young women. I loved how I was transported back in time to 1692 to the Boston area. Sneed described it perfectly and now I want to go there. I love how the main character, Bess Martin (also a fictional descendant of Susannah Martin in the book), is transported back in time. I really did enjoy *Salem Witch Haunt* and couldn't put it down. I spent many nights reading into all hours of the early morning, then struggling to get up to go to work. But that's not a complaint; just the hazards of a reader with a good book. – S. Knight

Salem Witch Haunt held me spell-bound from the beginning and then kept getting better and better. At the end, I found myself wishing there were more pages to read. Sneed is an excellent writer with a wonderful, engrossing story to tell. It has a clever, satisfying twist at the end. That she is a descendant of the people she writes about enriches the story. You can feel her love of the topic and personal involvement in these lives even though the story is fictional. Excellent read! – Jan M. Martin

I absolutely loved *Salem Witch Haunt*. I couldn't put this book down once I started reading it. The author does such a great job telling this story and the twist at the end was great. I really hope there will be a sequel. – Nathalia Goodwin

Salem Witch Haunt is amazing! It has an element of history that is often explored, but not really in depth. Theresa Sneed takes us into the world of Puritan Salem with a 21st century viewpoint, and it made me feel all the emotion of actually living in Salem at the time of travesty. This will keep you on your heels excellently, and it has amazing twists to it that you would never expect! I can't wait for there to be a sequel, and I would love to see it as a movie! – Amazon Customer

I loved *Salem Witch Haunt!* Well-researched, it kept my historical-fiction interest from beginning to end. I delighted in the author's family connection. Her reminders of 2015 (I'd like to see her with a tablet) amused me. Who should read it? Anyone interested in historic fiction. Way to go, Theresa Sneed! – Sheila Summerhays

Okay, so the first part of the time traveling to Salem was pretty scary. Though I would imagine that our time would be even scarier to them. After that *Salem witch Haunt* was a sweet romance with some surprises that I appreciated! I wasn't expecting the end! A great read! – T. Westhoff

A true adventure that takes twists and detours I never in a million years would have aligned with the Salem Witch Hunts but Theresa Sneed has woven the events into such a rich tapestry, one is left to question, how much of this story might be real. Fiction? Fact? Fantasy? Who cares, *Salem Witch Haunt* was FABULOUS! – Maliceon Books

Enjoyed this history, mixed with the romance and magic. Definitely recommend *Salem Witch Haunt!* - PEaton

Salem
Witch Haunt

Salem Witch Haunt, book one
Return to Salem, book two
Salem Bewitched, book three

Dear Reader,

I hope you enjoy reading the final installment in the *Salem Witch Haunt* series, book three, *Salem Bewitched,* as much as I enjoyed writing it! If you loved this book, please consider leaving a good review on Amazon, Goodreads, Barnes & Noble, and other social media forums. Your kind words might be the reason that someone else decides to read my books, and for that, I thank you in advance.

- Author Theresa Sneed ☺

Stay connected with new releases and free e-book offers by signing up at my website or from my Facebook author page at www.facebook.com/TheresaMSneed/

Salem Bewitched

Salem Witch Haunt
Book three

Theresa Sneed

Dedication

This book is dedicated to my ninth great-grandmother, Susannah North Martin, unjustly tried and hanged as a witch on July 19, 1692, and then later exonerated by the state of Massachusetts on Halloween, October 31, 2001, 309 years after her hanging.

Acknowledgments

Many thanks to Betsy Love for picking through this project with a keen eye for content and grammar. A special thanks to my thorough, excellent editor, Susan Knight.

They're fabulous!

Prologue

A piercing flash jolted her senses. Bess Martin felt her grip slipping and desperately clung to him. In an instant, Hezekiah ripped from her grasp, snatched away in a violent whirlwind. Screams electrified the air as their flesh dissolved into minute particles that swam before her frightened eyes. But like a taut, rubber band snapping back into place, the particles reformed, and their bodies flew haphazardly through the dark night, tumbling head-over-heels onto the frigid pavement—the very road they had just time traveled from. Only 323 years ago, the road was dirt. The cruel asphalt scraped the skin from her arms and scuffed the side of her face.

One

It Begins

My head felt like it was splitting in two, and maybe it was. Groaning, I struggled to stand, the acrid taste of blood seeping down my lips. I spit it out. Everything spun around me. I lost all sense of time and space. "Ha!" I chortled, my voice thick with sarcasm. Ironic. I, Bess Martin, who had traveled back and forth in time, like going through a revolving door at the mall, had lost all sense of time? I waited. Things settled. The distant sound of horses' hooves and panicked braying startled me—horses' hooves and braying? Nothing made sense. After a while, I could hear them no more and wondered at it.

I pressed trembling fingers to my throbbing forehead, but snapped them back. "Ouch!" Blood covered my fingers. I pulled myself up on my elbows, but fell back again. Pain shot through my arm. Funny, I should have been repulsed by it, but found myself a bit fascinated, like it wasn't my arm that was scraped and bleeding. A pitiful cry aroused my sanity, and I looked to my left.

The night air did not reveal much. I waited for my eyes to adjust, then wiped at the blood that fell across my eyelids. "Who's there?" Where was *there* . . . where was I? I fought to remember. The cold air felt good against my hot skin. The tangle of dress prevented me from rolling over and I struggled to release myself from it. Wait. Dress? I looked down at the long, tattered dress, and strands of my dyed blonde hair sticking to patches of blood.

Suddenly, it came back to me. The trials, the hangings, and the pursuit. Betty Hubbard, self-imposed leader of

Salem's circle girls, was chasing us! No. I shook my head, trying to clear the muddle suppressing my thoughts. Men on horses were after us. *No.* Yes.

"Ahh . . ." I moaned then glanced around. No. But it had just been day, hadn't it?

Confused, I stifled a sob, and, using my good arm, I pushed myself up. Wait? What's that? My fingers curled around the blue stones laying in a small circle the way they had been in the carriage. For a second, I was unsure of what to do, but then scooped them up and pushed them into my pocket. I staggered forward in the dark.

The groan sounded again. I froze. "Who's out there?" My voice sounded small in the dark night. What had happened? More of the pursuit returned to me . . . Betty's shocked expression when I foolishly revealed who I was, the dark cloud of dust approaching our coach, Hezekiah grabbing my arm just as—*oh, my gosh.* My mind cleared. We timed traveled. "Hezekiah!"

A weak sound came from farther down the road, but a much closer noise startled me.

"Lady Elizabeth. Help me!"

Holding onto my sore arm, I stumbled toward the distorted voice. "Mr. Hanson?" My heart pounded in my chest. Hezekiah's father was not supposed to time travel with us. Abner Hanson belonged in the past! Focus girl.

Abner was caught in a tangle of barbed wire. My eyes adjusted enough to see the line of fence posts he must have barreled into. "Can you roll toward me?" I worked with my good arm, pulling at his sleeve. He was covered in blood, nasty gashes ran across his arms and cut into his chest. Still, I had to wonder if it had somehow slowed down his acceleration into the future, catching him, like a safety net in time. Tugging together, we managed to clear the treacherous wire.

My thoughts turned to Hezekiah, and I called out for him again. Muffled moans from farther down the road frightened me. Low and eerie in the black night, the mournful sound was broken by long moments of silence.

Abner stood nearby, hand to his bloody chest. "What happened, Lady Elizabeth?" His eyes wild, he glanced around. "Where are we?"

"Ah, I'm not sure," I said, truthfully, though I was sure we were in the future.

Abner fell back against a post. "Is this?" He stuttered. "Did we leave 1692?"

My eyes met his. "Probably." Undoubtedly.

"This is unbelievable."

"Uh huh." A low moan filtered through the thick night. I scrambled up the hill toward it, afraid of what I might find. "Hezekiah?"

"Over here!" Hezekiah rushed up beside me, pulling me near. "Did you hear that?" he asked, his voice quavering. Peeling the prosthetic mask off his face, he stuffed it into a pocket. "What is that?"

Abner staggered over the knoll behind us. "You mean, *who* is that?" He pointed down the road past us. Hezekiah stared at his father.

All at once I realized who it must be—André. My shoulders sagged. I had just returned him to his own time, and now he was back in mine again? And hurt? No, I mustn't think that way. He's okay. Just a bruise or two. I gingerly touched my tender arm, fearing it might be much worse.

Conflicted and confused, I swayed in the night air. Of all the people to travel back and forth in time, it had to have been André. He had absorbed the future like a sponge.

Hezekiah ran toward the sound, and I walked as quickly as I could, a sudden rush of emotions choking me.

On the one hand, there was no better person to time travel than the scientist, André de Nostredame. On the other hand, there was no *worse* person. He couldn't exist in the past with what he now knew about the future. He would never be the same again. I inwardly groaned. What had I done? Snap out of it Bess, this is not about you. I shook my head.

Suddenly, a bright light appeared over the horizon, illuminating the road from a distance, outlining a crumpled body that lay across the double yellow lines. In a panic, Hezekiah turned to face me.

"Get off the road!" he yelled. Turning back, he sprinted like a bull toward the oncoming truck.

My heart sunk. He wasn't going to make it. He was too far away. "Get off the road, Hezekiah," I pleaded. "Get off! You can't save him!" The truck was almost to the body. Its brakes screeched, and the vehicle swerved from side to side. From out of nowhere, a dark form appeared. He grabbed the man's leg and yanked him from the oncoming truck, now squealing to a stop.

The lights from the truck splayed across the cold road. On the shoulder, the rescuer knelt over André's still form.

14

I clutched at my chest, fearing the impact from the time travel might have taken my friend's life.

The driver jumped from the truck. How strange to see a man using a cell phone—a modern device I had missed back in time. Hezekiah got to them before I did, and from where I stood, I saw the shock registered on his face. My hands flew to my mouth. André must be dead.

It wasn't something I wanted to see. Still, my friendship with André drove me to him, each step filling me with greater fear. I expected the worse, but then the rescuer turned, and I saw his face in the truck's muted headlights. It was André! He stood over the man, and it had been he who had rescued him. Relief washed over me, quickly replaced with anxiety for whoever lay injured on the ground.

I stayed back as Abner approached the man. His eyes widened, and he fell to the ground, grabbing his hand. "It's just like you to follow me, my friend," he said, his voice choked with emotion. He leaned over him. "Charles? Can you hear me?"

"Charles?" I gasped, stumbling toward them. Charles Fieldstone was driving the carriage when we time traveled. *Oh no.* I searched my memory, fearful that someone else had linked into my wild journey through time. No Bess. Everyone on or in the carriage was now accounted for.

The truck driver approached us in swift steps. "My phone's not working. Is yours?" Met by blank stares, he continued, "Well, this is a dead area." I knew he meant cell phone coverage, but wondered what Abner must have thought.

15

The truck driver stopped short when he saw Charles. "Whoa." He sidestepped and covered his mouth. "Whoa," he repeated. "Well, I," he pointed to his truck, "I can take him." He flashed his license long enough for me to see his name. Joe.

If Charles had been conscious before, he wasn't now. His chest rose and fell with each labored breath. With care, the men carried him to the truck and laid him on the narrow bed in the back of the cab.

I climbed in and sat behind Joe. "Um, where exactly are you taking him?"

He pointed down the road. "Why Boston, ma'am, about an hour from here." Joe adjusted his rearview mirror and looked at me. "Mind if I ask something?"

Aware of how odd we must look, all bloody and wearing torn, antiquated clothing, I stammered. "Sure."

"What happened to y'all?"

"We, uh, we," I glanced sideways at Hezekiah, wondering if he would still love me after he heard how easily I could lie. "We're part of a survival show—well, that's what we're hoping to be a part of at least."

"One of those hokey variety shows?"

"Uh huh." I nodded. "It's a show set back in the 17th century. We're," I swallowed hard, "we're escaping witches."

His eyes darted back to the road and then to me again. "What?"

"We have to practice it before we try out for it in Hollywood."

16

"Running through the woods in those clothes?" Joe shrugged. "Pretending your running from witches." He stroked his beard with his thumb. "Huh." Then he gestured in the back to Charles. "What happened to him?"

"Ah, well," my brain worked quick to fill in the blanks.

Hezekiah leaned toward the driver. "Charles has more energy than all of us put together. He darted out of the woods and into the road."

"Oh, I passed by a truck right before I saw y'all. Are you saying that truck hit him?"

"Uh huh." I gave a nervous nod—flying through time was every bit as dangerous.

Hezekiah stared at me. And there was that condescending, howbeit gorgeous, green-eyed look again. And even though he had aided and abetted me, somehow I knew I was going to get the blame for this, too. And I guess I deserved it.

Teenage time travelers should never mess with the laws of the universe.

.

Two
Mystery

Glancing over at Charles, I was relieved he had not gained consciousness. Weird to be grateful for something so horrible, but what would he do? How would he react? He'd not seen the pictures of the future that Hezekiah had shown his father. At least Abner had some prior knowledge of what he'd fallen into. Charles had none. Zip. Zero. Nada. I leaned my head against Hezekiah, who, despite the dire circumstances, looked stinking happy to have his father in the future. Dang. Abner looked pretty keen about it, too. Maybe it was a mean thing to do, but someone had to pull them back to reality.

"Um, excuse me," I said snidely. "Your dad," I turned to Abner. "Doesn't belong here. His place is with his wife—your *mother*," I added firmly. They grinned and ignored me.

"Excuse me!" I said more firmly, but when Joe glanced back, I pressed my lips together tightly. This conversation was going to have to wait. Although it was amusing to watch Hezekiah and his father exchange curious looks, no doubt realizing they couldn't speak freely around him, I was still nonetheless perturbed that they ignored me. Even André was engrossed in their silent exchanges of wonder.

I thought Abner would be sick from the jostling of the ride, but he didn't seem affected by the constant movement or from the loud, noisy engine. I wondered how that could be, until I saw him pull a silver flask from his pocket and take a long swig. Just wait until the morning when he finds out that this was *not* a dream. I smirked silently. I know.

Mean. I figured I'd better let him down gently. "Mr. Hanson, do you know where you are?"

"Why of course, Lady Elizabeth," he said, with a twinkle in his eye. "This is . . ." He became silent and a somber look saddened his jovial expression. He looked down, his body swaying with each jerk of the truck. "Why this is . . . your destiny, son." He looked into Hezekiah's face.

I felt two inches tall. He did understand where he was, and he probably knew the ramifications. He probably knew he couldn't stay, and he probably knew the quicker he returned, the better.

A long breath escaped his throat. "How will we get your mother here?"

"What?" It came out so quickly, I hadn't a moment to stop myself.

He laughed. "Just for a visit my lady," he said, with a smile.

"Why don't you bring the whole family?" I growled, but he just smiled wider, and the truck driver didn't help much either.

"That's a bit harsh, don't you think, pretty lady?" Joe turned back to the road, but then added. "The man just wants to be with his family."

My mouth fell open. I closed it with a snap and jabbed my elbow into Hezekiah who was grinning way too much.

"Bess," he said, gently taking my hand. It moved my sore arm, and I called out in pain. I pulled it back. He stared at me and then turned back to his father. Really? I held my sharp tongue. Sometimes I could be such a rotten person. I

20

mean, the most gorgeous guy in the world was my sort-of fiancé and his dad was just up for a visit. Twisting the topaz and diamond ring around on my finger, I grinned— a very long *up,* for a very short visit.

Charles's intermittent groans reminded me that he was there, too. And just how was *that* going to pan out? I fingered the stones in my pocket. A warm sensation rippled over me, and for a brief moment, I was back in 1692, staring at the scene we had just left.

A throng of angry men pummeled down the road, leaving a dusty cloud in their wake. They pulled up short, bringing their horses to a sudden stop. Gawking at the remains of the horseless carriage, they jeered and laughed, and then circled the broken wreckage.

"Where's the horses?" one man said, noting their absence. The men looked around, their own horses dancing skittishly on the dirt road.

"I dunno, Gustav. They must've been spooked and run for the hills," another man said. He swung off his horse and headed toward the carriage. "These ones won't be so lucky." A few chuckles from the men egged him on. The splintered door of the carriage lay open, and he stuck his head inside, and then snapped it out as if he'd seen a ghost. His face went white, and he pointed a trembling hand toward the carriage, backing up as he spoke. "There's no one inside!"

"Aw, come on, Stanley," Gustav scoffed, leaping from his horse. "They probably flew from the carriage. They must be laying on the ground somewhere."

"Like the horses?" Stanley said, still backing up. "This is too strange." He gasped. "The whole lot of them must have been specters—horses too!"

The others nodded, turned their horses back, and then took off at a gallop, leaving Gustav scrambling for his horse.

I opened my eyes. Hezekiah, Abner and André bent near me—yes, *all three* of them. Fear and astonishment filled their eyes. What? Can't a girl take a quick nap?

Hezekiah spoke low. I wasn't sure why. The truck driver had turned his radio on and it was nearly impossible for any conversation in the back. I strained to hear what he said.

He grabbed my hands, this time careful not to jostle my arm. "Bess," he said, with concern in his eyes. "Where were you just now?"

Oh. In my dream. "Back in Salem." I yawned. "Those men that followed us got quite a shock when they found the empty carriage."

Abner's eyes widened.

"Tell us more," André said, leaning closer.

I didn't know why, but maybe they just wanted to be entertained. I shrugged. "Well, the carriage split in two, and the men came up to it seconds after it crashed." I let out a tiny laugh.

"Continue," Hezekiah said, keeping me on track.

Okay, this was beginning to get weird. His intense look was freaking me out. "Why do you want to know my silly dream, Hezekiah?"

He shook his head. "Bess, it wasn't a dream."

I didn't think the truck could ever become so quiet. Even the blaring radio seemed somehow subdued. "Of course it was a dream," I stammered.

If the others weren't looking at me so curiously, I would've shaken the whole thing off. "It was just a dream," I repeated, returning their inquisitive stares.

"No, not a dream, Lady Elizabeth," André said softly. He looked at Hezekiah as if getting approval for him to continue. A nod propelled him forward. He leaned closer and touched my knee. "You left us, Bess."

The hum of the tires against the pavement and the oldies music on the radio pressed into my mind, blocking out his words. I must have heard him wrong. "What?" I whispered.

Abner slapped his knee. "You were here," he said sternly, but then his voice dropped low, matching the awestruck expression on his face, "and then you were gone."

It took me a moment to process what he'd said. Flabbergasted, I blurted out, "But, I'm right here!"

"Yes, Bess, yes." Hezekiah nodded.

The relief on his face told me that they had been telling the truth. I had slipped back into the past like stepping into another room. Drawn to that time, I was bewitched by the circumstances and the people, entranced by the trials and the hangings.

Giles Corey was next. A morbid fascination fell over me. Ugh. Why me? I didn't want to be there! And yet, I knew why. I had known all along. Someone had to speak for them, and I would, even if it meant my death.

I had a feeling I wasn't done with Salem, but kept those thoughts to myself. I pressed my hands into my lap, out of my pockets, away from the enticing stones.

We pulled into the hospital parking lot, and just as before, Dr. Sava met us at the entrance. His nonjudgmental appraisal of our bloody appearance and strange clothing calmed me. I had trusted him before, and once again, he took us in. Such a kind, gentle man.

The world wasn't nearly as bad as the media sometimes portrayed it to be. In fact, I was convinced that people would act kindly in most situations, if not fearful of retribution of some sort from this group or that. I was determined to never let anyone control or change me from who I knew I was. It saddened me to think that some people lose their very identities at the hands of others who would mold them into what they think they should be, or more especially, what they needed them to be for their own personal agenda.

Charles was still unconscious, and they took him right into surgery to mend his bones and gashes and determine why he was not awake.

It was obvious that Abner tried hard to overcome his anxiety at this new perspective of the future. His injuries were severe, but not life threatening.

With only a few scrapes on my head and arm, my injuries were the least of all, not counting André and Hezekiah's perfect landings. In a few hours, my arm was in a sling, and the cut on my head was wrapped in a bandage.

But who was going to mend my mind? I thought of little else than the experience I had just had. The men had been real and not a figment of my imagination. I must admit, seeing their frightened faces was gratifying. Still, I wondered, as they had, about the *horses*.

The panicked braying and sounds of horses' hooves I had heard when first reentering the present came back to me. *Oh*. The horses time traveled too! Flabbergasted, I drew my hands to my chest, hoping someone had discovered them and had taken them in, which had to have been the case. Horses running down the highway would definitely have made the news. I thanked the medical professionals and joined the others in the waiting room.

Hezekiah had wanted to remain with me, but I had assured him it was just a scrape, which it was. Back in the waiting room, he came near. It was hard for me to concentrate with him that close. I loved the attention, but the reality of the situation loomed before us. Things were broken that had to be fixed. I had broken things that I needed to fix. "So, Charles?"

Abner spoke up. "Not well, my dear . . . not well."

"Dead for two minutes," André said.

Dead for two minutes? That meant he was *alive*, right? I searched André's eyes for the answer.

"He died," he said slowly, "but they brought him back."

My heart raced. "Then he's okay? Awake?"

"No dear." Abner shook his head. "He might as well be dead."

I trembled. If Charles didn't return to the past, it could alter the future. What if he was the father of well . . . someone? "Does he have family?"

Abner scratched his nose. "Well, no, Lady Elizabeth, but he does have a sister in southern Maine, and one in England. They aren't speaking though. Some kind of squabble."

"No wife?"

"She died from the plague."

"Then he has no one?"

The room was silent. What a horrible thing—to have no one to worry about you, no one to return home to, no one to comfort you. I looked over at Hezekiah, who was busily engaged in conversation with André, and frowned. Didn't he know how much I needed him now? I shook it off, sure that my insecurities arose from selfishness. Time for a change. I excused myself and left the room.

No one really noticed anyhow. Approaching the front desk, I told a little fib—okay an outright lie. "My dad was brought in with me. Can I go see him?"

"What's your father's name?"

I'm sure my face went blank. I only knew him as . . . "Charles?" It came out like a whisper.

"Last name?"

Dang. I cleared my throat—acting classes from Danvers High setting in. Glancing around, I pretended I'd forgotten something. "My phone! Hold on. I'll be right back." Of course the illusion would have been much better if I hadn't been wearing a seventeenth century outfit. The receptionist looked at me strangely, while I dashed back into the waiting room.

I stepped over to the boys, and they acted like I had never left the room. "Um, I guess I don't even know Charles's last name," I said, interrupting their conversation.

Hezekiah paused, then said, "It's ah, Fieldstone. Charles Wendell Fieldstone."

"Oh," I said, feigning curiosity. I waited a few minutes and then slipped from the room again.

The receptionist saw me coming. "Excuse me ma'am, but your dad is asking for you."

My mouth fell open and for a split second I thought about my real dad, dead now for five years. "Um, oh, what?" I asked squinting.

"You are Charles's daughter, aren't you?" Her eyes ran the length of my long, tattered dress.

"Charles Fieldstone," I mumbled. While it was incredibly exciting that Charles had *finally* woken up, his brain must not be working right.

"Well, he's asking for you."

"Asking for me," I repeated, my eyes wide, but when doubt swept across her face, I added, "Yes, of course it's me." But it wasn't! Abner had just said that Charles had

had no children, least of all *me*. Still, the news that he was awake filled me with hope—hope for him and his quick return to Salem. I wondered how I could orchestrate that without him seeing too much of the future.

The stones seemed to grow ten times their size in my pocket. "Cut it out!" I mumbled, slapping my pocket. I smiled sheepishly at the receptionist whose eyes had widened at my sudden outburst. I supposed I did look a bit insane. Still, I was *not* going to go back to Salem again . . . leastwise, not right away. I needed to do lots of research first. It was sheer luck that I had returned from the past, but how did that even happen? I hadn't willed myself there and back, had I?

A cheery-eyed nurse approached me, her expression sobering when her gaze settled on my odd clothing. Not only was it torn and bloody, but the doctor had cut the sleeve from the shoulder to the wrist to clean my arm. I knew I would purchase clothing in the boutique or just wait until I got back home, but right now, I had other things on my mind.

The nurse led me toward Charles's room. She stopped just outside his door. "He's got quite a fever." She gestured for me to use the hand sanitizer pump on the wall. "Been talking kinda crazy too, like he's a bit out of his mind." Embarrassed, she stumbled over her next words, "Ah, sorry ma'am that was insensitive of me. But the doctors say he's got a touch of delirium, and I'm sure they'll be telling you that, too."

Oh. That explained the nonexistent daughter thing— maybe.

28

Opening the door, she motioned for me to enter, and then closed the door behind me. I glanced at Charles's antique clothing folded inside an open bag setting at the foot of his bed and then down at my own clothes. They must think us a strange sort, some kind of cult, or something. I suppressed a chortle. If they only knew.

Dimmed lights and the low drone of monitors gave the room an eerie feel, while the heavy scent of anesthetics mingled with ammonia accosted my senses, stinging my nostrils. But, what met my vision, far outweighed my other senses.

Wires and tubes stuck out from under Charles's hospital gown, and a wide bandage was wrapped around his eyes. What a strange, wonderful world was hidden from his sight, and how would I ever be able to calm his fears—the fears I knew he had to have.

"Elizabeth," he called through parched lips. It was hard to hear his soft voice, and I wondered how he knew I was there.

"Hello."

He jerked his head. "Who's there?"

"Um, It's me, Elizabeth."

"Elizabeth?" A sad sigh left his throat. "Impossible," he whispered. He turned away. "My Liza," he mumbled.

My eyes widened. Er, Liza? *His* Elizabeth? Who was I to him?

A sob erupted from his throat, as if he'd held it back and could restrain it no longer. "Oh, my sweet daughter, if only you were here."

I froze in place not moving a bit. He really did have a daughter! No, wait, it could be the delirium distorting his thoughts. I thought it best to stay quiet and let him continue.

He thrust his hand out, searching the empty air in front of him. "Liza?"

"Yes?" Apparently, I wasn't very good with the silence thing, but he just seemed so desperate.

Agitated, he stumbled over his words. "But how? Where?" He stopped and moved his sightless head around as if accessing his whereabouts. His hands went to the bandages, and he moaned. "What has happened to me, Liza? Where am I?"

Delirium was so demanding. I swallowed hard. "In a hospital."

He stiffened, whether from my continued invasion into his crazed thoughts, or from the mention of a hospital, I didn't know. He sniffed at the air. "Yes, hospital . . . but what is that odd sound?" He turned toward the beeping coming from the monitors.

I remained silent. I had no answer for him for that.

He sank back into the pillow. "She's *not here*. Liza is in Maine, content with her life." And then he looked straight at me, or at least where he had last heard my voice. A sob came from his throat, and I had an overwhelming feeling of my intrusion.

I had no right to pretend I was *his* Elizabeth! What if he wasn't delirious? What if she did exist? If I didn't find out, I wouldn't know how to help. Anyhow, I was wickedly curious.

A few minutes passed, and I thought he had gone to sleep, or slipped back into unconsciousness. "Charles?"

He straightened, obviously startled by my voice. "Please do not call me that."

"Father?" It slipped out before I had time to think.

Gasping, he reached out for me. "I'm hearing things, just hearing things."

I wanted to talk to him, to comfort him, to tell him who I really was. He'd appreciate a friend being near, but then how would I explain the ruse I had already begun?

He moaned and tried to adjust his head on the crooked pillow. I jumped up and repositioned it. His hand moved to mine.

Uh oh. Ruse over.

"Elizabeth," he breathed out. "My Liza," he sobbed. "I am sorry, I didn't know, my child."

I waited for him to continue, but didn't remove my hand. The silence was awkward, but what could I say? *Um, sorry Charles, but you don't have a daughter, that's just the fever talking.*

The words tumbled from his trembling lips. "You were an infant when I left—and so ill."

"What?" That did *not* sound like delirium, but like a confession. I snapped my hand away and in so doing, knocked his bag on the floor. "You *left me* when I was ill?" I bent over to pick up the bag, placing back on his bed. I couldn't believe it! How could he have done that? I had always liked Charles, but now I just wanted to smack him.

"It wasn't like that, Liza," he said, with a tired twinge in his voice. "You needed medicine—expensive medicine.

31

I went to sell some of my land to get the money for it. When I returned . . ."

"You came back?" Leaving me for *that* wasn't so bad. Wait. Not me. Focus girl.

"Of course I came back." His raspy breathing became choppy.

It didn't make sense. "I don't understand."

"When I got back, you were gone, you both were gone." He was talking to the wall. It seemed as though he didn't believe I was there after all, but that I was an illusion brought on by delirium. He clenched and unclenched his fists as if struggling with a horrid memory. And it was a memory, wasn't it? It seemed so real, the way he clung to each word, as if reliving the agony again.

"No reason to go on . . ." He stretched his neck, the effort forcing a gravelly wheeze, like something was caught in his throat. His chest heaved and then his face contorted. His legs thrashed, and he jerked from right to left. The heart monitor went crazy, beeping its ominous warning. Three or four nurses rushed into the room and stepped in front of me. I didn't have to be asked to leave, but as I left, my foot kicked something across the floor.

Bending over, I picked up a small portrait miniature and turned it over in my hands. The inscription *Elizabeth Fieldstone* burned into my hand as I flipped it over and stared into the face of a young girl of about seventeen.

Standing outside his room, I leaned against the wall, the miniature pressed into the palm of my hand. She was real. I stared at the door into the room, feeling a pang of remorse for not believing him. The man was dying, and I had wanted to question him?

A light flashed above his door. I moved farther down the hallway while Charles was wheeled out. I pushed myself against the wall as his bed rushed past me.

"Father!" My hand went to my chest and tears fell quick. I had called him father, when *Charles* had formed first on my lips. But was it enough for him to want to live? "Father! I came, Father!" I called after the gurney, as it disappeared around the corner.

From down the hall, Hezekiah and Abner appeared. Hezekiah reached me first. "What happened?"

I had lied about my identity sounded so lame, so I said nothing and slipped the portrait miniature into my pocket. I should've come clean when I had the chance.

"The nurse told us Charles's daughter was with him." Hezekiah tilted his head, his eyes bore into me.

I sniffled. "Um, well, Charles was asking for her, and they kind of thought that was me." I left out the part where I had told them I was his daughter before he had asked for me.

"A very kind thing for you to do," Abner chirped in, "but he has no daughter."

"Ah, well, yes, he does," I said, thrusting my hands on my hips.

"No, he doesn't, Bess." Hezekiah's eyebrows rose. "Wait. Why didn't he recognize you?"

"Yeah, about that." I told them about the bandages.

"Okay, that makes sense, but why did you pose as his daughter? When the bandages are gone, he's going to be miserable, Bess."

I was about to show him the portrait miniature, when Abner spoke up. "Where is he?" Abner poked his head in the now empty room.

Tears welled up in my eyes, and I pointed down the hallway toward the surgical center, an area we were well acquainted with, given our past escapades.

Hezekiah led me back to the waiting room. André was alone. He looked up at us and then back down at his book.

Leading me to a chair, Hezekiah pulled me down beside him. He seemed unusually attentive, as if he was worried about me, and then again, why wouldn't he be? I had the power to come and go through time. I could've left the present and had been back in the past when he found me missing a few minutes ago.

Hold on. I could go back in time and find Charles's real daughter. Being reunited with the real Elizabeth would help him to heal. My eyes shot open at the sheer absurdness of that thought. *No.* She can't come to the future. It'd be best to continue my charade and not bring another soul here from 1692.

And yet, I had time traveled in the blink of an eye a few hours ago. Was it that simple? Well, yeah. Evidently. No, Bess, evidently not! I had *no idea* how I had just time traveled, except that the stones had something to do with it, but to travel there and back in an instant? How?

I stared at the clock on the wall. If only I knew how to control time travel. How had I done it? I glanced over at

André, as he perused the pages of that ancient book. Hezekiah stood behind him, gazing down at its yellowed pages. André waved his hands as he spoke, as if excited at what he had read, and then he pushed the book into Hezekiah's hands, wildly tapping its pages.

They both looked at me at the same time. How could two men have identical expressions—gaping mouths, haunting eyes, and what I was sure was a look of sheer determination to not tell me what they had found?

THREE
Back Again

Hezekiah looked down at my pocket. Oh. I knew what they had been talking about—the *stones*. He wanted the stones! I took a step back as he approached me with the book in hand. "Oh, no you don't." I backed farther away and then bumped my sore arm on the door trim, quickly drawing it to my side.

His countenance softened. "I just want to see them."

"Why?" I asked coolly. If he thought for one minute that I was going to hand over the stones, he was crazy. Well, without a *good* reason, I thought, gazing into his green eyes.

"I would feel much better if I knew you weren't going to pop back into the past again."

He would feel much better? I was sure he had meant to say, I don't want you to be in danger, or I'd miss you terribly, or—anything but, *he* wouldn't feel good.

He took my hands, concern etched into his eyes. "Bess, how many times can one go to Salem and make it back alive?"

His voice caught on the word *alive*, so I forgave him on the spot. I stood up on my tiptoes and kissed him. Wrong move on my part. His hand slid down to my pocket, but I was on to him, and grabbed the stones first.

Fantastic blue-hued lights swirled around us, our very souls gyrating wildly out of control, as once again, we disappeared from the present.

I knew he was with me, because he hadn't let go. We toppled onto the ground and rolled to a stop. I hoped I hadn't reinjured my arm, and was surprised when it didn't hurt.

"Whoa!" Hezekiah glanced around, a bewildered look in his eyes. He helped me up. "Where are we, Bess?"

"I'm a Salem magnet, Hezekiah. Where do you *think* we are?"

"It's probably not a perfect science, Bess. There are too many unknowns. We won't know where we are until we look around." He thrust his hand out. "Give me one of the stones." He tilted his head forward and raised an eyebrow. "Just until we figure out what we're going to do."

I studied his firm lips and the stern look in his eyes. He was right. Separating the stones would prevent another unwanted time travel. If we were back in Salem, there was a reason for it. Still, my hand lingered over my pocket.

"Come on, Bess," he urged. "You can do this. Take out one stone, just one."

Reaching in my pocket, I took out a stone. "We could go back to the future right now," I whispered, rolling it around in my fingers.

He nodded. "It's your call, Bess."

But my heart wasn't into it. I knew why we'd traveled back to Salem, if indeed we had, and now I had to stay and finish the job.

Handing the stone to Hezekiah was like relinquishing a boulder, so heavy it felt in my hand. It was as if I betrayed it, and heavy guilt pressed into my mind.

"Bess?" He sounded worried. He pulled me close and held me tight. Kissing my forehead, he whispered, "For whatever reason, Bess, these stones have come to you." He scratched his head. "You really are a Salem magnet, and I think I know why." He looked down at the book. "You are a blood relation to one of the women hanged in Salem—a direct line."

I lifted my head and stared into his eyes. "Yeah, but so are thousands of other people."

"Yes, but you're different." He sat down and pressed his back against a tree. Reaching up for me, he guided me down beside him. "Samantha's senior project was on family history. She collected Reggie and Kenneth's saliva."

Though Hezekiah was actually their grandfather from the distant past, Kenneth, and his brother Reggie, were the closest thing he had to family in the future. "Oh, you mean that DNA genetic testing thingy?" I inched over closer to him.

"Yes, and you know what she found? Their DNA is as different as night and day, but both swear they came from the same parents."

"I've heard of that—the DNA we inherit from our parents is random, but what does that have to do with me?"

"I would bet your DNA is a *perfect* match of your great grandmother, Susannah Martin."

I tingled all over. "And?"

He opened the book and began reading in Latin, racing through the words.

I held my hands up to stop him. "And?" I repeated.

He read slower, translating as he went. "The stones answer to one who suffers the greatest misfortune of its time, but they belong to no one." His fingers ran over the words as he spoke, ". . . and are drawn to the most unlikely of characters."

"Okay, that sounds like me. I am definitely the most unlikely of characters, but—"

"There's more," he said, glancing back at the book and pointing to the words. "The stones know their master . . . their fears, their needs, their weaknesses."

"Um . . ." A little too weird there. "So, what does that mean?"

"It means, the stones are a part of you and though ancient, the era they seem to gravitate to is somehow important to you, too." He drew his knees up to his chest and wrapped his arms around them. "Why is that?"

He wasn't speaking to me right then, but I could see the struggle etched into his face as he flexed his fingers against his knees. He looked up at me. "Why is that, Bess?"

"What?"

"Why do you need to be here?"

There was a good reason. "Charles is dying, and it's my fault." I was hoping for an, *oh, it's not really your fault,* but he said nothing, further exasperating my anxiety. "Maybe his daughter can help him recover. We can't bring him back to the past in his condition, so we have to bring her to him."

"What?" Hezekiah drew his head back. "He doesn't have a daughter, Bess."

40

"Yes, he does." I held up the portrait miniature of Elizabeth Fieldstone.

"Where did you get that?" He took it from my trembling fingers.

"It's Charles's."

"Yes, I know." He handed it to me. "Charles showed it to me a long time ago. It's his sister."

Sister? My countenance plummeted. "Are you sure?"

"That's what he said." He pressed his lips tight. "If he had a daughter, he'd probably carry her picture instead, don't you think?"

I hated it when he was right, which was most of the time. "Yes, of course—"

Rattling and banging came from down the road. "Behind the tree," he whispered. We crawled behind it as the clanking grew louder. I held still. Anything could be coming down that road.

In seconds, a boy of about twelve appeared. He pulled on a rope tied about a mule, or rather the mule pulled the boy. Metal pots flung over the mule's back clanked and clanged.

"This way!" the boy urged, tugging on the rope.

Hezekiah approached him. "Do you need some help?"

"Yes, sir," he said.

"Where are you going?" Hezekiah slapped the mule on its rump and it went forward. He gestured for me to join them.

"I'm to lead this mule to the Fieldstone manner."

I looked quickly at Hezekiah and then back at the boy. "Fieldstone?"

"Yes ma'am. Lady Fieldstone bought it from my Mama." His face soured. "I'm happy to see it go."

"Elizabeth Fieldstone?" I asked.

He nodded. "Elizabeth Fieldstone Junior. She's a nice person. Mama says she don't need no mule, but she just likes to help us out. She could've bought the cow instead, but Mama says she knew we needed the milk."

I grew quiet as we walked, deep in thought, keeping clear of the rambunctious mule. What were the chances of winding up near the property of the very person I was searching for? The words in that old book began to take on new meaning. Were the stones really that locked into me?

We rounded a bend and came to a large estate. A girl about my age appeared in the doorway and met us halfway down the drive. A gray bonnet hid her face as she set a basket on the ground beside her.

The boy went about unhooking the pots and pans and another basket which was similar to the one at the girl's feet. He handed them to her outstretched arms.

She set the pots and pans on the ground and peered inside the basket. "Be sure to thank your mother for her fine work, Samuel." Reaching deep into her apron, she removed a small wrapped package. "Freshly-made biscuit bread for your walk home." Picking up the basket at her feet, she handed it to him. "Take these back to your mother for mending."

His face beamed as he hurriedly opened the small package, bit into the bread, and then slung the basket over his shoulder. "Thank you, Lady Fieldstone!"

She gestured toward the gate leading to the meadow. Samuel stuffed the bread in his pocket and coaxed the mule toward the gate. It wasn't a problem this time. The mule seemed to know she was home. Latching the gate, he turned on his heels, and then darted down the dirt road.

"Lady Fieldstone," Hezekiah said, with a formal bow.

She studied our clothing—mine, still torn and bloody, but Hezekiah's looking as regal as ever. Her eyes rested long upon bandaged arm, and I placed my hand over it, as if it would somehow hide it from her scrutinizing gaze.

She didn't appear too frazzled by it though, and I got a good look at her face. Without a doubt, she was the girl in the portrait miniature.

Hezekiah stepped closer. "I am Hezekiah Hanson." Apparently he hadn't seen the resemblance. "Your brother Charles has been in my father's employ for several years."

She blinked. "I am called Liza," she said, returning his greeting with a curtsey. "But, I have no brother nor sister." Her eyes darted from Hezekiah to me. "My father's name was Charles, but he died years ago."

"Charles Wendell Fieldstone?" I asked cautiously.

She looked surprised. "Why, yes, that was his name." She frowned. "He passed away when I was an infant."

"Hmm." I turned to Hezekiah, so only he could see my lips moved silently. "Told you so."

The front door opened again, and an older woman peered out. She looked to be in her late forties. It was obvious she was related to Liza. "Who is it dearest?" she asked. Upon seeing my tattered dress, she added, "We have no time for beggars but are in a hurry to leave for

Salem Town. I will have my sister Miranda bring you out some bread." She turned back toward the entryway and called for the bread.

"Salem Town," I whispered sideways to Hezekiah. Already, my brain was working, wondering to what year we had returned.

"No, Bess," he said. "Don't even think it." He pressed his fingers into my shoulders the way a concerned parent would a child, then stepped in front of me and faced the older woman. "You and Miranda are Charles Fieldstone's sisters, yes?"

The pleasant expression on her face hardened.

"My name is Hezekiah Hanson, and I have news of your brother."

She wavered. "Charles is dead." Deep creases etched into her forehead. She opened the door and gestured for Liza to go back inside. "Come along, Liza."

The door slammed, but shortly reopened, and a woman of about forty stepped out. It must have been Miranda as she was carrying a loaf of bread. "Here," she said, handing me the bread. "My brother Charles was a good man."

"Yes, he *is* a good man," I said, watching her closely.

Her eyes squinted, as she studied my arm. "Why do you speak of the dead?"

"He's our friend."

"From long ago?"

I shook my head. "I just spoke to him today."

Her eyes widened, and she backed away, tripping over her long dress. "Witch!"

I groaned. "No." I rolled my eyes. "Your brother Charles is as alive as you and I."

That seemed to agitate her more. "Tis not true," she scoffed. "I was there when they put his body in the ground."

Really? Feeling justifiably confident, I ventured forward. "Did you *see* his dead body?" Okay, a little brusque on my part, but dang, I'd just seen the man a few hours ago.

She flinched. "Of course!" She paused and then held a thumb and finger to her forehead. "Wait, I, uh . . ."

"You didn't see him, did you?"

"No . . ." Her eyebrows furrowed. "The village burned . . . they wrapped Charles in a burial cloth to spare us the sight." She shuddered.

Footsteps inside the house alerted us to Liza and the older woman coming near. "Follow me," Miranda said, leading us to a nearby shed. Spaces between the wooden slats allowed us to see them exit the house, get inside a carriage, and take off down the road.

"She's your sister?" I pointed at the carriage as it got smaller.

"Yes. Elizabeth is my sister."

"But she's not Liza's mother, right?"

"Heavens no!" Correcting her sudden outburst, she continued in a softer tone. "After Charles died," her eyes darted from me to Hezekiah, "Elizabeth took them in. Liza's mother Mary died not long after."

Elizabeth and Miranda were Liza's aunts. Both were Charles's sisters. "Why are they going to Salem Town?"

"Elizabeth is going to see old friends. I warned her against it and refused to accompany them to that dreadful town, but when she heard about the Coreys, she decided that she would be at their trial."

"Oh my!" At the mention of the Coreys, an exasperated breath left my throat.

"You know the Coreys?"

"No. I just know *about* them." Soon, one of the most horrific acts in all of history would happen. Giles Corey would be purposely crushed to death, one cruel stone at a time, in an effort to get him to plea to the accusation of witchcraft.

"Please believe us, Miranda," I pleaded. "Charles *is* alive, and he's asking for Liza."

She studied my face. Small traces of hope swam in her eyes, quickly clouding over with doubt.

"It cannot be. He is buried—"

I pulled the portrait miniature from my pocket and dangled it in front of her.

The color drained from her face. "Where did you get that?"

"It was on the floor beside Charles's sickbed."

She took it from me. "But how can that be? He would *never* leave them." She looked off in the distance. It was some time before she spoke again. "My sister raised the infant as her own."

I glanced at the inscription on the back of the miniature. "Elizabeth Fieldstone," I mumbled.

She nodded. "Charles and Mary named the child, Elizabeth, after my sister, but called her Liza for short. My sister added junior to Liza's given name and senior to her own."

Totally confusing for my era, but having a mother and daughter with the same name was common in the past. I studied the portrait.

"I do not understand. How could he do this?" Tears filled her eyes.

I didn't have the answer for that. All I knew was that he was dying and needed a reason to live. "Charles is asking for Liza. We just want her to know that. We want her to come back with us and see him." I felt Hezekiah stiffen next to me.

Miranda's face filled with wonder and then anxiety. "Why he did he leave us?"

I looked at Hezekiah. "He told me something about Liza being sick."

"Sick?"

"He said he went looking for a way to pay for her medicine."

Miranda's face filled with shock. She paced the floor. "*Elizabeth*," she whispered. *"What have you done?"*

Exchanging curious looks with Hezekiah, I forged ahead. "Charles needs to see his daughter. She's the key to his recovery—the reason he would fight to live."

She gasped. "He could die?"

I hadn't told her how serious his condition was. What was I going to say? Charles flew through time and crashed on an asphalt-covered road in the future?

"Um, he fell from a great distance and hit his head on a rock." True enough.

"Oh no!" She waved us away, while she fought to regain her composure. "Alive?" she muttered, throwing her arms in the air. "Dying?" She wrung her hands. Back and forth she parleyed, switching from obvious elation to misery. When she finished with what appeared to be an internal struggle, it wasn't a quivering Miranda that immerged. She was angry.

"Elizabeth lied to me. She told me Charles died at Pemaquid in an Indian raid!" With hands balled into fists at her sides, she paced the shed. She stopped in front of Hezekiah. "How far away is he?"

"Very far." Hezekiah reached into his pocket and removed the blue stone. "How badly do you want to see him?" Rolling the stone between his thumb and forefinger, he glanced my way again.

"No way, Hezekiah," I whispered sideways. I kept my hand far away from my pocket. I was shocked that he would want to bring Miranda back instead of Liza. Charles hadn't asked for Miranda, in fact, he'd never made a mention of her.

"Very badly," she snapped. "More than you could ever know."

Doubtful. Hezekiah knew well enough. He'd been separated from his brother by 300-some years. She'd only been separated from her brother by a few years.

"Yes," I said, "but he's asking for his *daughter*."

She looked down her nose at me. "Then there's only one thing that we can do." Opening the shed door, she pointed toward the meadow where a few horses grazed. A carriage was parked by the barn. "Go get her."

Yes! I refrained from doing a fist pump, as I was sure that wasn't a seventeenth-century gesture. Going after Liza was exactly what I wanted to do, but going to Salem Town during the trial and execution of Giles Corey was what I *needed* to do.

Four
Liza

Liza leaned her head against the small window, watching the meadows and farms go by as the carriage pummeled down the dirt road. With every jerk and bump, her temper rose. She didn't want to go to Salem Town. She wanted to confront those two strangers, but they were gone when they went back outside.

She glanced at her mother whose expression hadn't changed since they left—thin lips pressed together in a defiant scowl. She could read her so well. The grimace was from the encounter with the strangers earlier that day. Every time she'd tried to speak to her about it, she was met with that rigid glare.

"When are you going to talk about it?"

Her mother's silence magnified the muffled crunching of dirt under the carriage wheels and the soft thudding of the horses' hooves against the hard ground. Normally, Liza would have kept her distance, but the small carriage left no room to turn.

"He spoke as if he knew my father," she blurted out. "Did he work for the, um . . ." She twisted a strand a hair around her finger as she struggled to remember the name the stranger had mentioned. "*Hanson* . . . did he work for the Hanson's before his death?"

Elizabeth blinked. "Yes, I believe he did."

Finally, a confirmation from her mother. Determined to learn more, she pressed forward. "Did you know the Hansons?"

Her mother stared out the small window, her head bobbing with each sharp bump. "No."

Liza's shoulders fell forward. "Oh." Leaning back against the seat, she thought back to the strange encounter earlier that day. There had to be more. "Why did that man come to our house?"

Elizabeth threw a quick look that took the younger woman by surprise. "How am I supposed to know the answer to that?" she snapped. "He was probably someone wanting to claim part of your father's estate."

Though it wasn't much, her father had left a parcel of wooded land. Her mother had said that it was hers, should she ever want it.

"I wonder what interest anyone would have in that land. It's all trees. Maybe they want to cut it?" Liza had heard that King William III wanted the best of Massachusetts Bays' trees, but fear of Indian attacks had caused them to farm the trees closest to the shore instead of going farther inland.

Her mother met her eyes. "Yes, I suppose you're right." She turned back to the window.

Salem Town was the last place in the world Liza wanted to be. She'd heard all the stories and frankly, the whole thing frightened her. The Coreys had been friends of the family for years. She'd never seen anything odd about them. They were just two ordinary people, accused of an extraordinary crime—witchcraft. She shuddered.

Five
Giles Corey

The early evening air, though a bit cool, was refreshing—welcoming, especially considering where we were headed. Salem Town. How would we be received? We'd just been there one month ago, though to us, not even a day had passed.

I ran my fingers through my blonde hair, grateful I still had that disguise going for me, unless Betty Hubbard had blasted that one out of the water, too. We'd have to be cautious. I glanced sideways at Hezekiah. Even without the prosthetic mask, the gray hair dye and scruffy look hid his true persona. I didn't care, as my mind wandered to what he might look like forty years from now.

He broke the trance. "Hand me a chunk of that bread, will you?"

"Sure."

It had been warm when Miranda handed it to me, but was now cold and crispy on the outside.

I fell back into my thoughts, wondering what was going on at the Hanson mansion. With a month passing and no news of Abner, Hezekiah, or Charles, I imagined they were quite in an uproar.

At least, with the passing of a month, the mansion might not be under such a stringent guard. I now realized that was where we were headed, having passed right by Salem Town. I didn't second guess Hezekiah. Anyhow, I needed to clean up a bit, maybe redo my hair, before facing the threat of seeing Betty Hubbard or any of the circle girls again.

Down the long driveway, Hezekiah pulled the carriage off the road and hid it behind a cluster of trees. He unhooked the horses.

"Let's walk from here."

He grabbed my hand and led me and the horses through the dense trees.

Dusk hung over the land now thick with heavy fog, when we quietly made our way to the stables unnoticed.

Panning the grounds for unwanted men, my heart thudded deep in my chest. Not seeing anyone didn't calm my nerves. I wasn't about to let my guard down. I knew they could be lurking anywhere, hidden in the deep shadows.

The heavy barn door opened with a soft thud. After leading the horses to stalls, we sat on a wooden bench, both of us silent.

Hezekiah glanced at my arm. "How is it?"

I twisted it around. "It's fine." Peeling a corner of the bandage up, the skin was scraped and red, but healing over. I pressed it back down.

Movement from outside startled us. "Who's there?" a gruff voice called, the candlelight from a lantern bobbing closer. Hezekiah pressed his finger to my lips and waited. The dim light neared the opened door, giving the intruder an otherworldly feel.

I gasped.

Hezekiah however, chuckled. "Sigmund, my old friend." He spoke low, obviously wanting to remain clandestine to the outside, darkening world. "Shh!" he said, when the man jumped. He gestured for him to come inside the barn and close the door.

I was relieved to see that it was Sigmund, one of the Hanson's servants.

Once inside, Sigmund set the lantern down. "Well, I'll be. Master Hanson!" He grinned, obviously seeing right through our disguises.

"Yes, Sigmund." Hezekiah led him to a nearby stool. "Have a seat." He then proceeded to interrogate him while circling the stool. "Tell me, Sigmund, is everyone well?"

Sigmund hesitated. "They are distraught. Worried about you."

Hezekiah's eyes moistened. It looked as though he might dash to the house, but instead, he continued. "And the men that were to arrest me? Are they still about?"

"No, sir, they are gone."

He nodded. "Go before me. Tell my mother all is well, and I will be there shortly." He opened the door. "You are sure it is safe?"

"Yes, sir, the men left nearly a week ago. Everyone is convinced the she-witch killed ye." He winked at me reassuring me that he didn't feel the same way. And then he then turned and went toward the house.

Shortly, the barn door flew open and Sigmund rushed back inside. "She says if ye don't be a coming right away, she'll be out to get ye!" He pointed toward the house.

I lingered behind when Hezekiah went into the parlor. His mother gasped in relief, and then she asked, "Where is your father?"

Hezekiah pulled away from her grasp. "He is fine, Mother. He'll be home in a few days."

His mother, Victoria, glanced my way. "Come into the room, Lady Elizabeth," she said. With the tenderness of a worried parent, she pointed to my arm. "What happened?"

"I, ah, fell down. It's nothing."

"It is so odd looking." She studied the twenty-first century bandage wrap. "Especially this." Her fingers lingered over the metal clasps that held the bandage snug.

Fortunately, she already knew I was a time traveler, but others would question it. With reluctance, I took it off. Seeming to understand my century-hopping dilemma, she called for Sigmund to fetch a cloth bandage to cover my wound.

Placing her hand on Hezekiah's, she asked, "What of Charles?"

"He's not well. The carriage crashed—"

"Yes, I know," she said, cutting him off. "I personally went to examine the wreckage." Her eyes widened in wonder. "Poor Charles." She looked at Hezekiah and then at me. "How did you ever survive such a thing?"

Interesting question with no plausible answer.

"You went back to the future, did you not?" Victoria tilted her head toward her son. "And that is where Abner and Charles are?"

Hezekiah blinked, obviously surprised by her astute analysis. "Ah, yes, Mother," he stammered, "that is right."

She looked away. "And Abner made it through time just fine, but Charles, he did not." Her fingers went to her lips. "Poor, poor, Charles."

He drew his head back, surprised. "Yes, Mother . . . he is unwell, but we do have hope." He paused. "What do you know of Charles—his relations?"

She wiped a tear from her eyes. "Not much. A sister in the province of Maine and family in England, I believe."

"Did he ever speak of a Miranda?"

Miranda, Miranda," she said, seeming deep in thought. "Why no, not Miranda, but he used to speak of a Mary. She died during the smallpox outbreak in the mid-seventies. Mary was his wife."

"Hmm," I said, looking out the window at the starry sky, wondering how somethings that appeared so tiny were in reality, huge—and there were so many of them. I guess our life isn't as extraordinary as we think, and yet, maybe we're more like stars than we can imagine—greater and more infinite than we seem.

Hezekiah's voice brought me back to reality. "I've lost all track of time, Mother, what day is this?"

Victoria grimaced at the mention of time. "Why, it is Monday, the eighth of September, Hezekiah." She drew near and whispered. "How long will you stay this time?"

He seemed reluctant to answer and placed his hand over hers. "Not long, Mother. We leave for Salem Town in the morning."

Her hand flew to her mouth, and she gasped. "Oh, dear! Not that wretched place!" Sobbing, she buried her face in his chest.

I stepped aside, while he tried to comfort her. I knew we were going to Salem Town to find Charles's daughter, but how to tell his daughter that he was alive *in the future* sounded way too weird, even to me. We'd have to come up with a plan. My gaze fell upon the topaz and diamond ring on my finger.

Our staged engagement had been a ruse, and this ring was a family heirloom. Still, I longed to keep it, but it wasn't mine, not yet, at least. I twisted it off and set in on the fireplace mantel.

Staring out the window, I fingered the draperies while lost deep in thought. A rush of tingles swept up my back at the prospect of meeting up with Charles's daughter at the witch trials. I had been at all of the hangings to date and now would witness the last of the infamous trials of Salem. I dreaded it and longed for it at the same time. Was I that curious? Or perhaps, morbid?

I sighed. Maybe so—the fascinating tragedy of Salem consumed my thoughts. I wish I could change the horrendous past, but knew that the only thing I could do was *speak for them*. The tingles intensified. What better way than to *witness it,* before becoming a voice for the dead?

My thoughts turned to Giles Corey—the next victim. For the past five months, the eighty-one year-old man had been sitting in a cold jail in Salem awaiting his trial. I used to think of my near-perfect memory as a curse, but now was grateful I remembered so much recorded history throughout the annals of time.

Ugh. Time. Giles Corey had fascinated me. I even wrote a play about him while in junior high—a ridiculous skit, but nonetheless, fairly accurate, as I had used notes handwritten by Reverend Parris and Ezekiel Cheever.

Parris had been at the infamous Salem Witch trials and Cheever was a well-known Headmaster of the Boston Latin School during that era.

Of course, at the time we performed it, I had no idea what the girls looked like or how real everything would become to me. But Giles' first examination had taken place in April, and I had not witnessed it. I only had the words of Parris and Cheever to go by, which I used verbatim. I thought back to the play.

"Are you guilty of witchcraft, Goodman Corey?" The magistrate waved the papers in the air. "I admonish you to be truthful!"

Giles leaned over the bar separating him from the judges. "I hope through the goodness of God I shall, for that matter, I never had no hand in, in my life."

My friends had played the part of the circle girls. I shook my head in remembrance of their sloppy, dramatic performance. The only good actress was Samantha, Trent's, *er Hezekiah's* cousin. She played a great Betty Hubbard, who according to history could not testify against Giles because of violent seizures blamed on him. In fact, Samantha's portrayal was a showstopper, and knowing Betty better than I liked, it was spot-on.

I leaned against the window trim and looked out over the trees silhouetted against the darkening sky. The leaves would be turning in about a month, and all of this would be over. *Huh!* I scoffed. For many, the indignance and humiliation of being related to a witch would go on for years, not to mention the pain they would suffer while dealing with their loss.

Six
Changes

Hezekiah's brother, Gyles, dashed through the door. He crossed the room in wide, swift steps, until he reached his brother's side. "It is true!" His face beamed with exuberance and a mist of tears he did not hide. "You are back!" He grasped Hezekiah's hand and drew him to his chest.

Hezekiah's cousin Arabella was by his side and quick to hug him, but then she nestled back into Gyles. He gently took her hand. Hezekiah hadn't seemed to notice, but I grinned wide. I leaned against the wall, caught up in their tender display of sweet affection. She turned then and warmly embraced me.

She once was my former enemy. It was one of life's more pleasant surprises, when you judge someone as the villain, and then discover how wonderful they really are. I listened as Hezekiah answered their questions and told them we'd be off to Salem Town in a few hours, before the sun rose.

The door opened, and Arabella's sister, Gabriella, burst into the room. "Elizabeth!" she squealed and rushed toward me. "I was so worried about you!" Pressing a stubborn curl behind her ear, she scolded me. "A whole month you were away, and you couldn't have somehow told us where you were?" A spurt of air left her throat. "Not even a note?" Her eyes fell upon my arm, and she frowned.

It was apparent she knew nothing of our time travel. "I'm sorry, Gabriella. We wanted desperately to reach you." That was the truth. I felt some guilt, wondering how they took it, with the carriage in splinters and no bodies to recover.

Arabella spoke up. "They're here now, dear Gabby, and they're safe."

"Yes, yes, of course!" Gabriella patted my shoulder, but then she slapped it. "Don't you ever do that again!"

"Ow!" I rubbed my shoulder. Dang. I hated that it hurt her so much. There was a painful element to time travel, knowing that one day, we would leave for good—maybe even sooner than we thought.

Gabriella threw a nervous glance toward the window. "At least those diabolical men are gone."

"Yes," I said, "but Gabriella, we'll be off again soon."

Her mouth dropped open. "Tell me this is not true!"

Arabella frowned. "I wish it was not, dear sister, but it is."

Gabriella pouted. "Where are you off to now?"

I looked at Arabella for help. Her lips pursed together. "They are going to Salem Town before morning breaks."

Gabriella's hands flew to her face. "What? That dastardly place? You mustn't!"

"Believe me, I don't want to go," I said, covering my partial lie. "But it's important that Hezekiah and I rush—"

"Rush back into danger!" Gabriella interrupted, throwing her arms into the air. "It is a foolhardy thing to do."

"Yes, Gabby, it is," Arabella said, "But there are things you don't know—reasons why they must go to Salem."

Gabriella looked back and forth between me and Arabella. "Reasons important enough to risk death?"

I knew she was right. Under normal circumstances, we would never have come back here, but there wasn't anything normal about this. Charles was stuck in the future—dying. I had caused it, and I had to find a way to fix it.

Arabella looped her arm around my shoulders, and we stepped into the hallway. She gestured for Gabriella to follow us. "Come sister," she said. "Isn't it obvious what we must do?" She pursed her lips together. "We must change Elizabeth's identity."

That seemed to pique Gabriella's attention, turning it from somber to inquisitive. "Oh! Yes, of course!" She grabbed my arm and nearly dragged me to Arabella's room.

Shuffling through her wardrobe, Arabella removed two long dresses. "What about these?"

Gabriella shook her head. "No, those will never do, sister." She stuck her head into the wardrobe and pushed several dresses aside. "Ah," she said, pulling out an elaborate dress. "This one is perfect."

Deep maroon, with lace at its sleeves and around the neck, I had to agree—if she was trying to make me look different, this dress was perfect. It was way too classy. I was surprised I hadn't seen Arabella in it. Of course, I had been away for a month. Nonetheless, I doubted much occasion to entertain had come up after our hurried disappearance.

"Do you remember this dress, Elizabeth?" Arabella asked, holding the velvety material between her finger and thumb.

"No."

She sighed. "That, I do not doubt. You weren't paying much attention on our shopping spree for your supposed engagement party, whilst we tried to send your pursuers on that scavenger hunt."

Oh yes, now I remembered. I grimaced. That botched scavenger hunt had led them straight to me. I nodded and took it from her. "It's lovely." Glancing toward the hallway, I wondered why the simple dresses that hung in my room weren't good enough. I was about to protest, when Gabriella began unlatching the bindings from my tattered dress.

"However, it shall be you who wears it first," Arabella said.

Arabella and Gabriella worked my worn dress over my head, replacing it with the more elegant one.

Gabriella's face simpered as her eyes appraised the dress or more likely, me. I knew I needed a shower. Ugh— not a shower in this age—a *bath*. But still, her disdainful look was less than kind.

"Must you leave so soon, Lady Elizabeth? Can you not wait a few days? Salem Town will be swarming with those awful men looking for you," Gabriella whined.

Arabella smoothed the sleeve down on the lavish dress. "But Gabby, she won't look like Elizabeth has ever looked when we're done with her."

My lips twisted to the side. "Er, thanks," I said, knowing she hadn't meant that in a bad way. I really wasn't a high-styling aristocrat after all, but that was just what it seemed they intended to turn me into.

Gathering my hair high above my head, Arabella frowned and dropped the tresses. She stepped back and studied my face. "Your hair color." She grimaced. "It is all wrong next to Hezi's gray tones."

"I might be able to help with that," Gabriella said, twisting my hair through her fingers.

"How so, Gabby?" Arabella raised her eyebrows.

"Before I left England, I purchased, um," she cleared her throat. "I purchased the ingredients for hair dye."

I was surprised. "Really?"

"Of course, Elizabeth. I have recipes for gold hair." She glanced at my blonde hair and grimaced, "though not as bland as yours."

"Mmm." I held my tongue.

"I have recipes for white hair—as white as silver, and black hair, and even green hair, which I once saw a countess wear as she exited her carriage. Though it could've been a wig," Gabriella added, seeming deep in thought. She looked back at me. "White or silver?"

White would be too regal. Silver would make me look older, and it would match Hezekiah better. "Silver." They agreed, and then scurried off to Gabriella's room to mix the ingredients, leaving me in the room by myself.

Wait. How was I going to get this poofy dress off on my own? They hadn't buttoned up the back, so all I really had to do was work it off in reverse order. But trying to get the gathered material up the sides of my body was nearly impossible. I grunted and groaned, caught midway between the many folds of the dress. A faint knock sounded on my door.

"Do you need my help?" Victoria called through the door.

Ah, yeah, but where's the door? I couldn't see a thing. I pushed the thick fabric back down enough to see over it and shuffled toward the door. "Are you alone?" I really didn't want Hezekiah to see me contorted inside something that looked like ancient draperies.

"Yes, Elizabeth. What is the matter?"

I managed to open the door with my elbow, and she burst in, and then broke into laughter. "I did that only once." She chuckled. "It is nearly impossible to maneuver so many layers of material and lace over one's head by oneself."

While she helped, I thought back to an earlier time— my first time travel and the help I had received from Martha O'Brien, the woman who had befriended me in Salem Village.

Wondering where she was, I looked around. "Where's Martha?"

Victoria's countenance sobered, and then she forced a smile. "She left." She looked away, and I knew something wasn't right.

"When?"

"A few days after you and Hezekiah disappeared." She gathered the long dress up and over my head.

For some reason, I didn't believe her. Martha would never have left me. While Victoria struggled with the dress, a horrible thought came to me. They must have asked her to leave. No. They wouldn't do that, not so soon after the day we had disappeared. Would they? The dress came off with a pop, and I fell back against the bed.

A sick feeling swirled in the pit of my stomach. I pushed it back down, forced it away, but it festered and grew like a volcanic eruption at its brink. I pressed my lips tight. Why would they do such a thing? I fought to keep my quick tongue silent.

"They are filling the bath for you." Victoria motioned to the servant carrying a bucket of hot water down the hall. She wrapped a robe around my shoulders. "Come, Lady Elizabeth."

I watched them fill the tub, numb with grief. Martha had proven to be a valuable addition to the estate. Yet, I had known that the day might come that she'd want to return to her own home. Unable to restrain myself any longer, I grabbed Victoria's hands. "Martha is not safe in Salem Village!"

Her eyes widened, and she gave a quick nod. Tears welled up in her eyes. "Gyles—"

I jumped up. "Gyles sent her away?" I couldn't believe it. "Not Gyles."

"Oh no!" A sob caught in her throat. "Gyles didn't want to trouble you. We know you're in a precarious situation."

"Trouble me? With what?"

Her countenance stiffened. "Martha is a widow," she said, "and an Irish Catholic, Elizabeth."

"Um, what?" I folded my arms across my chest. How could she judge her? I knew that Puritans had a distain for Catholics, but the Hansons were not Puritans.

Then I remembered Ann Glover. Tried and hanged as a witch in Boston in 1688 because she was an Irish Catholic surrounded by Puritans. Goody Glover spoke little English and couldn't defend herself against mounting prejudices. I remembered reading the words of the Reverend Cotton Mather, ". . . the court could have no answer from her but in the Irish which was her native language . . ."

Seriously? She spoke very little English. And when asked to recite the Lord's Prayer, which at the time was a thing believed that a witch could not do, she did it *in Irish,* because she didn't know the English words. But they didn't accept her Irish rendition.

To make things worse, when they examined her house they found poppets, small dolls witches used to torment others. In reality, the dolls probably represented Catholic Saints, and as a practicing Catholic, Goody Glover would have them in her home. When she tried to explain that she prayed to them, they jumped right to the conclusion that she prayed to devils. Ugh. Catholics were detested by the Puritans—Irish Catholics, even more so.

My voice trembled. "Where is she?"

"They took her, Elizabeth." Victoria shook her head. "And there was nothing we could do."

I jumped up. "Of course there was—*is.*" I refused to believe there was nothing we could do to help Martha.

"No, Elizabeth," Arabella said firmly, coming into my room. Gabriella followed close behind, carrying a smelly liquid, slopping and splashing in a copper pot. Victoria cleared an area off the dresser for the noxious mixture.

"There was not a thing we could do without endangering ourselves."

That was true for anyone who wanted to help the victims. Once you spoke up in their defense, quite often, you became accused yourself. But how was she accused? How did the circle girls even know Martha? I glanced from Arabella to Gabriella and then to Victoria. How had they allowed it to happen?

"It doesn't make sense," I retorted, icily. "Surely, you could have prevented her arrest."

Arabella thrust her hands on her hips. "We couldn't do anything."

My eyebrows hardened in deep furrows. "Why not?"

A puff of air escaped her throat, but she didn't return my hard stare. Her eyes glistened with tears, "because she confessed."

"What?"

Victoria brushed at tears that had quickly appeared. "Those horrid men hounded us night and day. She couldn't bear it when you disappeared. She knew you'd be back, but how could you return with those men lurking around?"

My mind reeled, tossed about to and fro. Martha confessed as a witch? In shock, my words stumbled out of my mouth. "But why would she confess to being a witch? She was deeply religious and superstitious."

"Why do you think, Elizabeth?" Gabriella said, lowering her eyes.

Grimacing, I blurted out. "She's *not* a witch, Gabriella." I was irritated that she'd believe such a thing.

"I know that," she snapped back. She tapped her foot— a gesture she did when nervous or upset. "She was protecting you! Martha said *she* was the witch they were looking for," her voice dropped to a whisper, "and you were not."

I fell back against the bed. "What?"

"And her ruse worked, didn't it?" Gabriella pointed out the window toward the barn.

My heart sank. That was why the men weren't skulking around the estate. Martha had thrown them off my track and onto hers. I groaned and collapsed onto the pillow in a fit of sobs. Lost in agony, I mumbled, "Why did she do that? Why does anyone do something like that?"

Victoria placed her hand on my. "For the same reason that someone travels very long distances . . . for a friend."

Oh. Right. Charles. And it was why I wouldn't be leaving Salem until Martha was out of danger either. I sat up and squared my shoulders. Having a near-perfect memory crystallized my thoughts. History recorded more than one escape from the prisons of Salem during that horrendous time. One had to wonder how many more would have hanged by the noose had they not escaped. A daring plan began to brew in my mind.

By midnight, the hair color was applied and washed out, I had bathed, and my hair was almost dry. In the early hours of the morning, they finished my newest masquerade—my hopeful defense against Betty Hubbard, Mercy Lewis, and the rest of the circle girls.

After a fitful time trying to fall asleep, I awoke early and heard commotion in the hallway. "Bess, are you awake?" Hezekiah called through the closed door.

"Yes." I pulled myself out from under the warm blankets, went to the door, and opened it a crack. My eyes met his. Even with that prosthetic mask, how could he look gorgeous, so early in the morning? I ran my fingers through my disheveled, gray hair, pulling it up to my eyes. "Ugh," I said, noticing the flat color from the dim light of his candle bouncing off my gray mess.

He hadn't seemed to notice. "We need to leave as soon as you're able."

I nodded and went to close the door, but Arabella's dainty foot slipped between it and the door trim.

"Are you ready?" She stepped into the room, lighting the candle on my desk with hers. A flurry of footsteps from farther down the hall revealed a sleepy but resolute Gabriella.

Within minutes, they helped me into my dress. I had placed the stones in a small bag which I now slipped into the pocket of my dress. Then I sat down in front of the large dresser mirror while Arabella proceeded to comb through my tangled hair. I was more determined than ever to bring modern hair conditioner back with me, if I ever returned to the past again.

After a struggle on Arabella's part and endurance on mine, she finally arranged my hair in a small knot on the back of my head, with gray ringlets crowning my forehead and cheeks. A liberal application of a white mixture to my face, left it ghastly pale. She did nothing to my eyes, except a light dusting of white powder on the lashes, making them almost invisible, which was just as well. The gray hair and white face altered my looks quite enough. A string of pearls finished the effect. I really did look like an older and much more distinguished woman.

"Thanks." I reached for the two sisters with open arms.

Arabella backed away and grabbed Gabriella's arm. "Oh no, Gabby. Mustn't smear her face." Instead, she took my hand and squeezed it. Tears welled up in her eyes.

Gabriella stood nearby wringing her hands. "Are you sure about this, Elizabeth?"

Nope. "Of course, I am." I bit down hard on my quivering lip. I wanted to find Charles's daughter and bring her to him—a huge undertaking. And I wanted to rescue Martha—an even harder thing to do. But seeing some of the trial that was the biggest task of all. I dreaded the possibility of being recognized. I truly feared it. I had been able to travel through time in an instant and wondered if I would be able to do it again.

I swallowed as the thought pressed into my mind. What if I couldn't?

After handing us a basket with bread, cheese, and dried meats for our breakfast, Victoria pulled me aside. "I took the liberty and went through Charles's things. I hope this will help." She handed me a small leather book.

It seemed to be a ledger of sorts, though there were a few longer entries. "Thank you," I said, and slipped it in beside the stones.

I watched as Hezekiah once again said goodbye to his family. I wondered why the subject of Victoria visiting the future hadn't come up, but decided Hezekiah had finally agreed with me. It was going to be difficult for Abner, André, and hopefully, Charles, to return to a world without electricity or running water. Why make it hard on his mother, too?

She stood on the porch and waved, as we took off down the dusty road like we were just going off to the market on a sunny, September day. But for the worried look on her face, I would have thought so too, but I knew that look, as I keenly felt it myself. We were headed into unforeseen danger.

Sigmund drove the carriage. Gyles and Arabella had wanted to come, but Victoria and Gabriella had no desire whatsoever to go near the place. In the end, we decided that the fewer Hansons in Salem, the better. I settled back against the seat, across from Hezekiah, and stared out the carriage window. From the corner of my eye, I caught Hezekiah studying my gray hair. That would make any woman cringe, wondering what their man was thinking— worried that he might not like you, as an older woman.

"Get over it," I mumbled under my breath. "One day, I'll look just like this."

He grinned. "Hardly." He reached over and took my hand. "By then you'll have darling laugh lines etching the corners of your eyes."

He meant it as a compliment, but I could only envision the inevitable outcome. I knew it would be so. My mother had those laugh lines, and come to think about it, so did

Victoria. I smiled. If I grew up to be half as wonderful as they were, I'd be just fine.

I thought about Martha. She had to be around the same age as Victoria, but a hard life had carved deep etches into her tawny face. My stomach knotted thinking about her shackled in a dirty jail somewhere.

I knew at some point, I'd have to talk to Hezekiah about Martha and my plan to free her, but for now, I didn't want to think about anything. I just wanted to rest, as much as one could riding in a horse-drawn carriage on a bumpy road on an unusually warm day. I hadn't expected to drop off to sleep, but welcomed the reprieve from the agony swelling within me.

I don't remember much about the dream, except that it kept me restless, so that when I awoke, I bolted upright. "Oh." I blinked at Hezekiah's anxious face staring down at mine. "Um, how far away are we?"

He looked at me funny. "By my calculations, we should be in Salem in just under two hours."

I suppressed a chuckle. *By his calculations* . . . That was so Hezekiah, in both word and deed. The carriage rattled along, tossing me about over each jutting rock and uneven dip in the dirt road. But I was used to it by now. What was a rough road with what I was about to face? I was anxious to get there and just as fearful to arrive. Two hours away now seemed awfully close.

He wouldn't take his eyes off me until the look I gave him must have alerted him to the annoyance of it. He settled into reading, and I turned my attention back to the road.

As time passed, it grew hotter, and the small carriage became stuffy. I pushed at the lacey collar, trying to flatten it against my dress and get it away from my neck. Victoria had given me a small fan, and I pulled it from my pocket. "My, it's hot," I said, sweeping my hand to my forehead dramatically.

"Yes, it is." Hezekiah barely looked up.

I should have known that whatever had been bothering him would soon disappear when he turned his attention to that ancient book. He was immersed in it. I imagined André was just as shocked to see us disappear, as he was to see his book vanish in Hezekiah's time-traveling hands.

"Find anything interesting?" I knew he had. Knowing I was somehow connected with the stones was a bit eerie, but exciting too, and I wondered what else would be discovered within the pages of that book.

"Look, Hezekiah, the thing you didn't want to happen, has happened. I, er *we,* time traveled again. The least you can do is tell me why."

"*How,* you mean?" He flipped a page, keeping his concentration locked onto whatever mysterious thing he was perusing.

My lips twisted to the side. "Erm, okay, *how?*"

He lifted his eyes. "How what?"

"*Uh!* You are so wrapped up in that book." I lifted my hands in the air and then dropped them. "You don't even remember what you just said."

He closed the book. "Sorry, Bess. I'm a little preoccupied with where we're headed and what we are about to do."

And he didn't even know the half of it. Still, I was as worried as he was, didn't he understand that? I reached over and snatched the book off his lap. I'd show him.

He stared at me. "And just where do you think you're going with that?"

He was right. "Nowhere." I handed him back the book, but he waved it away. It wouldn't do me any good anyway. Even if I could read Latin, it was way too technical for me. I wished André was there. He'd explain it to me, if Hezekiah wouldn't.

"What *is it*, Hezekiah?" I waved the book in the air. "What other mystical thing do you not want me to know?"

"Too much knowledge could be a dangerous thing in the wrong hands."

I drew my head back. Wrong hands? I held my hands up and stared at them, moving them back and forth.

"I didn't mean it like that, Bess." The expression on his face softened. "You, of all people, must know every minute detail within the pages of de Nostredame's book."

"Oh." He did understand.

"But not until you grow up."

No, he didn't. "*Really?*" My eyes narrowed before slipping my hand into my pocket and wrapping my fingers around the stones.

Nothing happened. I glanced at Hezekiah, the blue stone glistening in his grasp. "To protect you, Bess," he said, his green eyes blazing, and I hoped I wouldn't have to resort to the only way I could get it back—thievery.

Seven
Child of the Sky

Wrapping my arms tight about my shoulders, I fought to hold my tongue. Decades of men suppressing women's voices probably meant little to Hezekiah who had grown up in a time where women were heard far less than men.

Shocked by that thought, I sat upright. Stop it, Bess. You know him and his family better than that. That calmed me some. It was true, too. In fact, I had met several strong-willed women in this time period. Some, including my great-grandmother, Susannah Martin, were hanged because of their sharp tongues.

I fell back into my thoughts, my eyes fixed upon the pocket Hezekiah had stuffed my stone into. *My stone.* Not his. Negative thoughts breed like maggots on manure. A sudden darkness descended upon me, covering me like a blanket of thorny, choking vines. This was a strange place I was slipping into—a dark, dreadful abyss.

I felt cold and alone. My heart pounded, angry and fast. Flushed, one moment I dripped in sweat. Chilled the next, I shivered. Back and forth they parleyed, until I thought I could take no more. I *needed* that stone in a way I'd never needed anything before. It consumed me. I wanted it. *Now.* I stole a glance his way, but he seemed unaware of the vicious struggle raging within me.

My hands balled up in tight fists at my sides. Why was he keeping it from me? This man I thought I loved— thought loved me.

Theresa Sneed

He looked my way, his tender eyes seeming to brim with worry. It caught me off guard, and a glimmer sparked within my breast.

The darkness broke, like the cresting of a moon over a dark night, or the rising of the sun after a troublesome storm. I shuddered. Where had those awful thoughts come from? How had they invaded my mind? I closed my eyes tight and fought back tears.

My heart pounded like a rabbit skittishly bounding back and forth to escape its impending doom. The stone. I caressed the bulge in my pocket. What would I do if I held them with the other he had hidden in his pocket? I stared out the window, once again fighting the urge to lash out at Hezekiah and his precious book.

But what of the mysteries contained within it? I looked down at it lying helplessly within the folds of my dress.

I felt smug, certain my presumptions were accurate. I sensed far more than even Hezekiah understood.

A pleasant tingle tremored across my shoulders. I recognized it, the wave of mild electricity that passed through me whenever traveling through time, though always at a much higher intensity. I breathed in deep, addicted to the sensation.

The gentle rhythm of the wheels rolling over the dirt road soothed me, but a sudden bump jerked me forward and brought everything back. My mind raced, struggling to put my disjointed thoughts together in a way that could make sense. With quivering fingers, I massaged my arm. Where had I just been?

78

Onida. The wind whistled through the carriage.

Meda, prophetess of the people? Startled, I stole a glance sideways—no one was there. I closed my eyes tight searching for her voice in the wind.

Onida.

Afraid to open my eyes, I waited. The wind tickled my nose, and I felt comfortable and at peace.

She stood before me in a meadow, green and lush, her hands outstretched. "Come with me child," Meda said, without moving her lips. I thought it all surreal—a nice dream, a perfect reprieve for my troubled mind, and I settled into it.

She said no more, but turned and walked through the tall, waving grass. I followed, immersed in the peaceful surroundings, when suddenly she spun around. Her eyes were no longer kind, and deep lines of anger etched her aged face. She raised her hand, in which a long staff had appeared. "Choose!" she said, this time the words forming firmly on her lips. Her eyes burned red. "Will you lead, or will you mock?"

Shocked, I backed up. Dreams could be so strange. I played along. "I do not understand." Which in reality, is what I would've said, if any of this had been real. Not the best thing to say to an angry prophetess. A wild wind swept through her gray hair swirling it like a whirlwind.

Her lips pressed together tight, as if I no longer deserved to hear her voice. Her eyes, full of fury, bore into me. *Onida, child of the sky, you have been most foolish!*

Um, yeah, that much was apparent.

You bring dishonor. Her face saddened and filled me with deep remorse, for what, I had no clue, but I wasn't about to ask again. Time passed. She remained still, eyes fixed on me, waiting.

No fair! How was I supposed to know what she meant? I hadn't been tutored by her. I hadn't any precious book in which to find ready answers. I didn't have any idea why the stones—I stopped short. That was it. The stones.

I ventured forward, the words tumbling out of my mouth, barely after they had taken root in my mind. "I have misused the stones." As the words gushed out, I began to understand.

Her countenance softened, and a slight nod from her confirmed it. *Their power is neither good nor evil, but both, and neither one is to be trifled with without consequences. Do not use them unwisely, my child.*

Eeks. She couldn't have told me that earlier? I swallowed hard. The wind died down and the sun set in the horizon, creating an ethereal effect surrounding the prophetess, or maybe it was her essence affecting the bleaker sunset. I bowed my head and let the words fall to the ground. "But how? How can I learn with no one to teach me?"

Instantly, she was gone, and I was awake, sitting across from Hezekiah. I would have thought it a dream, except that a brilliant halo flickered above Hezekiah's head, where no light ought to have been, and I knew. I knew who would teach me. As I watched, the light receded to nothing. Humbled, I settled back in the seat, a greater love and respect filling me for this most unusual man.

I couldn't help but wonder. Earlier, would I have left Hezekiah behind in 1692? I tried to keep my chin from quivering. No one knew much about time travel. What if my next foray through time was the *last time* it worked? Meda had said there were consequences.

Vivid imagery of the daunting years that would separate us stung me to the core. Hezekiah would have mourned my loss three hundred-some years before I would've even been born, and I would've continued on forever in my bitter loss, dying a crazy old woman, always regretting my foolish mistake.

I squeezed my eyes shut and began to tremble. Hezekiah was *so right* in taking the stone from my eager hands. I knew little to nothing about what I was doing or what might even be happening to my body each time I zapped through time.

A tear slipped down my face, and I reached up to brush it off, but Hezekiah's warm fingers beat me to it.

"I'm so sorry," I said, and placed my hand over his, not noticing how cold I was until my icy hand grazed his warm fingers. They felt like fire—too hot! I pulled my hand away.

"What's happening to me?" I gasped. "Time travel . . . it's changing me. It's like a drug to me." The last words came out like a whisper.

His lips pressed together, and he tapped the ancient book still on my lap. "According to this, Bess," he said solemnly, "you couldn't have said it any better."

"*Uh!*" My eyes locked onto his. I knew exactly what he meant, what I had forced myself not to look at, and what

Meda had alluded to. I thrust the book from my lap, as the carriage slowed down and pulled over to a stop. We'd have to talk about it another time. *Ha!* Time. I shuddered. We were there. How I dreaded it. How I loved it.

Eeks.

I would need a good therapist for sure. Hezekiah got out of the carriage and told Sigmund to stay nearby, and then he helped me out.

We had decided that if asked, I would be introduced as his wife, which was rather exciting to pretend, though I wondered how believable it would be.

I had thought about what I would say if asked how I'd arrived in Massachusetts Bay. . . Oh, I traveled through time. Hard to say exactly how. Quite a new thing, you know. Got to work out the kinks . . .

I grimaced, suppressing the sick feeling in the pit of my stomach.

The small town was jammed with people. The witch trials always drew large crowds of onlookers as well as the family and friends of the accused. I glanced around at the many faces, trying to guess who they were, seeing pain in some, abject curiosity in others.

Eight
The Accused

Morning rays caressed the horizon, giving the day a bittersweet feel. Looping my arm through Hezekiah's, we followed a small group of people pressing toward the building. We were some of the first to arrive. Before long, the crowd would grow much larger, and we would be lost in the sea of anxious onlookers.

"Hezekiah." A lump formed in my throat. It was never easy to take a stroll back into peril. "Betty Hubbard might recognize us, well, at least me," I said, staring at his wrinkled, prosthetic face.

He tilted his head and brought his hand to my gray tresses. "Probably not, Bess, but just in case." He pulled a folded document out of his bag and spoke low. "Boarding passes from England for both of us dated a month ago. Gyles and I worked on it all evening."

"Brilliant!" I said, clapping my hands together.

"If there's a problem, we show them our passes. In the meantime, answer any questions as a loyal subject to the King, who is visiting the Province of Massachusetts Bay." He put his hand in the small of my back and guided me forward, and then leaned down. "And act as if nothing is out of the ordinary," he whispered in my ear.

Act as if nothing was out of the ordinary in Salem Town? That would be much more of a lie than the fraudulent paper. To add to the ruse, Hezekiah took out spectacles and balanced them on his nose—a nice addition for my criminal-man.

We stepped into the building and opted to sit in the outside aisle in the middle of the room. Right away, the man next to Hezekiah started up a conversation.

"M'name's Dr. Crosby," he said, introducing himself. He studied Hezekiah's face. "You seem familiar to me. Are you from these parts?"

Hezekiah looked at him over his spectacles. "No, we just arrived from England," he said. He gestured to me. "This is my wife, Felicity."

Dr. Crosby tipped his head my way, and I tried not to be astonished. I hadn't given any thought to what my name would be and now wondered what last name Hezekiah had chosen for us.

Hezekiah seemed to sense my bewilderment. "Mathius Alby," he said, and reached for the man's outstretched hand.

Ah, so that made me Felicity Alby—okay, good thing to know. Their conversation soon turned to local politics which I was grateful for, as my opinion as a woman would neither be expected, nor welcomed in public. I deftly fingered the tassel on Victoria's fan and looked around.

Through the milling crowd, I thought I saw someone who could have been Liza, but when she turned, I saw more clearly that it wasn't. The room was filling up, and there was no sign of them.

A door opened at the front and a small group was ushered in. My heart sank at the sight of the accused. The only man in the group had to be Giles Corey, and the frail woman pressed near him, his wife, Martha. I was drawn to them. Though their hands were tied behind their backs, their tender affection for each other was evident.

"Tell me their names," I whispered sideways to Hezekiah and his new friend.

Dr. Crosby cleared his throat. "Well, the last two, they be the Coreys, and that there be the Easty girl." He pointed at the woman next to the Coreys. "Her sister was hanged last month."

I swallowed hard. "Rebecca Nurse."

"Ay yup," he said with a nod. "Ann Pudeator be next to her and then Mary Bradford. She be worse than Goody Martin."

My eyes widened. What a horrible thing to say, especially in front of her eleventh great-granddaughter, *me*. Susannah Martin was unjustly hanged from the gallows tree less than a month ago. I turned my face away from the man and clenched my teeth. The nerve of some people. A pat on my hand from Hezekiah calmed me down.

I was offended by this man's reference to Mary Bradford being worse than my grandmother, but it also brought a memory back to me from prior study. I had forgotten that part of history and now could hardly contain myself.

Mary Bradford was one of the accused witches that escaped from jail! I panned the front of the congregation, wondering who her future accomplices were, and how I could convince them to help Martha O'Brien escape, too.

"The other two be Alice Parker and Dorcas Hoar."

Dorcas Hoar was one of those people that you never forget, and perhaps, the only one on trial that actually looked like a witch. I saw her the first time I came to Salem. My eyes narrowed as I remembered that she tried to get my grandmother to confess to being a witch. Many of the accused confessed to avoid the gallows tree, but because the trials ended, and the hangings stopped, no one will ever know if the confessed witches would've hanged like the others.

I swallowed as I studied the small group of the accused—soon to be tried for crimes they did not commit. Only Giles seemed brave or defiant enough to look out over the gathered spectators. He knew what was coming. At least it looked as though he did. He appeared quite resigned and determined—lips pressed tight, head erect, eyes boring into the crowd.

For an eight-one-year-old man, he seemed much younger, and I assumed that years of rigorous farming had kept him healthy and strong.

A commotion in the back of the room caused many of us to turn and see who it was. My blood went cold, when I recognized the infamous Judge Hathorne strutting down the center of the aisle followed by Samuel Parris and two other men. He glanced my way, but paid me no attention.

I fought the urge to slide my foot into the aisle. Timed just right, his nasty fall might have been worth it, but an angry Judge Hathorne would be far worse than just an arrogant one. So I held it back and simmered as he walked by, his white wig bobbing with each hurried step.

"Let us get this going, I have a busy day ahead."

He had a busy day ahead, while the innocently charged were about to have all their days stolen from them.

Calm down Bess—your attitude could unleash your tongue. I opened the fan and swept it through the air, covering my sour expression, should he chance to look back.

He stepped behind the low bench and spoke in whispers to the other magistrates who had already gathered. Parris poised himself with an inkwell and quill, and the trial began.

Judge Hathorne shuffled through some papers on the bench and then cleared his throat. "I see that you have brought Goodman Corey before the court." With a wave of his hand, he gestured to bring him forward.

One of the men standing near the accused untied Giles's hands and led him to a small platform in front of the bench. His wrists were red and swollen, and I wondered how long they had tethered the aged man.

Hathorne cleared his throat. "Giles Corey." He paused, his eyes narrowing. "You are brought before authority upon high suspicion of sundry acts of witchcraft." His tongue clicked. "Now tell us, Goodman Corey, the truth in this matter."

Giles straightened. "I hope through the goodness of God I shall," he said firmly. "For that matter I never had no hand in, in my life."

"Humph," Hathorne grumbled. "Let us hear the evidence against him." He waved his arm for Giles to be taken off the platform. "Parris, if you will read the summons." He gestured toward the minister, who now held a paper in his hand.

Parris raised the parchment. "We command you to warn and give notice unto John Derick, the wife of Stephen Small, the Widow Adams, and Goody Golthite, that they and every of them be and personally appear at the present Court of Oyer and Terminer held here this day at Salem, forthwith here to testify the truth to the best of their knowledge on certain indictments exhibited against Giles Corey. Thereof make return, and fail not."

He stopped reading and looked out over the crowd. "Be ye present as summoned?"

Hands shot up in the front row, and several heads nodded, and then Parris presented the document to the judge. "All are present." He leaned forward. "But it appears that others would testify as well." He glanced at the first row.

"So be it," Hathorne replied. Shuffling through a stack of papers, he pulled one out, and placed it on the bench before him. "Here lies the deposition of Ann Putnam Junior." With an impatient snap of his wrist, he waved at the sheriff to bring her forward, and then he tapped his fingers together, until she stood before him.

Judge Hathorne picked up the parchment and read aloud. "Ann Putnam Junior testifieth and saith that on the thirteenth of April 1692, she saw the apparition of Giles Corey." He glanced up, cleared his throat, and then took a drink from a mug. "Parris, will you continue?" He shoved the paper toward him.

"It says, um," Parris read silently, until finding where the judge had left off. "The apparition of Giles Corey come and afflict me urging me to write in his book, and so he continued hurting me by times, until the nineteenth of April, being the day of his examination."

He took a breath and continued. "And during the time of his examination, the apparition of Giles Corey did torture me a great many times. And also several times since, the apparition of Giles Corey, or his appearance, has most grievously afflicted me by beating, pinching, and almost choking me to death, urging me to write in his book."

Parris wiped at sweat forming on his brow. He read on. "Also on the day of his examination, I saw Giles Corey or his appearance most grievously afflict and torment Mary Walcott, Mercy Lewis, and Sarah Bibber. And I verily believe that Giles Corey is a dreadful wizard, for since he has been in prison, he or his appearance has come to me a great many times and afflicted me." He handed the paper back to Hathorne.

From where I sat, I saw both Giles Corey and Ann Putnam's expressions etched into their faces—the older looked troubled but firm; the younger, unsure and nervous.

I languished over the fast-approaching outcome. Did he really think he could beat it—win this case? I knew some had thought he was trying to save his large farm, but he had already deeded it to two of his sons-in-law. Others believed he was merely taking a stand against injustice.

A former-day super-hero standing steadfast for truth. I liked that idea better. I sighed. It was probably for both reasons.

Hathorne's booming voice broke through my thoughts. "Do you own upon your oath this written evidence?" His hand slapped down on the document.

Ann brought her eyes up to his. With a shaky voice, she uttered, "Yes, I verily believe him to be a dreadful wizard."

The words were barely out of her mouth when Mercy collapsed on the floor in a frenzied fit, followed by several of the circle girls, including Ann. By this time, I was used to their performance, and yet, still not convinced that they were faking it.

From past experience, I knew all too well that some kind of spirit realm coexisted with earth. Yeah, I know, crazy. But I, *myself,* had seen things, and I'm not irrational nor senseless in the least.

I mean, where do spirits go after death? I refused to believe that they simply ceased to exist, and yet, I didn't think they interfered with earth either. Biblical passages speak of a great host of spirits being cast to earth with Lucifer—heaven's outcasts. What if that was true, demons on earth?

I shuddered at that irony.

Once again, Hathorne brought me back to the present, as his voice drawled out. "The deposition of Mercy Lewis, aged about nineteen years." He handed the document to Parris.

"Mercy Lewis," Parris muttered, scanning down through the words, "who testifieth and saith . . ." He paused and glanced up as Mercy was led to the platform. ". . . that on the fourteenth of April, 1692, I saw the apparition of Giles Corey come and afflict me, urging me to write in his book, and so he continued most dreadfully to hurt me by times, beating me and almost breaking my back, until the day of his examination being the nineteenth of April."

Parris cleared his throat, then continued, "During the time of his examination, he did afflict and torture me most grievously. And also several times since, urging me vehemently to write in his book. And I verily believe in my heart that Giles Corey is a dreadful wizard for since he had been in prison, he or his appearance has come and most grievously tormented me."

Seriously? Didn't anyone else see how similar her testimony was to Ann's? Of course it would be, because Mercy hadn't written it.

Hathorne pointed at Mercy. "Do you own upon your oath this written evidence?"

"Yes." She nodded, and then grasped at her neck as if gagging. "He is a dreadful wizard!"

Hathorne waved her off, as the afflicted cried out in agony, and then he handed Parris the next deposition.

Parris smoothed the paper out. "The deposition of Sarah Bibber who testifieth and saith that I have been most grievously afflicted by Giles Corey or his appearance and also on the day of his examination, if he did but look on me, he would strike me down, or almost choke me."

The deposition went, on almost identical to Ann's and Mercy's. The only difference was the addition of Corey whipping her and cutting her with his knife. She too confirmed the written words. And I wasn't surprised when she grasped her chest and blurted out, "I know in my heart that he is a dreadful wizard!"

Mary Warren's deposition was similar to Sarah Bibber's. She also testified that Giles' apparition, or spiritual body, had cut her with a knife. I wondered if Sarah and she had conferred with one another, or perhaps they had been in the same room when their testimonies were written down.

Two people who witness the same thing rarely see it the same way, and yet, the circle girls' testimonies were nearly identical. The way the testimonies were written was too similar to not have been penned by the same person. That person may have put the words in their mouths, urging their written testimonies to agree with one another. Especially beings several of the circle girls couldn't read or write and had signed their testimonies with an "X".

Elizabeth Woodwell's deposition was somewhat different than the others. Along with the pinching, she added that she had seen Giles's apparition appear in church, while he was physically in prison. Apparently, his spirit or ghost sat in the middlemost seat. Didn't they get how crazy that sounded?

Judges Hathorne and Corwin stared at the next parchment. Hathorne's mouth turned down in a frown. "Who took this deposition?" he asked, an edge to his voice.

Corwin pointed to the name at the bottom of the paper, and Hathorne grimaced. "Perhaps he was in a rush." He turned a glaring eye to the small group of circle girls on one side of the room. "Or perhaps, Elizabeth Hubbard had little to say on the matter?"

He scanned the paper. "Several times afflicted me . . . with several sorts of torments. Could not you have been more specific?"

I shuddered, as Betty took the stand.

"Yes, of course," she said smoothly, "but as you already noted, there was little time."

"Do you own upon your oath this written evidence?"

"Of course I do," she said without hesitation. And then the familiar words we'd heard before spewed out of her mouth in a dramatic screech, "I believe Giles Corey to be a dreadful wizard!"

A theatrically triumphant move on her part, as the congregation gasped, and pointed shaky fingers at the accused man.

"Yes, yes, of course," Hathorne said, seeming unimpressed but pleased at the same time. He waved her off, shooing her back to the circle girls.

Glancing at the summons, he scanned his finger down the names. I figured he was ready to hear more of their accusations, so was surprised when he said, "Is there anyone here that will speak in behalf of Goody Corey?"

It was a defiant challenge that required an even more defiant response. He then excused himself and left the room, which seemed strange to me, but must've been necessary.

A voice called out in the back. "I will speak for him." A gasp from the crowd echoed my own, and everyone turned their heads to see who had spoken. Who would be so brave?

Liza Fieldstone walked down the aisle. Our eyes met. The same kind of shock registered on her face that I know she must have seen on mine, but there was no way she'd recognize me in my elaborate disguise. If she had, she shook it off, returning to the task at hand.

"Yes?" Judge Corwin said, stepping in for Hathorne.

"Judge Corwin," Liza said. "I ask pardon for anyone I might offend, but I must be allowed to speak what I know."

Hathorne returned to the bench. "Yes, of course," he grumbled. The sour look on his face told me that if he'd been in the room just seconds ago, he wouldn't have let her approach the bench.

"Thank you." She returned his sour look with one that oozed kindness. I had to wonder if she was laying it on a bit too thick. No one was that nice to a man like Hathorne.

She ran her hands down the sides of her dress. "I have known the Coreys for all of my life."

Hathorne chuckled. "That long?"

Light laughter from the room mocked her youth. I inwardly scowled.

Her smile faded. "It doesn't take a long, wretched lifetime to know a person," she said.

Yikes! I wanted to shout, "You go girl!" and "Don't say that to a man with power" at the same time.

"You asked for someone to speak for him, and I can speak for both Giles and Martha Corey."

Hathorne lowered his eyes. "Go on," he said, with a pronounced frown.

"I have been in their home many times. They are no more wizards and witches than you are Judge Hathorne." She gave him a fleeting smile, and so did I, though I'm not sure either one of us timed it right.

Hathorne's response was quick. "And you are implying?"

"Exactly what you are thinking." Her voice softened. "It is far too easy to accuse someone of something so heinous. You are not a wizard and neither is he." She pointed to Corey. "He might be a little rough around the edges, as are you, dear judge, but he is a good man." A few people chuckled at that, but I was mortified that she'd be so bold.

Liza did not apologize, but forged ahead. "I give you my solemn oath, that I have never seen witchcraft in or around the Coreys."

"Yes, yes." Hathorne scowled and waved her off.

I was afraid that she would not sit down, but continue on with her justified tirade. I wasn't alone.

"Come along child," Elizabeth Senior called from the back of the room. "Do not speak another word." I heard her say under her breath, as she met her halfway down the aisle, and then escorted her toward the door.

I would have been amused, having heard that myself many times, but I was terrified. As they left, Betty Hubbard's scrutinizing gaze followed them out the door.

Calm down Bess, her name is never mentioned in the future, so she never became a victim. That thought soothed my nerves, until Betty turned her attention to Hezekiah, who was quietly talking to Dr. Crosby.

"The Court of Oyer and Terminer will take an hour recess," Judge Corwin said.

The crowd was quick to stand, and I was even quicker to yank Hezekiah to his feet. We had to leave before Betty made her way to us. My sharp tongue would not conceal my identity, regardless of the gray hair piled atop my head.

Hezekiah excused himself, then turned his attention to me. "Yes, I know we must go, Felicity." Holding his arm out, I looped mine through it.

"What? Oh, yes, of course, *Mathius*," I whispered. "But, we've got to leave *now*." I pulled his face down to mine. "Betty saw you."

It seemed he thought it was nothing, but he hadn't seen her arched eyebrows while she studied his face.

"She's coming!" That worked. He swept me out the door and into the dense crowd milling around the streets of Salem Town.

Nine

Travesty

Liza rushed out of the building. "Mother. Slow down." She pulled her long dress up and rushed up the worn path.

"Slow down?" Beads of sweat gathered at her mother's brow. "Did you not think, when you spoke so disrespectfully to Judge Hathorne?" She wiped the sweat off with a gloved hand.

"I, um, I guess not," Liza said slowly. "But Mother, you can't possibly think that anything will come of it."

Not often, nay never before had Liza seen her mother show true fear. A thin, red line edged her mother's eyes, like one who had not slept for many nights. It unsettled Liza.

"It's not Hathorne that I'm worried about," Elizabeth said. "These are strange times, my child."

She sounded so unusual. It wasn't comforting in the least. "Mother, everything is all right."

"Giles and Martha thought everything was all right, too." Elizabeth sighed, expelling a heavy thrust of air. "They did not believe they'd be accused of witchcraft either, Liza, and yet, there they are." Her hand shook, as she pointed back at the building where the Coreys awaited their verdict.

Grabbing Liza's arm, she hurried her along to the carriage. "Get inside, child," she demanded, glancing around. "Richard must be in the inn. I'll fetch him and the horses."

"Might we return to the trial to—" She didn't get the words out of her mouth, before her mother snapped back.

"We'll do nothing of the kind. We're leaving this wretched place."

Liza sank back into the hard seat. Her mother's words brought unpleasant truth. It was foolish to speak to Judge Hathorne the way she had, but she couldn't be silent. She closed her eyes tight. "More people ought to take a stand," she mumbled. "But then, they'd be accused themselves."

She sat up straight. "It is a vicious cycle of injustice. Those who should speak up for others are afraid for their own lives." She clenched her fists. "But it is too much power with too little culpability that I fear."

A shadow approached the coach. Glaring rays of sunshine blinded her vision, blocking the dark form coming near. The handle on the small door turned. Surprised, Liza drew in a quick breath and jumped back when the door popped open. "Hello? May I help you?" Her voice was thin and high pitched.

"I'm sorry to be so bold." The door blocked the sunlight, revealing an older woman with the voice of youth.

Bold and also rude. Her eyes squinted. She recognized the woman from the trial. "Do I know you?"

"Well, yes, and no," the woman said, adjusting her lace collar. "We met earlier." She placed her hands on her hips. "I have been looking everywhere for you."

"Really? Whatever for?"

"Well, um, see, it's like this," the woman said, placing her hand on the side of the seat. It looked as if she intended to hoist herself up into the carriage.

"Wait," Liza held her hand up, motioning for her to stop. "Where did we meet?"

"At your house, remember?" The woman looked down at her dress. "Oh, wait, you might not recognize me looking like this."

Liza's eyes followed the contour of the woman's pale face and high-coiffed hair. "I remember you!" She gasped. "You're the one who came to my house, but now you're . . ." Shocked, she gestured to the woman's white, painted face and gray hair.

She had heard about people that dressed incognito to trick others out of their money. It was just as her mother had said—they were liars and probably thieves. "Go away! Leave me alone!"

The woman drew her head back. She made a face and then threw her hands up in the air. "Fine, whatever."

Liza pushed her away and pulled the door shut. *What an odd way to speak.*

"I just wanted to talk to you about your father, but *apparently* you don't care."

Stunned, Liza sat still. "Father?" She wrung her hands. *What if they weren't liars and thieves?* "Wait!" she yelled, pushing the door open, but the woman was far away, walking a lot faster than any old woman she'd ever seen.

There was no time to think. Her mother would be back soon, and any chance of talking to that woman would be gone. She scrambled out of the carriage after her.

The courthouse was emptying and a few looked her way. Two or three exchanged excited expressions and pointed at her. It wasn't often that a young woman was bold enough to defy authority and now she worried if her brashness would get her in trouble. One of the circle girls broke through the crowd. Their eyes met and chills went down her spine.

A hand grasped her shoulder and whirled her around. Her mother didn't say a word, but pressed her hand into the small of Liza's back and ushered her into the carriage. "Quickly, Richard. Quickly, now!" She climbed in beside Liza and shoved a basket onto her lap. "Eat, my child. We've a long ride a head of us."

Liza stared out the window, until her mother released the tie on the curtains, and they swished back into place.

Ten
Stay Put

I didn't get too far down the street when I realized I hadn't tried hard enough. Rude or not, I needed to talk to Liza Fieldstone. I turned just in time to see Betty glaring at her and Liza's mother guiding her back to the carriage.

"Did you find her?" Hezekiah said, catching up to me. We had agreed to split up to look for Liza and then meet at the stables.

I pointed to the carriage taking off down the street. Betty had disappeared into the growing crowd exiting the building. "Yes, but she freaked out on me." I almost smacked him when he rolled his eyes. "Only because she thought I was going to rob her or something weird like that." Again with the smug look. "What?"

"Think about it, Bess." He smirked. "If you told her you were that young, cute girl this morning, how do you think she would react?"

I was stuck on "young and cute" and grinned at his appraisal, but he wasn't smiling. My eyes narrowed. "What do you mean?"

"Seriously Bess, we're not in the twenty-first century anymore. People can't change their looks at random."

"Yeah, well we did."

"And you're not from the seventeenth century, are you?"

I opened my mouth to retort, but he was right. She must have thought it incredibly strange for me to be a teenager one day and an older woman by the next morning. "I blew my cover, huh?"

He nodded. "But it doesn't matter. After Liza's outburst, I'm sure they're headed home."

My shoulders slumped forward. "What are we going to do now?"

"We're going to follow them."

Away from Salem? I bit down on my thumb. No. Not yet. I had something else I had to do first. If I had never time traveled, Martha would not be in jail for witchcraft. I had to right the wrong that I had created.

"Hezekiah, we won't want to follow them too closely. I mean, after all, we're driving one of their carriages. Can we eat something first?"

He studied my face. "Sure." He pointed down the street.

"You go and bring something back. I want to rest and soak in some rays." I tilted my face toward the sunshine.

He gave me a funny look. "Seriously? In that dress?"

He was right. I'd be sweating in seconds in this monstrosity. But still I said, "Uh huh."

He frowned. "Okay, but stay put." He looked back at me several times, which was annoying.

I glanced up and down the street. My friend Martha, and Mary Bradbury—the woman whom I knew would be making her escape sometime in the near future—were probably being held captive in the same jail that had imprisoned my grandmother and my Native American friend, Honovi. It wasn't too far from here, less than a ten-minute walk. Struggling with rushing toward the jail, I forced myself to lean back against a hitching post instead.

Hezekiah's words wouldn't leave me. "Stay put."

Why? Didn't he trust that I would be right back? My eyes narrowed. Did he really think I needed his permission to take a short walk?

Stay put.

Tiny pricks of dark blotches appeared in my vision, much like from the tension headaches I used to get if I didn't get enough sleep or food while in high school. I pressed my fingers into my throbbing temples. I had to get out of the sun—out of this awful dress! Shorts—I needed my shorts and tank top.

Stay put.

Feeling a bit weak, I trembled against the post. I would simply tell Hezekiah about Martha—why hadn't I already? He'd understand. He'd help me rescue her. I turned toward where I'd last seen Hezekiah. Just the movement of turning, sent my head into a spin. I grasped the post tighter and waited for the dizziness to pass.

Onida.

What?

Onida. Meda's voice wafted through the air.

I turned my face toward the sound, but only saw a small crowd of people retuning to the courthouse, and overheard their faint whispers, as if I walked beside them.

"I will not let them kill her," an old man said.

"Nor I, Papa," said a younger woman, about the age of my mother.

"Father!" someone called from across the street. He approached them swiftly and grasped the older man's shoulders. "It's all arranged. We will free Mother soon." They scuffled up the steps and into the building.

103

I gasped. Were they the Bradburys? I had to talk to them! I released the post and tumbled to the ground.

"Oh, dear!" I heard footsteps approach.

"What is the matter?"

Bodies surrounded me, and voices spoke all around.

"Help her up."

"Is she alive?"

"I wonder who she is."

I stirred and then opened my eyes.

"Are you all right?" The Reverend Parris asked, helping me to my feet.

"Yes," I said, leaning into him. "It's just the heat." My head was clearing, but the dark blotches remained.

"Come along," he said, leading me to the steps of the meeting house. "Let's get you out of the sun."

"Reverend Parris," I said in a whisper. I had met him once before, the first time I had traveled back in time to 1692. He was a key player in the Salem debacle and a man who had wisely removed his own child from the circle of crazed girls accusing the innocent.

Betty Parris was the first afflicted and the youngest accuser at the age of nine. I shuddered when I remembered seeing her writhing on the bed with her cousin Abby, like something straight out of the Exorcist.

Abby—Abigail Williams—was the young woman the playwright Arthur Miller had wrongfully cast as a jilted lover. According to Miller, she caused the witch hunts to pay back the guy who rejected her, John Proctor. Of course, Miller had portrayed Abby as older, and Proctor as younger, because in real life, Abby was only 11 years old and Proctor was 61. Wow.

I looked up at Parris, a sudden sadness engulfing me. He would survive, as would his daughter, but survive to the degradation of his career and reputation, and then to live with the knowledge that he was involved in the death of innocent people.

"Thank you," I said softly. "You go on, I'll be fine." The blotches had cleared, and I felt better.

He helped me back up, and I watched him enter the meetinghouse. My thoughts turned back to the small group of people planning what I was sure was Mary Bradbury's escape. I had to go into the building and talk to them. I started up the steps after Parris.

"Whoa there, girl," Hezekiah said, coming up behind me. He put his hand firmly on my shoulder.

Eleven
Standing Mute

I waited for his words. "Stay put" like an obedient dog. I inwardly growled. "Your first mistake was telling me to stay put."

His eyebrows twitched. "And my second mistake?" he said grimly.

"Waiting to see if I would."

His green eyes bore into me, and I was glad he hadn't trusted me on that point. I mean, I would've found him again. I did before. I frowned. I almost hadn't. A strange, cold feeling gripped me.

"That, Bess, was not a mistake, but a safety precaution," he said, with a sad face, "for the years that could separate us should you inadvertently time travel without me."

Oh. Of course. My heart sunk.

He walked me down the steps and to a fallen tree on the side of the dirt road. "What were you doing, going back in there?" He sat down and pointed to the meetinghouse where court had probably already begun. "The truth, Bess."

A puff of air escaped my throat. I sank down beside him. The words tumbled out between sobs. "Martha . . . jail . . . my fault," I blubbered. "And then when I remembered that Mary Bradbury had escaped . . ."

"Whoa, hold on! Martha Corey is in jail, we know that, but—"

"No, not her. *My* Martha—Martha O'Brien."

"Oh." He drew his head back. "But how is that your fault?"

I explained it out to him, ending with, "She's risking her own life, because she lov—loves me," I burst into tears.

He pulled my head to his chest and ran his fingers across my tears. "So this is what's been bothering you?"

I nodded, between sniffles.

"Mary Bradbury," he whispered, deep in thought. "I've known the Bradburys practically all of my life. I read about her in the future and thought it was excellent that her family and friends had helped her escape."

"You know the Bradburys?" I pulled away, stunned. "You mean, all this time, we could've been planning Martha's escape together?"

He cupped my face in his hands. "One of these days Bess, you're going to have to trust me completely, and stop acting so . . ." He didn't finish.

"Juvenile?"

"No," he said, dropping his hand. "So afraid." He pulled me up.

I walked beside him, my mind in a whirl. I was somewhat perturbed at his ridiculous observation. I'm not afraid. All at once, I realized where we were headed, back toward the meetinghouse the Court of Oyer and Terminer was taking place in. "Why are we going back there?"

He looked down at me. "Because the Bradbury clan are probably sitting in the back row, where they were before the Court took a break."

"Oh." Smart guy. My heart thudded in my chest—had I seen them earlier? We stepped back into the building and found a seat in the back row. "Where are they?" I whispered glancing about.

Hezekiah jerked his head to the right. He leaned into my ear. "Last three men in this row up against the wall and two women beside them."

"Oh." I leaned forward and caught the gaze of the older man I had seen earlier, obviously Captain Thomas Bradbury. He gave me a curious look. I didn't pull my gaze away and wondered if he had seen the pleading in my eyes, the worry etched into my face, and the fear gripping my heart. The trial was in full swing, and must have been for some time, as the judge announced the gentleman leaving the platform as one of the last witnesses against Giles Corey.

I was riveted to the platform as Hathorne called Giles Corey back up. "What ointment was that your wife had when she was seized?"

One of the things Martha Corey was accused of was making witches potions. I wondered what old Salem would think about essential oils in the future. *Dang.* Couldn't a woman, or a man, use natural remedies?

"Untie him," Hathorne demanded.

I hadn't noticed he had been tethered again and supposed they must have done that during the break. They unloosed his hands and one fell forward.

The instant his hand was released, a piercing scream erupted from one of the girls, followed by several more screams from the others. I covered my ears with my hands to block the eerie sounds. Still, my eyes were drawn to the front.

Giles dropped his head to the side and the heads of the afflicted did the same. He sucked in his cheeks and theirs did, too. Weird. Weird. Weird. In fact, I wasn't sure anyone could suck in their cheeks that deep—it was totally unnatural.

It ended before long, and passed like a dark cloud through a windy sky. I shuddered.

Hathorne patted the pile of depositions on the bench. "The Reverend Samuel Parris has brought in the written examination of Giles Corey. We have looked it over."

He pointed to Corey. "Upon hearing the same, and seeing what we did see at the time of his examination." He paused. "We ask Goodman Corey, where he stands. Will you state guilt or innocence in response to the sundry charges of witchcraft?"

Giles stood taller and pressed his lips tighter. He was like stone—not to be moved nor acted upon. He would not plea if his life depended on it.

Yikes. It did.

I think Hathorne saw what I did. He continued, "Then, together with the charge of these afflicted persons against you, we commit you to our majesties' goal."

I swallowed hard. I knew that Giles Corey now had days to live, soon to join those who had been wrongfully hanged, only his death would not be so merciful.

Twelve
The Bradburys

Though her hair was disheveled, and she was thin and forlorn from cruel imprisonment, it wasn't hard to tell that the stately, white-haired woman was Mary Bradbury.

"Goody Bradbury," Corwin said, ushering the eighty-year-old-woman forward.

I glanced at the Bradbury clan's faces, each one looking distressed from worry.

Judge Hathorne tapped the bench. "Who testifieth against her?" A few people stood in the crowd. Captain Bradbury jumped up, lurching at her accusers, but two of his sons quickly pulled him back down.

If Hathorne had seen it, he didn't acknowledge it. "Samuel Endicott," he said. "What is your claim?"

A thin and jumpy sort of man, Endicott held his hat tightly to his chest. "I bought butter from Goody Bradbury for my voyage, but it turned rancid and maggoty," he said, not taking his eyes from the judge.

Incredulous. Over time, unrefrigerated dairy products would decay, and flies would lay eggs that would eventually hatch into maggots. Cause and effect. I wondered how long something simple like decay would hold an aura of mysticism to the uneducated. Ugh. Come on, even these people had to understand rot.

"And then," continued Endicott, "during a violent tempest, the ship lost fifteen horses. All of 'em drowned in the raging waters."

Really? A ship losing horses during a storm, and he was blaming it on Mary?

"I saw her shape on the vessel," he clamored.

It was the way he said it, almost as if he had added that part to his testimony for believability. Maybe he realized how lame it had sounded up until then.

"When I was a boy," Endicott continued, "my brother Zerubabal, my father George Endicott, and Richard Carr," he paused, pointing to one of the men that had stood up earlier, "they saw Goody Bradbury enter her gate, then go around a corner, and then a blue boar ran out of the gate and charged them."

Hathorne raised his eyebrows. "And?"

"Why we saw it dart right into Goody Bradbury's window!" He wiped his hands on his shirt. "My father was glad we'd seen it as well as him. He always thought she'd transformed herself into a boar." He sat down, and the other man stood.

"Name's James Carr," he said to the judge. "When I was courting the same woman one of Bradbury's sons was courting, I was taken in a strange manner, as if some living creature run about every part of my body ready to near tear me to pieces."

"Yes, that is true," Dr. Crosby said. "I can testify that Mrs. Bradbury is a great deal worse than Goody Martin."

I remembered when he had whispered those words in the crowd, and I liked him even less after spewing them aloud in the court.

"Seemed to go away after I struck back at a spectral cat," James said, turning back to speak to the doctor. He faced the court again. "My kin and I believe that our John died because of Goody Bradbury cursing him in his courtship of her granddaughter. She said she was too young, but John grew sad, and by degrees, much crazed."

"Now wait, James," another man said, standing. He introduced himself to the court as William, another one of the Carr brothers. "I never heard John complain of Mrs. Bradbury. The death was more likely natural, James."

"What about John's ghost appearing at Mrs. Bradbury's examination? Our niece, Ann Putnam," James said, pointing to one of the circle girls, "she's been tormented by Goody Bradbury's specter since May."

The room was quiet while Ann was escorted to the platform. She blinked a few times, and then spoke to the crowd. "She killed my father's sheep . . . and that horse he took such delight in."

A sharp scream erupted from her throat, and she collapsed on the floor in a frenzied fit. Shortly, she stopped writhing and returned to the small group of accusers. I know they didn't "high-five" back then, but I was sure the smug expressions on Betty Hubbard and Mercy Lewis's faces had the same triumphant meaning.

"Is there any who would speak for Goody Bradbury?"

I was elated that many more stood for her than those who had stood against. Of course her husband Captain Bradbury stood, along with all of her large family, several neighbors, her minister, and even local magistrates. There were nearly a hundred people who stood in behalf of Mary Bradbury's reputation and character. I was absolutely stunned that it wasn't enough.

It was crazy that spectral evidence held more credence than good, honest testimonials. I suppose it was a big reason why the Salem witch trials only lasted a few short months.

Truly after a while, they must have come to terms with how morally wrong it was to hang someone who could no more leave their body in a ghostly appearance to go about pinching someone, than physically leave the jails where they were bond and sometimes gagged.

After a long pause in the procedures, Judge Corwin took a parchment from Hathorne and read from it. "We find Martha Corey, Mary Easty, Alice Parker, Ann Pudeator, Dorcas Hoar, and Mary Bradbury to be guilty of sundry acts of witchcraft. You are sentenced to death by hanging."

Shock registered on the accused faces. "Let me speak!" Ann Pudeator jumped forward. The magistrates walked toward her. "I protest! Why dost thou use the altogether false and *untrue* testimony of John Best Senior? Dost thou not recall that he was whipped and likewise recorded for a liar?"

Noise from the crowd rose in pitch, and a voice called out. "Tis true, 'bout a decade ago, Goodman Best was whipped for lying about the Beadle brothers running a burglary ring to finance their taverns."

"Aye, aye, he speaks the truth," another recounted.

Mary Easty, whose sister, Rebecca Nurse, had been hanged in July, timidly stepped to the platform. She held a parchment in her hand. Unfolding it, she spoke in a soft voice, "I have written this and would like to read from it." She looked to the bench for approval. Hathorne said nothing, but a slight nod from Corwin edged her forward.

"Knowing my own innocency . . . and seeing plainly the wiles and subtlety of my accusers, I cannot but judge charitably of others that are going the same way of myself, if the Lord steps not mightily in. Therefore, I petition not for my own life for I know I must die, but that if it be possible, no more innocent blood may be shed, which undoubtedly cannot be avoided in the way and course you go in. I question not but your honors for you would not be guilty of innocent blood for the world. But by my own innocency, I know you are in the wrong way."

The crowd was silent. By their faces, I could tell that many were moved by her words.

Corwin leaned forward. "Save your life, Goody Easty," he pleaded.

"She cannot confess, because she is in the Devil's snare," Hathorne snapped, slapping his hand down on the bench.

She looked directly into his eyes, not turning away. "I cannot, I dare not, belie my own soul."

Hathorne swept his hand through the air, as if he was sweeping off a pesky bug, gesturing for her removal.

Dorcas Hoar was next. I had seen her a few months ago, speaking to my grandmother. But she had a full head of short, gray hair then, completely shorn off now, and very odd for a woman in this time period.

Corwin must have read my mind. He held up a snarled lock of dark gray hair, at least four and one-half feet long. "This was coiled under her cap," he said.

My eyes narrowed. *That* was coiled under her cap? I shuddered. Dorcas must have pulled wisps of gray hair down to make it look like she had short hair.

"It was ordered cut off her head, but she protested that she would die without it."

Very weird. Wait. I thought legend had it that a witch's hair couldn't be cut. The long matted tresses were pretty gross. I realized that it was just folklore that imps nested in such places, but looking at the tangled snarls made it somewhat believable.

"I be a witch!" Dorcas screeched, raising her fist to the air. "I be a witch!" There wasn't a sound in the room, not even from the circle girls. If it hadn't been for Dorcas calling out the names of other witches in the community, I'm sure they would've removed her right away.

Hezekiah took my hand and leaned in. "Mary Bradford is being led from the room."

I was so engrossed in Dorcas Hoar, that I hadn't seen them retie Mary's hands. Movement behind me was sure to be the Bradburys leaving the meetinghouse.

Hezekiah waited until they were gone. "Come along," he said, helping me up. Once outside, the Bradburys were nowhere to be seen.

My heart sunk. "Where did they go?"

"I don't know."

We spent the next hour walking around, but didn't see them. We went by the jail several times, but they weren't there, not even when the magistrates brought the accused back to the jail. Hezekiah and I watched from across the street.

"You've known them all of your life. Should we just go to their homes and visit them?"

He smoothed the side of his prosthetic mask, deep in thought. "They live about twenty-five miles from here in Salisbury."

"Well, that means no then, because history states that right around this time is when they broke Mary out of jail and took off. They won't be going home tonight."

"No. You're right. So, that means, they must be in an inn or somewhere in the outskirts of town." He looked at me. "Where would *you* hide?"

I'm sure he meant that as a compliment. "I guess I would want to be close to the jail."

"Uh-huh."

"Somewhere I wouldn't look out-of-place in."

"Yep."

"I'd hide in the jail."

"What?"

"Look," I whispered, pointing toward the back of the jail, where the whole lot of them gathered—the Bradburys, hidden in plain sight.

"Of course," Hezekiah breathed out. "No one would suspect the Bradburys in the *daylight*." Captain Bradbury was talking to a short, balding man.

I tugged on Hezekiah's sleeve. "Isn't he the jailer, Colin O'Donovan?" It didn't surprise me that the captain paid him off, as we had paid the same man to release Honovi earlier on.

"Yes, he is. Stay put, Bess." Hezekiah squeezed my shoulder.

"Uh." A short breath escaped my throat, but I followed his wishes, and watched from afar.

Hezekiah approached them in broad, swift steps. After what looked like an awkward introduction, he grasped the captain's hand and pulled him into an embrace. The jailer took a step backward, but a firm word from Hezekiah pulled him forward again—just a friendly, neighborhood chat, outside the walls of a jail wherein lay the victims of the witch trials, and the love of the captain's life.

I was so jealous. I wanted to be over there, too. I imagined they spoke of Mary, the captain's wife, and how they planned to rescue her.

The band of Bradburys broke up, leaving just Hezekiah, the jailer, and the captain. One of the Bradbury's sons, the man I had seen earlier, lingered by the corner. I wondered what he was looking at, his face grim, his eyes hard and piercing. I followed his gaze and knew right away what caused his anger—Samuel Endicott.

Endicott didn't see Bradbury until he was nearly on top of him. Grabbing his shoulders, he thrust him into the wall. "Butter? Rancid butter?" A rustle of footsteps rushed past the nook I was nestled in.

"Let Endicott go, Thomas!" a woman called out. "Come on, Thomas. We don't need this!" She grabbed his arm. "Let him be," she urged.

Thomas snapped his arm away. "Let him be, Jane? While our mother languishes behind those walls, awaiting the noose about her neck?"

He pointed a finger at Samuel. "Listen you," Thomas said, between clenched teeth. "You might feel safe right now, but I'll be waiting." He pressed his finger into Samuel's chest. "Behind every corner." He pressed harder. "In every dark alley." Another nudge. "I'll be there, when you least expect me." His breathing was heavy.

Samuel took a step backward and then brushed at his shirt with a shaky hand. "That sounds much like a threat, Thomas."

Thomas glared at him, before Jane led her brother away. "Goodman Bradbury?" Samuel blubbered.

My heart thudded. I wondered what had happened to Samuel Endicott. In my near-perfect memory, I had read how Mary Bradbury had broken out of jail before the September hangings took place, but Endicott simply disappeared. He left his home one night and never returned again. He was declared legally dead after seven years.

I was so preoccupied in watching the two men depart in opposite directions, that I didn't hear the light footsteps approach, until they were upon me.

Thirteen
Forevermore

"Good day." Mercy Lewis's voice sent a shiver up my back.

Calm down Bess—gray hair and white makeup, remember? I turned to her slowly. "Good day," I said, trying not to shake.

"Have we met?"

I blinked. "Of course not child, where would I have seen you before? I only arrived a fortnight ago." Pleased with my British accent, I was sure she'd be appeased.

"You are much like a dear friend of mine," she said. "You have her eyes." She studied them and then pouted. "Only she was recently pronounced a witch and has fled Salem on her stick."

"I'm sorry?" I retorted. I reminded her of *me*, and she thought *me* a witch? What a hateful thing to say. Calm down Bess. Curb your tongue, remember? "Then, I do suppose thou art lucky, that I am not," I said curtly.

"Are you not?" she said wryly, "Pity." She turned and walked away.

It was times like this that I wished I was a witch. I fought the urge to retaliate and imagined a dropkick into the small of her back.

She screamed and fell forward tumbling to the ground. My hands flew to my face. I had only imagined it. I had only thought it. Surely, I hadn't caused it! Stop Bess, of course you hadn't. I hurried toward her, even as a man approached. He got to her first.

"You've got to watch where you're going," he said, pointing to a deep pothole in the road.

"Oh," I whispered, backing away. Pothole, Bess, not you after all. Still, I couldn't help but give her the evil eye when she looked my way. One of these days—soon, I hope—I'm going to learn to not antagonize the likes of Mercy Lewis.

"Witch!" she screamed, waggling her finger at me.

"Shush, child," the man said, leading her away. "It was just a pothole, dear."

I was thankful that only he had heard her nerve-wracking scream and unsettling accusation against me.

"What was that all about?" Hezekiah said coming up beside me. "Was that Mercy?"

"Uh-huh." I shook all over. Most people are never called a witch, but for me, it was pandemic, like a widespread malady narrowed down to one person—me. Of course, that was a bit ludicrous. I was within feet of several incarcerated victims awaiting their cruel, unjust death by hanging.

Hezekiah nudged me forward. "Are you okay?"

"Yes." No. The dizziness hadn't returned, but I still felt a little weak. "I should probably eat something."

"I agree." He led me to the open doors of a nearby inn. After seating me by the window, he pulled a chair in beside me. "Bess," he whispered in my ear. "I know how they're getting Mary out."

"Oh?" I leaned closer. "They're going to knock a hole in the wall?" I imagined that scenario in my head. "Or dig under it?" I glanced around, fearful that someone was listening, but no one looked our way. "Oh, I know," I whispered, "cover her in dirty laundry and bring her out in a barrel?"

I was pretty proud of all the ways I had imagined we could rescue Martha and wondered if one of them was how the Bradburys would successfully free Mary.

He smirked. "No." Taking a handful of coins from his pocket, he spread them on the table, and then he grinned.

My eyes widened. Oh. Of course. They paid the jailer. I grabbed his hands. "Can we? Can we, too, for Martha?"

"Already done." His face sobered. "But now, what will she do?"

My smile faded. It was a good question. I tugged on his sleeve. "How long do we have before she's freed, Hezekiah?"

"It will happen sometime before the next hangings."

Eeks. The next hangings were September 22, more than a week away. And just a few days before the gruesome death of Giles Corey that would haunt Salem forevermore.

"So, we wait?"

He didn't seem pleased, but nodded. I suspected he wanted to get on with our business—convincing Liza to come with us to the future—but in the meantime, new responsibilities prevailed. Where in the world were we going to send Martha? And how fair was it to uproot her from her home, because of me?

"We could change her name and relocate her to any of the small towns up the coast," he said, seeming deep in thought.

Martha was about to be treated like she was part of a witness protection program, but what was the alternative?

"Yeah, okay," I said glumly. After all, she wasn't alone. Anyone that escaped the witch jails of Salem was lucky to get away.

If Mary Bradbury hadn't escaped, her life would've been strangled from her, hanged alongside the others on that fateful day. I pressed my eyes tight—that day was soon approaching.

Fourteen
For What It's Worth

Liza closed her eyes, not because she was tired, but because she had to think. Nothing made sense. The world was upside-down with neighbor against neighbor, lobbing cruel words with nary a second thought for their deathly recklessness.

She could see the truth of it in her mother's eyes, who up until a few short weeks ago had seemed happy and at ease. Now every small sound or sudden appearance startled her. Liza wondered what frightened her so.

She didn't question her mother's goodness, and yet the Coreys were the epitome of uprightness, and look at them now. Did her mother fear the same could happen to her? *That must be it.* Any sane person would fear the bizarre happenings of Salem.

She wanted to talk to her mother, to ask her of her fears, to tell her of her own. The carriage rattled on, and Liza thought back to the woman who had disguised herself as old—the same woman who had come to her house in Maine as a young woman, asking about her father.

She opened her eyes a slit, hoping now would be a good time to talk. Her mother's eyes startled her—wide and frightful. It alarmed her to see her bizarre expression. "Mother?"

Elizabeth snapped out of her trance. "Oh," she said, with a quick shake of her head, "yes, dear, what is it?"

Liza squinted. "It's just that you were staring at me in such an odd way." She waited for an explanation, a reason for her mother's strange behavior.

Elizabeth blinked. "Oh, really? I guess I was deep in thought."

That much is obvious. Liza leaned forward. "About what, Mother?"

She twisted in her seat. With nowhere to go in the small carriage, Liza's mother parted the curtains and stared out. "I believe it might rain."

Liza refused to relent. "About what, Mother? What were you thinking?"

Elizabeth's eyes darkened. "Nothing."

You are not getting away with this, Mother. It would be much harder to get her to say anything once they arrived home. "I find that hard to believe, Mother."

"Find *what* hard to believe?"

Be calm, Liza. "That you had nothing on your mind just now."

Her tongue clicked. "Don't be ridiculous. Of course I have something on my mind."

Liza sat up straighter. *Finally.* "And what is it?"

Elizabeth's eyes softened. "Why you, dear—it's always you."

Liza fought the urge to lash back. It was a nice thing to say, but clearly an evasion of truth. Her mother was hiding something. Her frightful eyes moments ago revealed that something was wrong.

Her mother reached over and placed her hand on Liza's. Her voice wavered, "I fear it is the last we will see of dear Martha and Giles." Pulling her hand away, she stared out the window.

Oh. She had been wrong in judging her mother. It had been all about the Coreys—her mother's strange, unnatural fear of late was tied into the upcoming slaughter of innocents.

Hezekiah brushed the coins off the table and into his hand and then dropped them into a small bag tied to his belt. I was relieved that he had already begun the process of releasing Martha, but I was curious of the exact details, when and how it would happen, and where she would go from there.

I nudged the side of his foot to get his attention, which appeared riveted on something in the far corner of the room. All chatting stopped, and I followed everyone's gaze to the source of the sudden silence.

Judge Hathorne had entered the room.

Imposing in and out of the courtroom, the judge had a strong sense of power and authority. He sauntered through the room, stopped in front of our table, and then turned to the one beside us. Sitting down, he gestured for the small group of men who had followed him to do the same. I recognized Judge Corwin and thought the other man might be Judge Sewall. I'd seen him from a distance before and it looked like him.

A sharp glance from Hathorne caused the crowd to return to their activities, and the chatting resumed. I, for one, was not so calm. I bit down hard on my lip and stared at Hezekiah, who was facing the Judge's table. Seated with my back to the judge, luckily, my angry face couldn't be seen.

Hezekiah cleared his throat. Tilting his head toward me, I got the message—calm down and listen. So, I did.

"He's a stubborn man, John," Corwin said.

"Aye," Hathorne replied in a gravelly voice.

"He won't plea on his own."

It was silent behind me, and I wondered what they were doing. A stern look from Hezekiah told me to stay still.

The other man spoke up. "One word, John . . . *Clitherow*."

"Aye, aye, Samuel."

Oh. So the other man was probably Judge Samuel Sewall after all, but I searched my memory and couldn't find anything on Clitherow.

"It's not been done in Massachusetts Bay, Samuel. T'was a cruel way to die," Corwin said, in an urgent tone.

"Pfft." Hathorne shifted in his seat. "Only if he doesn't yield." A fist banged on the table. "He need only speak, "yea" or "nay". Otherwise, we'll coerce him into entering a plea."

"Is that really necessary?" Corwin retorted.

"We think so," Sewall said. "Corey must be brought to justice." A rustling of papers and then he spoke again. "I received this letter from Thomas Putnam." He read it aloud.

"The last night my daughter Ann was grievously tormented by witches, threatening that she should be pressed to death, before Giles Corey. But through the goodness of a gracious God, she had at last a little respite."

A long pause, with some mumbled words that I couldn't make out, and then Sewall resumed his reading.

"Whereupon there appeared unto her a man in a winding sheet; who told her that Giles Corey had murdered him, by pressing him to death with his feet. But that the devil there appeared unto him, and covenanted with him, and promised him, he should not be hanged."

Sewall cleared his throat. "The letter goes on to tell how the apparition claimed that Corey would have to die, because Corey had killed him. "And that," he paused, and then continued. "Giles Corey was carried to the court for this.""

"Yes, yes, I remember that well." Hathorne huffed.

Sewall read on. "The Jury, whereof several are yet alive, brought in the man murdered. But as if some enchantment had hindered the prosecution of the matter, the court proceeded not against Giles Corey, though it cost him a great deal of money to get off."

I tapped my fingers against the tabletop. This was straight out of a badly written movie. You seriously, can't make this stuff up.

More rustling of papers, and I imagined Sewall was refolding the parchment and stuffing it into something.

I remembered reading that letter while in junior high school, but it wasn't the same as having it read by the person it had been actually addressed to. It was incriminating evidence at the most. At the least, it was a well-written letter filled with presumptions.

"So, it is agreed that if Goodman Corey stands mute, and refuses to plea so that his case cannot continue, we will use "strong and harsh punishment.""

"Peine forte et dure—strong and harsh punishment," I whispered. The words stunned me.

Giles Corey would lay on the ground with his arms and legs secured by cords tied to nearby posts. A board would be laid across his chest and then piled with heavy stones, increasing the weight, until his body wouldn't be able to withstand it. Oh, cruel injustice! I fought back the tears.

The men left, leaving Hezekiah and me alone, facing each other. I wasn't hungry and pushed my potatoes around on my plate.

"Take a few bites, Bess," Hezekiah said. "You need to keep up your strength."

"Okay." But I couldn't put the food into my mouth. "Hezekiah, what is Clitherow?"

His lips pressed together, and he spoke low. "Not what, but who—she is a Catholic Saint. Well, she isn't yet, but she will be."

"Oh."

"She refused to plead to the charge of harboring Catholic priests in her house. She was trying to protect her children from being tortured to reveal evidence against her."

"That's horrible!"

"Yes, but it's even worse than that. They put a sharp stone under her back, and the door from her own house on her chest, before piling it with about 700 pounds of heavy rocks."

I felt bile rising in my throat, and drew my head back in shock. "She . . . she couldn't have lasted long," I said, barely breathing.

"Fifteen minutes. And then they let her lay like that for another six hours." He reached over and took my hand. "She was pregnant, Bess."

My body weaved. Hezekiah jumped up and helped me to my feet. He grabbed the warm bread and put it into his bag, before leading me from the room. I'm sure I looked as sick as I felt.

At least Salem hadn't done that to John Proctor's wife, though even as I thought it, I imagined her a pregnant widow, imprisoned, awaiting her own hanging—a hanging that would gratefully never happen.

While I appreciated Hezekiah being upfront with me, the timing was off. I already felt woozy and weak and that story didn't help at all. Still, truth is truth and no matter how difficult it is to hear, it needs to be known, so that history doesn't repeat itself.

But as with Giles Corey, sometimes history has to repeat itself several times before the ramifications sink in and society corrects itself. Ha! I scoffed, knowing that wicked men and women would always exist. Nonetheless, they would walk the earth alongside good and upright people, too. That, I had to believe.

Hezekiah and I walked by the jail on the way to the courthouse. As always, one or two men stood outside its walls. The judges had left before us, which meant the rest of the trials had probably already begun. The meetinghouse room was nearly full. We took our seats in the last row, one row behind the Bradburys.

Judge Hathorne shuffled through the stack of papers until he found what he was looking for. He pulled it out and waved it in the air. "Alice Parker," he said, looking up at her, as they led her to the small platform. "You are brought before authority upon high suspicion of sundry acts of witchcraft. How do you plead, Goody Parker?"

"I deny being a witch."

Hathorne dismissed her with a sweep of his arm. "Who testifieth against her?"

"I do," a woman called from the front of the room. She was led to the platform that Alice had just vacated. "My name is Margaret Jacobs." Rather than facing the judge, she turned to face Goody Parker and boldly declared, "You appeared to me in apparition—a ghost—in Northfields last May." Having said all she'd apparently planned to, she stepped off the platform and returned to her seat.

"Yes," the judge said, seeming wearied, "is there another who testifieth against her?"

A man raised his hand and was ushered to the front. "I am Marshall Herrick," he said gravely. "When I arrested Goody Parker, she yelled out, 'there were threescore witches."

I leaned into Hezekiah, "threescore?"

"Sixty," he whispered back.

Goody Parker's hand shot up an inch or two and then slowly raised to her shoulder.

Hathorne motioned for her to speak right where she stood.

"I do not remember how many I had said."

Oooo, too much information, girl. Better not say it that way. It was almost an admission of guilt.

"Well, I remember!" A tall man strode down the aisle. "Name's Louder—John Louder. I remember it well. I overheard her say threescore." He growled, then pointed at Alice. "Her specter chased me across Salem Common!" When the judge stared at him, he turned and stormed back to his seat.

Hathorne pushed a few papers aside then tapped one of them. "Mary Warren," he said firmly. "What dost thou testify?"

Immediately, Mary Warren fell to the floor in a fit of convulsions. It seemed as though the crowd never tired of it, but I did. Really? Get up already.

"My father," Mary began, pulling herself up off the floor, "promised to harvest her hay, but he didn't get to it for lack of time. But she—" her eyes glazed over and the fits came strong.

After a few minutes, she regained control, and continued as if she'd never been interrupted. "Goody Parker came to our house and said, he'd better be done with it. Not too long after that, my mother got sick and died."

A series of sobs brought on more convulsions. "And my sister, she couldn't talk at all!" She brought her finger up to Alice, but kept her eyes on the judge. "Goody Parker brought poppets and a needle and threatened to run it through my heart, if I didn't torment the poppets!"

Slowly, she turned to Alice, looked her in the eye, and convulsed.

133

Goody Parker's eyes widened. "God will open the earth and swallow me up if one word of this is true!"

Her words shocked the audience and it was quiet for a moment. I suppose they were waiting for a hole to open up in the floor, but when it didn't happen, all eyes riveted on a man approaching the judge.

"May I speak?"

I recognized him as Reverend Nicholas Noyes, from my grandmother's trial and hanging. I knew that what he had to say would not be good.

He stepped closer to Alice and put his foot up on a stool. Cradling his chin in his hand, he rested his elbow on his knee. "Do you not remember, our conversation while you were ill?" he questioned her coolly. "I spoke then with you about various witchcraft rumors. What was it that you said?"

Her face was like stone. "If I were as free from other sins as from witchcraft, I would not need to ask God's mercy."

Hathorne drew his head back.

I mean, I got it, why didn't he? She was saying that she was not a witch, but I think what got her in trouble was the way she said it. I had a feeling that whenever the words "mercy" and "sin" were in the same sentence, one had to concede to the one over the other. One who didn't need mercy under any circumstance was a bit pompous.

Mary Warren's convulsions took on a whole new dimension. I'd only ever seen a cow stick their tongue out that far. I nearly threw up when I saw it. Parlor tricks are parlor tricks and though sometimes hard to explain, they always did have an explanation. But odder than odd, right before our eyes, her tongue turned black.

Okay, this is where I wanted to leave the room—*right now*. Hezekiah grabbed my hand and held me still. Apparently, I wasn't the only one so affected—a few were vomiting in the aisles.

Beyond herself in agony, Alice screamed. "Her tongue will be blacker than that before she dies!"

Eeks. Again, keep it to yourself, Alice. Your words condemn you.

"Why do you persist in afflicting the innocent?" Hathorne demanded.

She seemed resigned. A long breath escaped her lips. "If I do, the Lord forgive me." The room was quiet as they led her away.

Hathorne turned to the last one left to face the court, Martha Corey. He gestured for her to come forward, and, immediately, several of the circle girls fell writhing to the floor.

As soon as the girl's fits subsided, Hathorne said, "Goody Corey, explain yourself." He gestured to the girls.

"Pray, give me leave to go to prayer," she pleaded.

"We do not send for you to go to prayer," Hathorne scoffed. He leaned forward. "Tell me why you hurt these girls, Goody Corey."

"I am an innocent person." She looked out over the crowd. "I never had to do with witchcraft since I was born." Folding her hands in front of her, she continued, "I am a gospel woman."

Hathorne tilted his head toward the afflicted. "Do you not see these complain of you?"

Martha cast her eyes to the heavens and clasped her hands together. "The Lord open the eyes of the magistrates and ministers. The Lord show his power to discover the guilty!"

"Sounds like a prayer to me," I whispered to Hezekiah. He nodded in reply.

"Tell me Goody Corey, about Cheever and Putnam's intention to check your attire a few months back. Did you not mention your clothing with no apparent foreknowledge of their intention?"

"I knew, because the men said my clothes had been mentioned."

"You oughtn't to begin with a lie," snapped Cheever.

She stumbled over her words, "My husband said the children identified specters by their clothing."

"You speak falsely," Cheever barked. "Ann Putnam was blinded by your specter that day so she couldn't see what it wore."

I nearly gagged. Were they kidding? Ann could see that the specter was Martha Corey, but she couldn't see what she wore? Evidently, the plan was to match the specter's clothing with the living counterpart. Argh. I missed the future where things made more sense.

"You are under oath, Goody Corey!" Hathorne barked. "How come you to this knowledge?"

"I did but ask."

"You dare thus to lie in all this assembly? You are now before authority. I expect the truth. You promised it. Speak now and tell who told you what clothes."

"Nobody."

"How come you to this knowledge," he said, his voice rising in pitch and volume. The room went quiet. I'd not seen Hathorne this agitated, and I'd witnessed his wrath before. He stood now and banged his fist on the table. "How come you?"

A sigh left her parted lips, as if exhausted from the struggle of words. "I guessed," she finally admitted.

I inwardly groaned.

Hathorne's eyes narrowed and his voice dropped low, "but, you said you knew so." He raised his head triumphantly, like he had scored a point.

The afflicted circle girls' demented fervor intensified. They jabbed their fingers at her. "The devil whispers in her ear! He whispers in Goody Corey's ear!"

With both hands on the table, Hathorne leaned forward. "What did he say to you?"

"We must not believe all that these distracted children say," Martha pleaded wearily.

"Cannot you tell me what that man whispered?"

"I saw nobody."

"But did not you hear?"

"No."

One of the girl's screamed and pointed at the empty spot beside Martha. "It is the trussed and impaled apparition of someone roasting over a fire!" She screamed again. "Goody Corey did it!"

Another girl cried out, "I am bit!" Clenching her arm, red teeth marks suddenly appeared.

I wasn't sure if she had done that to herself, earlier maybe. It was all too weird to be true!

"Her specter stabbed me!" Yet another of the afflicted fell to the ground, writhing in agony.

"Confess, Goody Corey! If you would expect mercy of God, you must look for it in God's way—by confession!" Hathorne implored her.

"It is indeed wrong to lie," she said, glancing at the afflicted. "We must not believe distracted persons."

"Did you not say our eyes were blinded and you would open them?"

She blinked. "Yes. To accuse the innocent."

Hathorne turned to the first row. "Crosby, come forward." He gestured to the man. "Here is your stepson-in-law, Henry Crosby. Let us hear what he has to say on the matter."

Henry sent a nervous glance her way. "She said, neither the girls," he tilted his head to the accusers, "nor the devil could stand before her, and that she would open the eyes of the ministers and magistrates to the truth."

"What did you mean by that—the devil could not stand before you?"

"I did not say that," she replied.

Reverend Parris stood up. Until this time, he had been sitting and writing down the proceedings with quill and ink. "We have had three others testify that they heard Goody Corey say those very words." He waved a parchment in the air. "Sober witnesses, not the afflicted."

A few chuckles came from the audience, but I was fuming. If he really believed there was some skewed validity between the afflicted and the sober witnesses, then why accept any of the circle girl's testimonies?

Martha groaned. "What can I do? Many rise up against me."

Hathorne smirked. "You can confess."

"So I would, if I were guilty."

"Here are sober persons. What do you say to them? You are a gospel woman," he said snidely. "Will you lie?"

"When all are against me, what can I help it?"

"Now tell me the truth, will you?" Hathorne seemed put out. "Why did you say that the magistrates and the ministers' eyes were blinded, and you would open them?"

A nervous laugh erupted from her throat. "I did not." The words trailed from her lips to a whisper.

I felt bad for Goody Corey. She seemed disoriented and confused, and well may she be, hounded by the likes of John Hathorne.

"I never harmed the girls." Raising her head high, she continued. "I am a gospel woman."

"Ah!" the girls chortled in unison, "she is a gospel witch!"

Goody Corey's eyes widened in near hysteria. "Ha!"

Hathorne leaned forward. "Do you not believe that there are witches in the country?"

"I do not know that there is any."

He drummed the table with his fingers. "Do you not know that Tituba confessed it?"

"I did not hear her speak."

She bit down on her lip and the afflicted girls screamed, many biting down on their own lips.

"You are ordered to stop biting your lip!"

"What harm is there in it?" She clenched her hands and at once the girls screamed, showing new bruises forming on their arms. She slumped forward and the girls cried out in pain.

Yeah, the bruises were convincing. My stomach turned, and I pressed quavering fingers into my abdomen. I had seen enough and was ready to go. The proceedings were nearly over anyhow.

I turned to Hezekiah. His eyes were round with fear—not something any woman wants to see on her man's face. I followed his gaze back to the circle girls.

When Martha Corey shifted her feet, the circle girls feet lopped around like mindless puppets thundering against a stage floor, their bodies falling this way and that, unable to keep up with the involuntary thrust of their feet.

I grabbed Hezekiah's hand and squeezed hard. I would have a hard time getting those images out of my head. There was no way in this world that what they were doing was orchestrated!

Hathorne stood. "I believe it is apparent that she practiceth witchcraft. There is no need of spectral images."

You think? I found myself nodding, even though I didn't believe such a thing.

I know, again with the demonic-host-that-followed-Lucifer-to-the-earth thingy, an explanation that made sense, if you believed in that sort of thing, which I was finding I was believing more and more each day.

Their thundering footsteps stopped and a strange eeriness settled over the room.

Now that their feet were stilled, one of the girls called out, "Goody Corey covenanted with the devil for ten years and only four remain!"

"And I saw a yellow bird suckle at her fingers and witnessed the devil whispering in her ear," another of the girls said. "She brought me the book and tried to make me sign it."

"What book?" Goody Corey asked. "Where should I have a book? I showed them none, nor have none, nor brought none."

The girl froze in place then lifted her finger to the door that led outside. "Do you hear it?"

"Yes!" cried some of the girls. "It is a drum beating assembly. The witches are gathering outside!"

An audible gasp came from the room as everyone stared at the door. Okay, now I wasn't about to leave. Even though it was daylight outside, that scared me enough to keep me right where I was.

Hathorne rose from his seat. "Who is your god?" he demanded.

Goody Corey's chest rose and then fell. "The God that made me."

"She pinches me!" One of the girls screamed and fell to the floor.

"And me!" Another girl grabbed at her arm whirling around as if trying to escape the invisible pinch.

Hathorne swung his arm out toward Corey. "Bind her!"

How convenient that the pinching stopped once her hands were bound. Don't get me wrong, as convincing as everything was—wasn't it her physical hands that were bound and wasn't it her unbound, spectral hands that did the pinching?

"Felicity," Hezekiah said, loud enough for those near to hear.

The name took a few seconds to register. "Yes, Mathius?"

"I'm not feeling well. Do you mind if we go?"

"No, of course not." I gathered my things, grateful for his well-timed ruse. I had had enough too, but still, when we left the building, I couldn't help but glance around once or twice for that throng of gathered witches the girls had seen.

Finding it quite clear, we went to the carriage.

Fifteen
Neither Good nor Evil

I didn't question Hezekiah when he headed toward his parents' estate. It seemed the logical thing to do. We needed to be somewhere safe—somewhere where we could relax. Traveling incognito wasn't as easy as it sounds. I struggled with the stiff collar that had been annoying me all day.

They were ecstatic to see us, and I was thrilled to hear the words. "Fill her bath!" A long, hot soaking was high on my to-do list.

"Take your time. We don't expect dinner for a few hours." Victoria beamed. It was obvious she had been waiting anxiously for our return and perhaps wondering if we would.

Hezekiah took me aside. "We've been together all day, but hardly had a moment to ourselves." He looked up. "And it doesn't look like we are going to now, either." He gestured toward Gabriella who had just entered the room.

"Oh, Elizabeth!" Gabriella squealed. She lifted her arms to throw around my neck, but when she saw how scruffy I looked, she pulled them away. A quick peck on the cheek was an acceptable replacement, for both of us.

Now, back to that alone time with Hezekiah. Nope. Not going to happen as Gabriella saddled up beside us. "I was so worried. Salem of all places," she said, clicking her tongue in obvious disapproval. "Well," she said curtly, "was it worth endangering your lives?"

We hadn't convinced Liza to come with us yet, but we had secured Martha O'Brien's escape. "Yes, I would say it was somewhat worth it."

"Somewhat is not enough to risk your lives in that horrible place," she said, a pronounced pout on her lips.

I nodded. My minor infraction with Mercy had turned out okay. As luck would have it, I hadn't seen her again, up close, at least. She had been at the courthouse, but, fortunately, I had been blocked from most of the circle girls' view.

Sigmund appeared in the doorway. "Your baths are ready." With one hand, he gestured toward the staircase leading to my room, and with the other, towards Hezekiah's.

Mrs. Fayette, one of the servants I had met the first time I came to the estate, helped me get out of my dress. After a few minutes of chatting, which I had to encourage on her part, I dismissed her, so I could be undisturbed in the warm bath. There were things that troubled me, and now it was time to face them. I put my wet feet on the lip of the tub and stretched my legs out.

I had placed my blue stones on the table beside the tub and now picked them up, turning them around in my hands. Hezekiah had the missing stone, and without that one, they were useless. I plunged them into the water. They sparkled and shimmered and cast blue rays up through the water.

"Whoa!" It startled me, so I fished them out, and dried them on a nearby towel. Maybe they weren't so useless after all.

Meda's words came back to me. Their power is neither good nor evil, but both, and neither one is to be trifled with without consequences.

I flipped the towel over them, sank into the water, and groaned. Somewhere in the distance, or perhaps it was just deep in my mind, I heard doleful, rhythmic drumming. On some level, I realized that I was as crazy as the circle girls. I closed my eyes and slipped beneath the water.

Embryonic in nature, the water comforted me as I focused on what I had tried not to feel. Crazy. Yes, maybe that's what I was. Maybe I'd wake up and discover none of this was real—not even Hezekiah.

No. No. I shook that thought away. Yet, how many people had time traveled, repeatedly, to the same place? How many people had magic stones or a fantasy love affair with a good-looking guy—a rich, good-looking guy, 320 years older than them?

Yep. I was crazy. Actually, everything I had just listed was oddly the real part. The crazy part was at the surface of my thoughts, just within my reach—the slow deterioration of my mind.

I pushed my head above the water, gasping for air, shaking all over. I glanced at the bulge under the towel— the beautiful, beguiling stones. Meda had said there were consequences to time travel, and yet, I had at least one more that I had to do—return home to the future. How was I going to do everything that needed to be done with just one time travel?

I could stay here, in 1692. I glanced around at the lavish room. I could live without the modern amenities of the future, especially if it meant keeping my sanity. There was just one more set of hangings left, along with the *peine forte et dure* of Giles Corey. Then life could get back to normal.

Squeezing my eyes tight, I forced myself to not think about anyone else but me. I would marry Hezekiah and live out the rest of my days comfortably and in love. What more could a person ask?

For peace. I clutched my hands to my chest. Tears slipped down my face. I knew no matter the cost to me, returning things to where they belonged was essential to not only my peace, but to others as well.

Reuniting Charles with his daughter, while nice, was playing god. Getting him back to 1692 was the right thing to do. But trapping Hezekiah, Abner, André de Nostredame, Honovi and his sweetheart Magena in the future was unfair.

I think.

I really struggled with that one. Magena would be dead in the past had I not rescued her and taken her to the future. And the scientist André de Nostredame would not be able to leave the modern technology he was devouring in the future to go back to the barbaric past.

Too many things had already changed. Unless there was a way to go back to the beginning and never time travel at all, there was no use in trying to put things back the way they were before I came along and messed them up.

And then there was Hezekiah. I couldn't even bear the thought of leaving him in 1692.

What was the answer? There had to be a good outcome. But maybe there wasn't. Most people experience fleeting moments of peace and joy mingled with passing trials, like stepping stones on the pathway of life. Maybe my outcome would not be so pretty, but whatever might come, whatever might be, I would live for those fleeting moments of peace and joy.

I sat upright and reached for the towel. Slipping my hand within its folds, I removed one stone—just one. I would have faith. The stones had chosen me.

Instinctively, I placed it on my forehead. It grew warm against my skin and a vivid image opened in my mind. Odd that it wasn't my thought, nor my choice of imagery either.

It was a little girl with long flowing hair wearing a knee-length, yellow dress. She reached out for me. Taking my hand in hers, she led me through a lush green garden, at the end of which was a beautiful wrought iron bench nestled amongst rows of bright red tulips.

On the bench sat Hezekiah. He was holding a little boy with curly dark hair and bright blue eyes. They both looked up at me at the same time. The little girl brought me to them and placed my hand in Hezekiah's, and then both children placed their hands on top of ours.

I sucked in a breath and opened my eyes, their images fading to nothing. Tears welled up in my eyes. Was this my answer? A happily ever after? I groaned softly. I was crazy. You're not crazy, Bess. Don't believe it. I forced myself to get dressed and reenter the world of 1692.

Hezekiah was waiting for me in the hallway. I thought it a bit strange, but not as strange as what I had just experienced. He was dashing in his high-collared shirt, tailored coat, and fancy breeches. For a moment, I relished in the imagery I had just witnessed. Oh, how I wanted to be his wife and the mother of his children! That thought made me blush, and I covered my smile with my hand.

But he had seen it and grinned. Okay, normally I wouldn't want him to see me looking at him like that, but at the moment, I wanted to forget the world and only be with him—which would have been ideal, had the room been empty. Apparently, everyone had been waiting for me to come down so they could go to the dining room. I curtsied and reached for his outstretched arm, looping mine through his.

We walked quietly through the halls until we got to the dining room. Magnificent, with its high ceilings, rich tapestries, oil paintings, and ornate trim, the room held a sense of romantic charm. I smirked. Yeah, romantic charm with the whole family sitting around. Wait. Where were, "Arabella and Gyles?"

"Coming!" Gyles called from the hall. "Here we are." He put his hand to the small of Arabella's back and guided her to her seat.

She looked radiant. Her eyes twinkled as she panned the room, but when they rested on me, they popped wide-opened. "Elizabeth! You are back!" She pushed away from the table and hurried to my side. "It is the second most important event of the day!" Before anyone could question her, she flashed a ringed finger around the table.

Victoria jumped up. "You are married?" She stared blankly at the ring.

"Now, Mother," said Gyles, giving Arabella a stern, but playful look. "It happened so suddenly. I know you are disappointed, but with all the craziness around us, we thought it best to take matters into our own hands." He moved beside Arabella and kissed her on the cheek. "Come, my dear," he said gently. She smiled and followed him to her seat.

It was no surprise to me. I had seen the oil painting of them in the future. But now I was sad, knowing that it would be all we would have left of them. Unless I stayed.

Stop, Bess. Mustn't think like that.

After dinner, we took a stroll in the gardens. Hezekiah held me near as we walked, and I wanted nothing else in the world. "What do you suppose your father is doing?"

He looked at me strangely. "I don't know. Is he doing anything?"

"What do you mean?"

"Well, when you were here the first time, didn't time sort of freeze for you in the future?"

"Oh, yeah," I said, thinking back. "I returned to the exact moment I had left." I stopped walking. "So that means that . . . oh, it's so hard to imagine."

"Yes, but Bess, don't think too long on it. The book explains . . ."

"Oh, that book," I grumbled, gritting my teeth. While it revealed many interesting things, once we broached the subject of that ancient book, Hezekiah was lost to me for hours. I tried to understand his theories and explanations, but they were way too technical for me.

Still postulating his theories, he led me to a bench. Side by side, I let my imagination wander, while he droned on about the book, the time continuum, or something or the other. Running my fingers down the sides of the wrought iron, I gasped, and jumped up, startling Hezekiah.

"This is it! This is it!" It was the bench in my vision earlier. I was going to stay in 1692!

"Yes," he said slowly, a quizzical expression on his face. "Don't you remember it? It's one of the few things that survived time. It still stands in the gardens in the future. Though," he added, seeming thoughtful, "I believe it is situated on the other side of the garden."

"Oh." So, my vision could be now or later—no prophetic help there, if it was even prophetic at all.

It was getting late and we had a busy day tomorrow. Sometime between now and the next few days, Mary Bradbury would make her escape—hopefully with Martha O'Brien. The plan was for the two women to stay together. Evidently, the jailer had been paid a little extra to move Martha into the same cell as Mary. The rest, Hezekiah had planned with Captain Bradbury.

I remember reading that Mary Bradbury had returned to Salem after the witch hunt was over and eventually died of old age in her own home. I had to hope that the same would happen for Martha O'Brien.

Approaching my bedchamber door, I wondered if Gabriella or one of the servants might appear. For the moment, it was just the two of us. Hezekiah seemed to realize it, too.

"Bess," he said, his voice soft. Taking my hands in his, he kissed my fingers and then my lips.

I could've died right there and my life would've ended perfect.

He grinned, perhaps sensing my thoughts. "I'll see you before the sun rises."

I lingered in the doorway and watched him turn the corner farther down the hall. Then, I spun around and entered my room.

Sixteen
A Fleeting Gesture

The carriage rolled to a stop and Richard opened the door for Liza and her mother. They had driven all through the night. The morning sun crested the hills in a soft blanket of gold. Miranda met them at the door, a perplexed look on her face. Liza thought it was very unlike her aunt, who always seemed to have a smile or a kind word to give.

What troubled Liza more was how her mother walked by Miranda with nary a word. It was clear to Liza that Miranda was upset.

She approached her aunt resolutely, determined to sort through what beset her. "How are you?" Placing her hand on Miranda's arm, she leaned forward and kissed her on the cheek. But it was a fleeting gesture, as Miranda kissed her back, and then darted after Elizabeth, leaving Liza alone in the foyer.

What has my mother done now? Running her hand along the banister, she went up the steps, and into her room. Even though she had slept through most of the night, the bumpy road had not allowed for peaceful sleep. Weary, she laid down on her bed.

Startled by a sudden noise, Liza sat upright and then hurried to her bedroom window. One of the smaller carriages was laden with boxes tied together like the ones she had seen taken to the ships in the harbor. She watched as Miranda stormed to the carriage. Elizabeth stood nearby, her face like stone. Miranda and Elizabeth's eyes met, and both seemed filled with anger.

Harsh words flew between the two sisters, and then Miranda swung around to the carriage and hoisted herself onto the perch. The carriage pulled out, and her mother turned and walked into the house.

Farther down the road, the carriage pulled off to the side. Miranda got out and went into the woods that lined the long road. She weaved her way back, staying behind the first row of trees.

Liza stumbled from the window. Hurrying down the stairs, she checked the hallway for her mother, and then went through the kitchen and out the front door. She dashed toward the barn, then took a sharp turn toward the trees.

After a quick glance toward the house, she rushed into the thick foliage under the tall rows of maples and oaks. Before long, she heard rustling and snaps in front of her. "Miranda!" she whispered loudly. Nothing.

"Miranda! It's me, Liza!"

A head peeked out from behind an oak tree. "Liza!" In seconds, Miranda's arms wrapped around her in a tight embrace.

Her sudden rush of tears was unexpected and left Liza puzzled and confused. She pushed her distraught aunt away. "I don't understand, Miranda. Please tell me what's wrong."

Miranda grabbed her by the arm and yanked her forward. "Come with me, quickly!"

Miranda's wild eyes startled her. She resisted and pulled back. "What are you doing, Miranda?"

Miranda's grip tightened. "You must come with me, child."

Her strange behavior escalated, and Liza fought to get away. "Stop, Aunt Miranda! What are you doing?"

Miranda's face went blank. She dropped her arms. "Of course," she said, "Of course, you've no idea." She mumbled, "I must be cautious." Facing her full-on, she said, "I will tell all. That I promise you, Liza."

Liza's heart pounded in her chest. "Yes, you must." She pushed a wisp of loose hair away from her eyes. "Please, Aunt Miranda, tell me what's happening between you and my mother."

Miranda took her hand. "Will you trust me, child?"

She studied her eyes. Miranda had always been a part of her life, and she loved her dearly. "Yes, I trust you."

"Then you must come with me now." She tugged on her arm.

Liza pulled away. "No." She shook her head. "You're not making any sense, Aunt Miranda."

A heavy sigh left Miranda's lips. "I know, I know." She turned to the right and then the left, a great struggle evident in her frenzied demeanor.

No matter how bad the disagreement was between the two sisters, it was absurd to expect Liza to leave because of it. "I cannot go, and you shan't either." She gestured back to the house and took a step toward it.

Miranda pointed a shaky finger toward the house. "I will never go back there!"

"Whatever happened between you and my mother, we can work it out."

155

"No! She lied to me. I *believed* her." Miranda slammed her fists into her sides.

"Lying *is bad*, but surely not bad enough to leave."

"This lie is." She brushed at tears streaming down her face. "I have to find those two strangers who appeared here last week."

Liza drew her head back. She'd just had a strange encounter with one of them in Salem Town and was convinced they were thieves and liars. "What do they have to do with all of this?"

"They told me," Miranda said, sputtering. "They said your father . . ." She paused, her face filled with anger.

Liza's chest constricted, and she could barely breathe. "What did they tell you about my father?" She staggered. She didn't want to hear about some mysterious part of his life before his death.

"Elizabeth lied to both of us." Miranda stepped near. She cradled Liza's face in her hands. Sadness filled her eyes, as she studied Liza's. "Your father is not dead."

She pulled away. "Impossible! He died in an Indian raid!"

Miranda shook her head. "That's what Elizabeth told us."

Liza's knees buckled beneath her, and she grabbed a nearby tree for support. She knew Miranda had no reason to make up something so outlandish. She'd never spoken an untrue word. Liza's mind was in a spiraling whirl of shock, fleeting hope, and anger. "Surely you must be mistaken! The strangers—they're telling lies."

156

"I believe them, Liza. Come with me, we will find them and hear them out, and then you can decide for yourself whether or not you want to go back there." She lifted her chin in the direction of the house.

Liza nodded. If it wasn't true, then she could always return home, but if it was true, that would change everything. She would never be able to forgive her mother.

Placing her hand in Miranda's, she stepped forward, toward the carriage, the strangers, and hopefully, the truth.

Seventeen
The Last of It

Just as Hezekiah promised, we were up and out of the house before sunrise. It had been hard to say goodbye again, especially not knowing the future. I gagged on that. Hezekiah drove the carriage, and I nestled beside him. The cool morning air was crisp, the kind of fresh air you love to breathe in, but still chills you to the bone. I wrapped the wool blanket about my shoulders.

Before long, we pulled alongside the inn where we always ate. Funny how things were beginning to feel like home to me. It filled up as travelers arrived for a hot breakfast.

"We are close to my cousin's home," Hezekiah said. He pointed out the window and down the street.

I had been thinking about that too, but owing to the complications of showing up in disguises, and perhaps being recognized by one of the circle girls, a visit was out of the question. I saddened me knowing Hezekiah would suffer true loss of family if he returned to the future with me. Stop, Bess. Not *if*—only *when* he returns with you.

Conflicted, I stared down at the burnt potato slices and greasy bacon piled next to a couple of fried eggs. Yum. I wasn't a big fan of potatoes, except for fast food hash browns. Those were great. I wondered when ketchup would be invented. Ketchup fixes everything. If I stayed, I was so breaking the rule on that one. I'd made tomato soup with my mom, so ketchup . . . I frowned. There was the dilemma again. I could never leave my mom and little brother. Never. And I expected Hezekiah to leave his family? He leaned closer and took my hand.

"What's wrong, Bes—*er,* Felicity?" He jerked his head toward the other side of the room.

A glance to my side explained his odd behavior. Betty Hubbard was cleaning off one of the tables. I decided I'd better not draw any attention to myself and simply shrugged. Putting my head in my hands, I shielded my face. It was fine. She didn't look our way, but continued on into the kitchen. Our cue to leave.

"Good morning Mathius, Felicity!" Dr. Crosby said, as he pulled up a chair beside us. "On your way to the courthouse?"

We sat back down. "Yes, for a little while," Hezekiah said.

"Seems like a long list on the agenda today."

It might have been a long list of the accused, but only four out of the nine scheduled today would actually make it to the gallows tree. If I remembered correctly, which I generally did, the ones on trial today that would be hanged were Samuel Wardwell, Mary Parker, Margaret Scott, and my old friend Wilmot Redd.

Wilmot had cured my illness the first time I had time traveled to Salem. Reputed to be ill-tempered, I had found her to be kind and very knowledgeable about curing aliments with natural remedies.

"We were just about to leave," Hezekiah said, glancing toward the kitchen.

"Aye," Dr. Crosby said. "But have you heard the news?

Hezekiah tilted his head. "No."

"Goody Bradbury is gone, and no one knows how or where she is."

He seemed please to spread the news to someone who hadn't heard it yet. "Would've thought it an act of witchcraft, meself, but she took her servant with her, too."

"Servant?" I said, unable to contain myself.

"Aye, an 'ol Irish washer woman who shared her room in the jail."

Covering my wide smile with a kerchief, I jumped up and gestured toward the door.

"She be in a hurry to get over to the meetinghouse, eh?"

"Yes and no," Hezekiah said, trying to cover my sudden movement. "It's a woman thing."

My eyes widened. At least the good doctor left us alone, and I could go somewhere and scream in delight. Martha O'Brien had escaped.

Everywhere we went, we heard talk of the jailbreak. Some thought she'd paid the jailer off herself, which he adamantly denied. The greatest part was the family members who gathered at the jail demanding to know where she was—what a marvelous act to throw the authorities off. I imagined they had farms to take care of, crops to harvest, and the like, and so couldn't go into hiding with her. I also knew that Mary was well hidden and had escaped a probable death because of the bravery and courage of her family and friends.

Hezekiah took me aside. "She's safe Bess. You know that, right?" He studied my eyes. "So, now, we can take care of Charles's daughter."

161

I nodded and felt the word yes form on my lips. "No." It surprised me as much as it surprised him. Unsure of where that came from, I opened my mouth to find the rest of the words, but was interrupted by a noisy crowd pushing their way through.

"We caught the one—the Irish woman!"

My heart sunk. No! It couldn't be! Hezekiah and I worked our way through the crowd. Two men, boisterous in nature, thrust the old woman forward. I gasped. It was not Martha O'Brien. Relieved that we had failed, but anguished as well, I sobbed into Hezekiah's shoulder.

"Stay put," he said, and then when he saw the twisted look on my face, he added, "please."

I found a large rock under a shady tree and properly sat, fanning myself with Victoria's fan. I wondered what had gone wrong. I imagined all kinds of scenarios, but all of them ended the same.

Martha O'Brien was still incarcerated.

I wondered if I could see her. Hezekiah was nowhere to be seen, and the jail was right there, across the street. I could be in and out without ever being missed.

I approached the counter in the main entryway. O'Donovan, the jailer, had his back to me, and the ledger lay open on the counter. I scanned the list of prisoners, searching for Martha's name.

"Good day," I said politely, when he finally turned around. "I am sorry to bother you, but I, um, I wondered if I might take a look around. I am very curious."

He scowled. "No ma'am, this be a jail not a shop. Ye can't be a lookin' around at 'em like they were on display."

I sighed. "I suppose you're right, kind sir. I'm just terribly curious." I pulled out a hand of coins I'd had in my bag and placed them on the counter.

He looked at me suspiciously. What? Only men could do that? I controlled myself and said sweetly, "Why, for your kindness, sir. I don't want to infringe upon your time. I know how valuable it is."

O'Donovan grunted, pulled the coins across the counter into his empty hand, and then jerked his head toward the stone entryway leading to the cells. "Just a quick look. That'd be all—no more than a quick look."

"Of course." I curtsied, then rushed toward the entryway before he changed his mind.

The stone hallway was rank with feces and urine smells so strong I had to cover my mouth and nose with a handkerchief. Cold-hearted cruelty met my eyes. Four or five people were packed into each small cell with no food or water. Some were tethered to posts, and some walked freely in small circles within their filthy rooms. But search as I might, I didn't see Martha in any of the rooms.

Hurrying back to the front, I asked about her. "Did you not receive a woman named O'Brien?"

He scratched his nose. "Aye, I did." He tilted his head and stared at me. "Why do ye ask of her?"

No more lying. "She befriended me when I needed it most."

O'Donovan's eyes softened. "She be in the Boston jails, not here. We moved her there a week ago."

"Oh." I quickly left the jail and rushed back to my "stay put" spot. Tears ran down my face. How were we to get her out of the jail in Boston? I put my face in my hands and sobbed.

"What's wrong?"

I looked up to see Hezekiah's cousin, Zebulon and his wife, Sarah staring down at me.

"Oh, I just . . ." Pointing toward the jail, I dropped my hand to my side.

"You needn't say more," Zebulon said. "We are all concerned with the happenings in our small town."

"Good day," said Hezekiah joining us.

Zebulon chuckled. "Good day, Hezekiah."

Eeks. I guess he saw right through the disguise.

Sarah leaned forward. Apparently, she had not recognized him. "Hezekiah?"

"Yes, Sarah, my love," Zebulon said. "'Tis my long, lost cousin." Upon seeing both Sarah and my puzzled expressions, he continued. "I ran into him just moments ago, and though he tried to conceal his identity, his eyes belied him."

"Meaning?" I said, stepping beside Hezekiah.

"They twinkled with mirth upon meeting mine," he said with a grin.

Oh, yeah, I guess it would have been difficult for Hezekiah to not show affection to his cousin.

"You need not explain your disguises, Lady Elizabeth," he said grimly, "For we have heard about your unfortunate encounter with Betty Hubbard." He grimaced. "But pray tell, what names go ye by now?"

"Mathius," Hezekiah said, "and Felicity Alby."

"Oh? You are married?"

I blushed. "No!"

"Soon," Hezekiah said, at the same time. He paused at my abrupt answer, but then put his arm around my shoulder and pulled me closer. "Soon," he whispered in my ear, and I could think of nothing else, until he asked them about Martha O'Brien.

Yanked back to reality, I groaned. "What did you find out?"

Hezekiah looked at me, as if he suspected I already knew the answer to my own question. I imagined he'd be far less disappointed if I admitted it rather than covered it up. So, I blurted out. "Yes, I went inside the jail, and she's not there."

His eyes widened and his lips parted, apparently quite surprised with my confession.

"Um, I know you told me to stay put, but I, um, well . . ." I thrust my hands on my hips. "I'm not from around these parts, and where I'm from a woman can do pretty much what she pleases." Oops. Too much information there. I did notice that Sarah suppressed a smile, though—we would talk later.

Hezekiah sighed. "Yes, I guess I need to refrain from telling you what to do, but old habits are hard—" He stopped talking and stared at the jailer who had come to the door of the jail. "Excuse me, please," he said, "Stay . . ." he caught himself in midsentence and just waved me back.

Okay, I understood that. It was best for O'Donovan to not make any connections between the two of us as he had taken both of our money without any results.

We could hear their heated argument from where we stood. "That would be most unwise, Goodman Alby," O'Donovan said, between clenched teeth.

"As it would be for you, O'Donovan."

O'Donovan's beady eyes glanced from right to left. Finding no one but us near, he bellowed, "So be it!" and stormed back into the jail. Hezekiah followed him.

I gasped. "Oh, no." I lurched forward, but Zebulon grabbed my arm.

"Wait," he said calmly. "He knows what he's doing."

Within minutes, Hezekiah stepped out of the jail. In long strides, he made his way over to us. He held a parchment in his hands, and thrust it in our faces, the ink still wet.

Martha O'Brien
Boston Jail #5
Prisonkeeper: John Arnold

"Ready?" he asked, taking my elbow in his hand.

"We are going to Boston to pay Goodman Arnold off?" I asked.

"Yes."

My eyes narrowed. What was I not seeing? My near-perfect memory pulled up the ledger laying open on the counter in the jailhouse. "Stay put," I said to Hezekiah, with a slight grin. Before he could stop me, I took off toward the jail.

"Goodman O'Donovan." I approached him and boldly spoke. "I've just one question for you, and I have no more money to give." Keeping my eyes on him, I hoped to show the confidence I was struggling to find.

He seemed more curious than amused, though both expressions were on his face. "Aye?"

Good. An affirmation. I sighed. "Captain John Alden, kind sir," I began, "Is he not in the jails of Boston?"

He stared at me, but then went to his ledger. "Aye, he be there."

"Might I implore which cell?"

He smiled. "For ye, my Lady, anything." He ran his thumb down the page and then tapped it. "John Alden."

My heart raced—I knew Alden's story well.

O'Donovan turned the page and read the rest of the entry. "He be in the same cell for fifteen weeks now—number four." He looked up. "What business have ye with the likes of 'im?"

Not that it was any of his concern, and because there wasn't any truth in it, I replied with a sigh, "He owes my husband money."

O'Donovan nodded, and I left the jail. Outside, my accomplices waited. "Yep, she's in Boston all right."

Hezekiah looked annoyed, until I widened my eyes and gestured toward his cousin who was temporarily distracted.

Zebulon looked up. "We're going to have to go. Sarah needs to rest."

She did look a little piqued. "Is something wrong?"

Her countenance saddened, and she patted her flat tummy.

"Oh." Instantly, I remembered that she had been pregnant the last time I saw her. I threw my arms around her. "I'm so sorry."

"It is fine," she said, pulling away. I could tell she was trying to be brave. Her chin quivered. "There will be another."

"Come see us," Zebulon said.

"I might just take you up on that, Zebulon," I said. Noting Hezekiah's puzzled stare, I added. "Hezekiah needs to go to Boston, but I'd like to stay here a little longer."

"Oh, the trials," said Zebulon, already nudging Sarah forward.

"Yes. Oh, and I don't need any fussing over. In fact, don't even plan for me, I may not show up at all." I said that to free Sarah from thinking she had to cook or do anything for me.

After quick hugs, we watched them walk down the street. Hezekiah turned to me. "Okay, Bess, what did you *really* do?"

He knew me so well. "Do you remember reading about one of the accused, Captain John Alden?" I smirked. "I saw his name on the ledger."

His inquisitive look changed to surprise. He slapped his hand against his head. "Yes, of course." Grabbing my shoulders, he exclaimed, "He escaped from the jails in Boston. You're brilliant, Bess."

"Yep," I said, pleased with myself.

John Alden was accused by one of the circle girls who at first had identified another man's specter as her tormenter, but after promptings from an officer, she changed her story. The officer had pointed out Alden to her. She said she'd never actually seen Alden in the flesh, and had mistakenly accused the wrong man.

How different would his specter be from his actual body? If that were true, then how had any of the specters been identified with their mortal counterparts?

My vivid imagination conjured up specters showing spiritual passports to cross over from their underworld to ours, and I sneered. Please. Really?

Hezekiah dropped his hands. "But, why stay here, Bess?"

He had to ask? I glanced toward the courthouse.

"Oh, I see." He seemed to struggle with the next words, I could tell by the anxiety etched into his green eyes. "Please change your mind. I would feel better if you were by my side."

"Yes, I would too," I admitted. "But, you can do what you have to do without me. And you'd have to come back this way anyway. I really want to see this through."

Morbid, huh? I was no better than any of the thronging spectators, hungry for a good show. Stop it, Bess. This is way too personal for both them and you. Most everyone was there to support not condemn, all too afraid to voice their opinions.

While my mind was on Salem, Hezekiah's was somewhere else. His eyes bore into my soul. He grasped my face, which shocked and delighted me, and then he pulled my lips to his with such tenderness that I felt weak in his arms, and would have collapsed, if not for his firm hold.

He pulled away and stared at me. There were no words. I mean, seriously, no words were spoken by either one of us. He just gave me his infamous grin and walked away.

Now I had no desire to stay and only wanted to be with him, but with the remaining trials looming between us, my legs would not move.

That incredible kiss was just the beginning of our love, right? There would be many more. My insecurities flared. What if this was the last time we were together? Ugh. I have to stop thinking like that. Throw something else out to the universe.

"I love you!" I called after him, but he was already too far away, mingled in with the gathering crowd.

I looked down at the small bag he had pressed into my hand during that kiss, grateful that he had thought to replenish my coins.

Eighteen
Indignation

I slipped into the crowd entering the building. Inside, I made my way to a spot where I could sit behind a broad shouldered man, concealed from the circle girls, who were now entering the meetinghouse from the front.

Once the girls were seated, the accused ones stumbled through the door, herded in like cattle at an auction. All nine were tethered together with one long rope looped through their individual restraints. One of the jailers untied the rope and pulled it through the restraints, which were left tied around their wrists.

I overheard a man beside me listing the accused's names. "Ann Foster, and beside her is Mary Lacey Senior, and then Wilmot Redd, and Samuel Wardwell," he paused, while probably considering the next person's name. "Mary Parker, then Margaret Scott, Rebecca Eames, Abigail Faulkner, and the last one is, Abigail Hobbs."

I leaned forward to get a better look at Margaret Scott, as the man added, "Goody Scott is seventy-seven years old, and she ought to be allowed to sit."

I agreed. It was cruel how they were made to stand.

The judges now entered. Everyone around me stood. Not to draw any attention, I stood, too, while the judges took their places. One of the magistrates gestured for us to sit. Reverend Noyes came forward and said a prayer, and then the judge spoke.

"We have nine cases to hear. I expect the truth each one of them," Hathorne said sternly. "Goody Scott, we will begin with you, and then you will be removed from the court so you can sit."

Finally, some compassion.

"In the jail."

So much for compassion.

Hathorne held a paper out for Reverend Parris to read.

"Margaret Scott, you are brought before authority upon high suspicion of sundry acts of witchcraft."

Hathorne swept his hand through the air in a small circle as if prompting Parris to add more.

"We, um, expect to hear the truth from you." Parris glanced over at Hathorne, who gestured for him to continue. "What say ye to these charges against you?"

"I am innocent of witchcraft."

"We have here," Parris glanced at the pages Hathorne had given him, "a complaint from Daniel Wycomb." Looking out over the audience, he pointed at a man who stood up in the front.

"I am Daniel Wycomb." The man approached the judge.

Hathorne studied him. "What does thou testifieth?"

Wycomb scratched his head. "It was 'bout five years ago. Goody Scott came by to glean my field. But seeing I hadn't got to harvest yet, I told her to wait until I got the corn in first."

"Understandable. It is the right of the poor to glean another's crops once they've been harvested. Go on," Hathorne said.

"She seemed a bit put out, and she snapped, 'You will not get your corn in tonight.'"

My eyes narrowed. I would've said something like that too, if I felt my need was more urgent than his—kind of like, 'even you have no intentions to harvest tonight, let me get a few ears, and I'll be off.'"

"Well, I told her I would get it harvested right away. I insisted I would."

"And?"

"She wouldn't leave, until my frightened wife gave her some corn." He shifted his weight and continued, "I went right out to harvest the field. Filled up my cart, too. But something spooked those oxen. They would not pull the cart forward, but only backward, or any direction 'cept the right one!"

Okay, that did sound a little freaky.

"I left it right there, I did, all night long, and in the morning, the oxen were just fine."

Hathorne leaned over to Corwin and whispered a few words at which Corwin gave a nod. He turned back to Wycomb. "And your daughter, Frances, how is she?"

Wycomb shuddered. "That is the worst part." He pointed at the aged woman. "Goody Scott's specter hurt her badly—pinching, and poking, and biting!"

Apparently Goody Scott's specter was much stronger than her frail, seventy-seven-year old body. Even now, she quivered with physical weakness.

Hathorne nodded and scratched something down with his quill. "Thank you, Goodman Wycomb." He gestured to Parris to call the next witness.

"Thomas Nelson." He waited until Nelson stood before the judge. "What does thou testifieth?"

"Goody Scott came a lookin' for some firewood."

"From you?"

"I owed her ten shillings."

I calculated the amount to be about $1.20. I think.

"I offered her ten shillings worth of wood to clear my debt, but she wouldn't accept it. Wanted more, she did!" He scowled. "And wouldn't you know, right after that, two of my cows died, one rearin' on her hind legs right before she dropped dead? And the other found dead with her head stuck under a plank."

Ew. Thanks a lot for that visual.

Goodman Nelson continued, "And then there was Robert Shillito." He paused and bowed his head. Looking up, he continued, "Afore he passed on, he told me and my wife many times how Goody Scott's specter hurt him. He declared to his last breath, that as long as she lived, he would never be well."

Hathorne spoke quietly to Corwin, and then gestured to the jailer to take Goody Scott away.

The proceedings continued with Ann Foster and then Mary Lacey Senior. It was all pretty much the same with little variation. I sat patiently through Rebecca Eames, Abigail Faulkner and then Abigail Hobbs. As I knew they would be fine—yeah, right, if sitting in a jail for months after the hangings ended was fine—I was more focused on the last three to be tried, Mary Parker, Wilmot Redd, and Samuel Wardwell.

"Goody Parker," Parris said, gesturing for her to come forward. No sooner had her name been read, then three of the girls fell writhing to the floor.

Mary Parker looked to be in her early sixties, a plump, and otherwise lovely lady. I imagined she had lots of friends. She had such a pleasant demeanor about her. With the girls comatose on the floor, her gentle countenance seemed clearly shaken. Hands to her mouth, great tears rolled down her face.

"Poor Mary," a woman whispered beside me.

"Poor indeed," the man next to her scoffed. "Her late husband left her well provided for."

She jabbed him with her elbow. "That's not what I meant, Samuel."

Several minutes passed, while the girls lay as if dead. Finally, the judge gave Mary an order. "Touch them."

I inwardly groaned. The "touch test" was pure witchcraft. Using witchcraft to prove witchcraft was like trying to prove you weren't a witch by plunging you underwater to see if you would sink or float. Floating was bad. It meant you were a witch. Sinking was, well, death to a mortal, but at least you died innocent of witchcraft. Yep. Lame.

In the touch test, the afflicted miraculously recovered if the supposed witch touched them. Sort of moronic when you think about it. A witch that could heal just by touch seemed more saintly than evil.

I remembered reading about a pair of girls in England in 1662 whose fists were clenched so tight that not even a strong man could pry them apart. The authorities were convinced that two elderly women were witches, had them touch the girls, and then the girls' fingers opened easily. But when they blindfolded the girls, and they were touched

175

by other members of the court, they unclenched their fists anyway. Aha! Caught deceiving, one would think, but they hanged the two elderly women anyway.

If they truly believed in the touch test, then perhaps they should have examined the lives of the members of the court who revived the girls. Right? It's called a witch hunt for a reason—a cruel, bloodthirsty reason.

Still, it was amazing to see the girls spring up at her touch, though it startled Mary, a reaction a true witch would not have had. A true witch would have not only dreaded the results, but expected it.

Parris said, "Goody Parker, you are brought before authority upon high suspicion of sundry acts of witchcraft." He paused while the girls returned to their seats. "Please, tell us the truth in this matter."

"I am not in the devil's snare."

One of the circle girls screamed, "She hurts me! She hurts me!"

"Bring the girl forward," Hathorne demanded. "State your name."

"Martha Sprague," the young girl said, shielding her face from Mary's.

"I did nothing to hurt this child," Mary stammered.

Martha kept her hands in front of her face. "She hurts me! She hurts me!"

With a sigh, Mary looked directly at Hathorne. "I am not the only Mary Parker. There is another who shares my name."

The woman beside me gasped. "She would incriminate her own sister-in-law to protect herself?"

That was a little weird, and I decided that maybe Mary Parker wasn't so sweet after all.

Mary glanced at the girl, who had uncovered her eyes, just as Martha stole a look her way. She screamed and fell to the floor, followed by three or four of the other girls. The room was in a frenzy, as terrifying screams hung in the air, like the soulless bodies of the hanged crying out for revenge.

I covered my ears.

The screaming stopped, leaving the room silent and eerie. The hairs on the back on my neck pricked. A new and horrifying scene took its place. One of the circle girls, Mary Warren, convulsed, a tidal wave of blood gushing from her wide-gaped mouth, like in the exorcist, only red.

I felt faint, and I had no one to hold onto. I looked down to see the woman beside me clutching my hand tight. Grateful, I clutched back. One of the guards ran up to Mary Warren, thrusting a sheet to her mouth. "She is stuck!" he cried out, pulling a pin from her hand.

The judges jumped from their seats, while guards dragged a resistant Goody Parker over to Mary Warren.

"Touch her at once!"

Goody Parker fought it, and who wouldn't? Mary Warren was quite a spectacle—a bloody mess. I wouldn't want to get near her either. They yanked Parker's hand out and brushed her fingers against Warren, and upon Goody Parker's touch, the bleeding stopped at once.

Mary Warren heaved and then coughed out blood that had settled in her throat. "It is she. She is the Mary Parker who tormented me!" She gasped and pointed up to the ceiling with a bloody finger. "There! Perched on a beam! Do you not see her specter?"

I found myself ducking and looking up at the ceiling. Stop it, Bess! This was the same nonsense said at my grandmother's trial. Seriously, how could Mary Parker's spirit leave her body and perch itself on a beam without her empty body collapsing on the spot? Still, I had to wonder if she truly did see *something* up there.

Mary Parker sobbed. "I have nothing to do with witchcraft. I am innocent."

Judge Hathorne waved her away, and she went to stand with the others. Her sobbing could be heard for minutes after, but the trial proceeded nonetheless.

Things had calmed down, and I patted my new friend's hand. "Thank you," I whispered, and pulled my hand away. She gave me an understanding nod.

"Wilmot Redd," Parris said. He pointed at her and then at the small platform by the judge.

"The town witch," my new friend said.

I couldn't get mad at her. After all, she had just given a complete stranger much needed comfort. Anyhow, I had already heard the rumors about Wilmot months ago. She healed with herbs and ointments. Strange that even in the future, using natural remedies to cure aliments was mocked and looked down upon by the so-called learned.

Wiping a sudden string of tears, I stared at Wilmot with sadness. I would never forget her kindness months ago, when I lay in a sickbed at the Hanson mansion. Apparently, the circle girls must have tired. Not a scream nor a fit ensued at the onset at least, but when Wilmot made it to the platform, they began anew.

"She bites!"

"She pinches!"

After the fervor died down, Judge Hathorne rose. "Are there any among you who testifieth against Goody Redd?"

With some reluctance, three women who had been sitting together in the same row, stood up and approached Hathorne. None of them would look at Wilmot though, and I understood why, when my friend explained that they were Wilmot's neighbors.

"They ought to be ashamed," she added.

I agreed.

One of the women spoke. "Five years ago," she began, "a neighbor had a quarrel with Goody Redd."

"Over missing linens," piped in another of the women. "Charity Pitman says, that Mrs. Syms says—"

"That's me," said the third woman, slightly raising her hand. "I'm Charity Pitman."

It was getting hard to follow who was who, and I could tell by the expressions on the judges' faces that they were having difficulty, too.

"You're Mrs. Syms?" Corwin asked, jabbing a finger her way.

"No, I'm Charity Pitman," she repeated. "Mrs. Syms said that she was sure that Goody Redd's maid, Martha Laurence, had stolen them."

I bit my lip. She said—she said, but the actual person that said it wasn't here to testify. That's called hearsay, right? Great proof in a court of law.

Charity continued, "Well, when Mrs. Syms threatened to tell Justice Hathorne," she paused and smiled sweetly at him.

I felt like gagging.

"Anyhow, when she threatened to tell him, Wilmot cursed her. She said, if you do, you will never mingere nor carcare again." She coughed and covered her grin.

Sporadic laughter rippled throughout the room, but I didn't get it. My friend leaned in. "Use the outhouse," she whispered.

"Well, she came down with distemper of the dry belly-ache, and she couldn't go for months." Charity nodded at the chuckling audience and then returned Hathorne's grin.

I didn't find it funny at all. It didn't make any sense that Wilmot's curse could come to pass. It must have been a coincidence. I glanced from Charity to Wilmot and then to the judge's grim face. It didn't look good for Wilmot.

The smile slipped off Charity's face. "But her words condemn her the most. I heard she wished a "bloody cleaver" be found in the cradles of other people's children." A sob caught in her throat, and she drew her hands to her chest. "I saw the cleaver hang over my child before it sickened."

Weird. Charity acted like she'd really seen it, and maybe she did. It didn't seem like something *anyone* would ever make up about another neighbor.

Someone called out from the crowd. "And don't forget that our milk turned like snarly blue wool."

"Perfectly good milk," Charity added, a quick frown Wilmot's way.

180

Um, yeah, well, moldy milk can turn to blue cheese, right? No witchcraft there.

Hathorne grunted. With a wave of his hand, the jailer removed Wilmot from the small platform, and then led the last of the accused, Samuel Wardwell, to the front.

I was a little more informed about Wardwell, having written a paper on the men accused as witches in high school. He was well known for his panache for fortune telling. In fact, a lot of what he foretold happened. I couldn't explain that, other than super-lucky guesses.

Hathorne leaned into Corwin and whispered a few words, at which Corwin excused himself, and left the room. The judge cleared his throat. "Goodman Wardwell. You have already confessed before the court. Repeat your confession, please."

"Repeat it? But I renounced it."

As if expecting Wardwell's reaction, Hathorne thrust a paper toward Parris. "Perhaps this will bring it back to memory."

Taking the paper in hand, Parris read, "I am but a carpenter and a farmer. Owing to the amount of work before me, I bid the devil take stray beasts that trampled my fields."

I remembered that Wardwell had originally claimed that he'd seen ghostly cats, and the form of a man, presumably the devil. This man had called himself the Prince of Air, and he promised Wardwell that he would live comfortably and be the captain of the militia if he honored and served him. Wardwell said he had signed the devil's book with a black square. Wardwell had good reason to want to go retract his words—this was really freaky stuff.

Parris continued reading. "I agreed to covenant with him until the age of sixty." Parris looked up at him again. "You are the age of forty-nine?"

Wardwell struggled with speaking, then blurted out. "I do not claim my words."

"You do not claim your own words?" Hathorne scoffed. He gestured for Parris to continue.

Parris read, "About a week later, the man reappeared with the same words and promises that he had not yet fulfilled."

Hathorne nodded. "Nor does he ever."

"Please," Wardwell cried. "What I said before, I now renounce."

"Of course you do." Hathorne sneered. "Thomas Chandler, where are you?" He looked out over the audience. "Ah, there you are. Come forward. Tell us what thou knoweth to be true."

Chandler stood before the judge. "Goodman Wardwell was much addicted to fortune telling, and made quite a sport of it." Glancing around, he seemed to gain confidence from the nods coming from some of the people in the courtroom.

"Last winter," Chandler continued, "Wardwell told John Farnum that he would take a nasty fall from his horse. He predicted that the girl he hoped to marry would say no, and that he would take a trip south."

Those things were highly suggestive and Farnum could've caused them because he was expecting them to happen.

"Wardwell said that John would get shot—have himself a terrifying bullet wound, which he did. They all happened—the girl, the fall, the trip south, and the bullet wound—just like he said they would."

Eeks. The bullet wound was harder to explain. No one would step in front of a bullet on purpose.

"Yup," said a man standing two rows back. "I'm James Bridges, and that man," he pointed to Wardwell, "told me things about myself I'd never revealed to anyone in my life. I wondered how he could tell so true." He sat back down.

Hathorne glanced out over the crowd of spectators. "Are there more who testifieth against Goodman Wardwell?"

"Aye," said a man with a short, white beard. He sauntered down to the front and stood before the judge. "Good day, Judge."

"Good day, Constable Foster."

"My sister-in-law, Dorothy Eames is sure Wardwell be a witch—knowing the future as good as he does." His eyes widened. "Wardwell told my wife she'd have five daughters before she had a son." He nodded and looked out over the crowd. "I thought my son would never come."

The audience laughed, while Foster scratched his head. "But sure enough, he did, right after our five daughters." Foster pointed at Wardwell. "He'd take a look at a person's hand like this." Foster held his palm out for the court to see. "And then he'd cast his eyes to the floor before givin' his prediction." Foster stepped sideways then returned to his seat.

Corwin returned with Giles Corey. He brought the old man to the platform in a third attempt to get him to confess or deny. Not a sound was made, making Corey's silent defiance all the more surreal.

A man stood up in the front. I had no idea who he was and looked sideways at my friend for help.

"He's a good friend of the Coreys—Captain Gardner," she whispered.

Captain Gardner didn't go to the judge, but went straight to Giles. "Please say something, Giles. Think of your family. Your friends." He grunted softly. "For two days, I have pled with you." He sighed. "Not speaking is near same as denying, Giles."

Giles looked at him for the first time, but his lips remained pressed tight.

"Giles," Gardner sobbed. "Please, dear friend." He stared at him for a few moments. I could almost hear the inward pleadings of those in the room, who like me, hoped for his deliverance.

Hathorne cleared his throat. Gardner looked over at him and then back at Giles. He grasped Giles's hand and shook it, like he was just saying goodbye for the moment, and then turned away. He didn't go back to his seat, but walked up the aisle, and out the door.

Hathorne took control. In a loud voice he said, "Giles Corey, by standing mute, the court has no other recourse but to call upon English law. Under the new charter, I now condemn you to piene forte et dure!" He slapped his hand down on the bench. "May God have mercy on your soul!"

It was quiet while Hathorne wrote a few things on the parchment in front of him, blotting the ink as he went. Upon finishing, he waved his hand over it probably to dry the ink and then handed it to Corwin.

Judge Corwin looked down at the paper and sighed. "The Court of Oyer and Terminer finds Ann Foster, Mary Lacy Junior, Wilmot Redd, Samuel Wardwell, Margaret Scott, Rebecca Eames, Mary Parker, Abigail Faulkner, and Abigail Hobs to be guilty of sundry acts of witchcraft. You are sentenced to death by hanging."

No one screamed, but many eyes were wet. The crowd stood to leave. The circle girls seemed as unaffected by it as if we were just leaving a Sabbath day service. They chatted and laughed merrily, no doubt happy to have the rest of the day to do whatever they wished.

But my eyes followed the accused, now being led out of the room and down the road to the jail. For five of them, it would be the last time they walked down a street in Salem Town.

Nineteen
The Journey

Miranda and Liza wove their way through the thick underbrush. In no time, they were at the carriage and climbed aboard. Miranda's angry face and tight grip on the reins startled Liza, and yet, she felt a similar anger of her own. If all were true, her mother had kept her away from her father—a father she'd thought dead for almost all of her life. *No. My mother would never do that. The strangers are the liars, especially that girl dressed like an old woman.* She wondered why Miranda would ever believe strangers over her own sister.

Liza kept glancing backward at the dusty road behind them, fearful that her mother's carriage would pummel the road after them.

Her mother had a unique way of punishing others that Liza had witnessed on more than one occasion. Should you make a mistake in any way unacceptable to her, she would not speak to you, or even look at you, for days. Running off with Miranda would make that condemnation much more severe than just a few days of cruel silence.

Still, she had to find out the truth, and then she would face her mother. "My father is alive?" she mumbled. Even though the noise from the road muffled her words, Miranda must have heard them.

"Yes, I believe so," Miranda said, keeping her eyes on the rough road. She said a few words under her breath and then slammed her hand down on her lap.

Liza's eyes widened. She pressed her fingers to her forehead and then squeezed her eyes shut. "You know this to be true, because why? You have seen my father?"

"No." Tears streamed down Miranda's face.

"What?" Liza gasped. "You haven't seen him, and yet we are embarking on a journey that will certainly divide our family." It wasn't too late to turn back. She quickly looked behind them again.

Miranda slowed the horses down to a trot. She turned to Liza. "After you and Elizabeth left, I had the occasion to speak privately with them."

Liza wondered what lies had led them to this. "I am not sure they are to be trusted, Miranda. The woman was at the trials." She wrung her hands on her lap. "She disguised herself as an old woman."

"Really?" Miranda looked over at her and then back at the road. "How strange. I wonder why?"

The woman was one of the two strangers her aunt had based everything on—a woman who dressed in a clandestine manner for no other reason than to trick people, she was sure. "I don't know why she changed her appearance, Miranda, but it was very peculiar. She frightened me when she told me she had met me at our home. I knew right away that it was true. I could tell it was the same woman who'd been at our house earlier. Her voice, her eyes . . . a convincing masquerade." She shivered. "She wanted to talk to me about my father."

Miranda wiped at her face, wet with tears. "Yes." She sniffled.

Liza threw her arms up in the air. "How can you believe an undeniably deceitful person and a complete stranger?" She shook her head and folded her arms across her chest.

Miranda pulled off to the side of the road. The early morning sun filtered through the tree-lined road. Not another person was in sight. Miranda's chest rose and then fell. "I did not believe her at first." She rearranged the reins on her lap. "But she insisted she had just been with him."

"You cannot believe everything you hear." Liza repeated words she had heard her mother say many times and groaned.

"Yes, I know that." Miranda fumbled with something in her handbag and pulled out a portrait miniature. "Until she gave me this."

Liza took the small portrait from her. She was stunned. "This is me. Is it the same as the larger one at our house?"

"Yes, Elizabeth had it made. You were ten years old in that portrait."

Though the larger version of it hung in their dining room, Liza had never seen the miniature. "Why haven't I seen it before?"

Miranda shook her head. "That is the mystery, my dear child. I only saw it once myself. On the day that is was delivered, it disappeared. Elizabeth," her face soured, "thought it had been bewitched."

Why did it always come back to that? Obviously, it was not bewitched. "How did the woman acquire it?"

"She said she found it on the floor."

"What floor? Where?"

Miranda clenched the reins tightly. "She said she had found it a few days ago, at the feet of Charles's sickbed." A sob caught in her throat.

Liza didn't know what to say. If it were true, she'd just get her father back to find him in a sickbed? "How sick is he?"

Miranda's wild eyes frightened Liza. "I don't know! Ahh!" Her long wail filled the empty woods.

This was too much. Her aunt was insane. Liza fought the urge to flee, but to where? They were in the middle of nowhere.

"I'm sorry, child. I'm sorry." Wiping her hand across her face, she dried the tears. "I'm a bit out of sorts," she said, brushing a finger against her nose. "It will take me some time, but I will be fine."

Liza swallowed. At least her aunt was admitting to her strange behavior. She turned the portrait miniature around in her trembling fingers. If he was alive, the deceit was devastating. She hesitated to speak of him, but she had so many questions. She stole a glance at Miranda who stared ahead at the road, her breaths becoming steadier, and her demeanor returning to normal.

"How far away is he?" Liza asked.

"They told me far."

Liza's breath stopped. "How far?

"I don't know how far, child, but we shall find out." Miranda picked up the reins. "Ya!" she called, pulling the horses into a gallop.

The long trip from Maine to Massachusetts Bay would take the better part of the day—farther away than that seemed impossible to imagine. She shuddered and wondered if this was really the best idea. If all of this were true, why couldn't her father just come to them? *Oh, yes, he's in a sickbed.* She sighed and settled back into the hard seat as best she could.

It was late into the night when they arrived at the inn in Salem Town. A weary Liza looked up at the boxes tied to the carriage. "Are we leaving them out here?"

"Oh, no my child. My whole life is in those boxes." Miranda unloosened one of the ties. "We'll take the lighter ones and have someone inside help with the rest."

"How long shall we stay here?" Liza hefted a box on her hip.

"That depends on how long it takes to find Hezekiah and that strange woman."

"Hezekiah? Oh, yes, that was his name. Hezekiah Hanson." Liza felt vindicated that Miranda saw the woman as strange, too. Maybe there was some hope in convincing her to turn back and find out the truth another way. She followed her aunt into the inn and up to their rooms on the second story.

The rooms were nice—two large bedchambers and a front room. Liza was too tired to explore more and took the bed her aunt did not. She hadn't questioned Miranda when she gave the innkeeper fictitious names, nor when she asked him to secure the carriage in a barn rather than out in the open.

Miranda was obviously worried that her sister would follow them to Salem Village. Liza hoped she would come after them. It would be a lot faster to come to the truth that way. She crawled into bed and within minutes was fast asleep.

A loud pounding startled Liza, and she sat upright. Crawling out of bed, she rushed to the window. Using a mallet, a man hammered a notice on one of the posts then moved down the road to the next.

Glancing around the bedchambers, Liza did not see her aunt anywhere. Though Miranda's bed was already made, it could not have been very late. The sun was just cresting the horizon. The door opened and her aunt rushed in, clearly flustered. She waved a paper in her hand.

Liza took it from her and read, "Notice of forthcoming peine forte et dure . . ." She gasped. "What is this?" Her eyes searched the document. "Hear ye, Hear ye, Salem Village, on the day following, Giles Corey will be publicly executed by strong and harsh punishment, pressed to death for standing mute."

Liza's mouth fell open. "This is barbaric!"

Miranda stood as if in shock. "I thought we had left this kind of torture behind us in England."

Liza rushed back to the window. She had a good view of the jail and the empty field beside it where a few men laid some planks on the ground and tied them together.

Miranda joined her beside the window. "They are building the platform for him."

"What can we do?" Liza was frantic. "There has to be something we can do." She grabbed Miranda by the arms. "Come on, we have got to stop them!"

Miranda would not let her pass. "Stop them from what? Building a platform? Hanging the notices?"

"I do not know, but something."

"Be reasonable, child. What can we do?"

Liza's chest heaved. She broke into sobs and fell into her aunt's embrace. "Nothing?"

Miranda's words were laced with sorrow. "I do not believe so, child."

What could they do in a town encroached with superstition and fear? To change the minds of the many, when only a few had the fortitude to oppose the horrific happenings of Salem, seemed a daunting task. But she was not going to sit idly by. How could she live with herself, if she did not at least try?

A loud knock on the door startled them. Miranda put her finger to her lips.

"Lady Nash?" the innkeeper called through the closed door, using the fictitious name Miranda had given him.

She opened the door part way.

"A woman come lookin' for someone ye age, and the age of the wane," he said, pointing toward Liza. "I told 'er no one come to the inn by that description. Just thought ye ought to know."

"Oh, my," Miranda said, reaching into her pocket. She dropped a coin into his hand. "Thank you."

"I can see why ye hide from the likes of 'er. Not a pleasant one." He shook his head and turned the coin over in his hand. Then he gave it back. "No need to pay me, m'lady."

"Then, might you bring us up something to eat and drink?" She removed a few more coins from her pocket and handed them to the innkeeper. "Thank you," she said, after he took the coins and turned away. She closed the door. "What are we going to do?"

Liza tried not to show relief that her mother was somewhere in town looking for them. *If I can just get the two to sit down together. Mother will forgive her once she hears of the strangers' deceit.* She thought if Miranda knew her true intentions, she'd never let her go outside on her own. She came up with a plan. "She will be looking for two women. We cannot travel outside together. Whoever goes out, has to stay two steps ahead of her."

Miranda rolled her eyes. "It won't be you, Liza."

It was insane that Miranda had placed all her belief on complete strangers. Liza circled the room, bringing the conversation back to the person who had caused all the trouble. "We don't even know if that strange woman is still here." She glanced out the window.

"Strange or not, she is the key to unraveling this mystery."

Liza looked down at the street. A few people strolled from one side to the other and an occasional carriage bounced down the dirt road, but other than that, it was quiet. The small town was still waking up for the day.

Miranda joined her at the window. Situated on a triangular corner lot, the unique position of the inn gave them a wide view of the town from different angles. "The best we can do, until we come up with a better plan, is to watch from here," Miranda said. "It is a perfect spot. This inn is central to Salem Village and diagonal to the jail. Perhaps we will be fortunate enough to see Hezekiah and his friend walk by."

"Or my mother," Liza mumbled.

"I have some knitting," Miranda said, untying one of the boxes. "That will keep us occupied."

Liza frowned. She took the knitting and pulled a wooden chair to the window that faced the jail. In no time, she was lost in her thoughts, wondering if her father was really alive, what he was like. She had no memory of speaking to Miranda about her brother. The subject had been nipped in the bud, whenever she tried to talk about him. Over the years, she stopped asking.

If my father has been alive all this time without contacting me, then, what kind of a person is he? She wasn't sure she wanted to meet him. Her mother probably had a good reason to avoid talking about him altogether. She should've spoken to her mother first, before taking off with her aunt. Putting her elbows on the window sill, she stared outside at the people passing by.

"He must be a horrible man," she said aloud, though she had meant it just for her own ears.

"Charles?" Miranda said, looking shocked. "Not at all."

Liza glanced at the floor. "Then why hasn't he come to see me? What kind of a father lets his sisters raise his daughter and never comes by to check on her?" Her voice escalated in pitch and fervor. "What kind, Miranda?" She pressed her lips tight, fighting back tears. "A villainous scoundrel."

Miranda laid her knitting down. Her face hardened. "Do not talk of him like that."

Liza gave her aunt a quizzical look. Miranda was being unrealistic. If the man was alive, he had to be simply wretched. "What was my father like growing up?"

Miranda's lips pressed together tight. It was obvious she was still offended by Liza's harsh appraisal.

Liza let out a quick breath. "I'm sorry, but how would you feel if you found out that your father had never come see you?"

Miranda dangled the portrait miniature in front of Liza. "He must have come at least once."

"You never saw him." Liza's eyes narrowed. "Are you implying that Mother gave that to him and sent him on his way?"

"Yes." Scowling, Miranda balled her fists up to her sides. "It sounds just like something she would do."

Confused, Liza frowned. Her mind was in a whirl. Miranda seemed so convincing, and her mother did have a sour disposition at times, but would she do something so hateful? So altogether wrong?

Miranda's demeanor softened. "In answer to your question about his deportment, Charles was quiet, hardworking, and honest."

That did not sound like the qualities of a scoundrel. Liza had no memory of him. She was an infant when he died.

"You remind me of him," Miranda said. Tears welled up in her eyes. "Your passion for what is right." She tapped the notice. "He would have felt the same." She cleared her throat. "That is why I am convinced he would not have stayed away, not a day."

"But he did."

"Yes, he did," Miranda said, with a long sigh. "I must admit, that does trouble me."

Finally. It was the first time Miranda conceded that Charles might have been wrong.

"But let us wait and hear from him first before we pass judgment."

Though it would be difficult to do, it seemed fair. Liza nodded. She would try not to judge him until she had the whole truth. Standing, she took her aunt's hands. "I had wanted to go out on my own, but I think we should both walk about looking for Hezekiah and his friend." Miranda started to object, but Liza forged ahead. "If we run into Mother, then we will stand firm in our resolve to find my father. She can either join us, or step aside and get out of our way."

Miranda studied her face. "I have never heard you speak this way."

"I do not mean to be disrespectful, but I am tired of hiding when time is so precious." She looked down at the notice.

"That is true." Miranda said. "After you eat and dress, we shall look around Salem Village for those unusual visitors."

"Agreed." She threw her arms around Miranda, relieved that her aunt's craziness had seemed to lessen from the prior night, and most eager to get out of the inn and continue on with their journey.

Twenty
Awakening

In the deep recesses of my mind, a pounding started, faint at first, and then it grew to a voluminous distortion. It jarred me awake, and I sat upright. "What?" I glanced around, not recognizing my surroundings at first. "Oh, oh yeah," I said, with a yawn. "This is Zebulon and Sarah's house." After yesterday's trials, and with the circle girls triumphantly stalking the streets, I had come straight over here seeking refuge.

The pounding continued. I gathered a robe around me and hurried out of the bedchamber. Sarah stood by a front window looking out.

"What's going on?" I asked her.

She looked at me oddly. "We do not know. Zebulon has gone to read the placard." Gesturing for me to sit, she sat on the bench by the window. "Pray tell about your gray hair. Zebulon mentioned the witch accusation."

"Yes," I said, running my fingers through my disheveled hair. I had taken the stage makeup off the night before, and I must have looked a mess. I knew the truth was in order, well, not *all* the truth. "I'm trying to not be seen by the circle girls, and others, who think me a witch."

She nodded. "Tis an elaborate disguise, Elizabeth." She smiled. "But a good one. I had to look twice before I recognized you."

"I am relieved that it has worked so far." And scared to death that my luck will run out.

"You are safe here, but just in case," she said, studying my hair. "May I?" Sarah picked up a brush and the hair pins I had taken out the night before.

"Yes, please do."

Her touch was gentler than Gabriella's. I hardly felt the knots being worked out, as she brushed through the tangles, and then styled it on top of my head. She held a small piece of flattened copper in her hand. Though intended as reflective, my image in it was quite blurry and hard to make out, but my hair, I'm sure was adequate. I thanked her and then excused myself.

I went into the bedchamber and got back into yesterday's clothes, and then as carefully as I could, I reapplied the makeup. Of course, I cheated a bit and used a tiny mirror from the future that I had hidden in the bag. Returning to the front room, I joined Sarah in the kitchen. She still seemed a bit tired. The door opened, and Zebulon rushed in, his face perplexed and worried.

"What is wrong?" Sarah asked.

"They've gone and done it," Zebulon said gravely. He placed a folded paper on the table and spread it out.

Bess read quickly through the announcement.

Notice of forthcoming peine forte et dure.
Hear ye, Hear ye, Salem Village,
On the day following,
Giles Corey will be publicly executed by
strong and harsh punishment,
pressed to death for standing mute.

"What?" I jumped up, the blood rushing to my head. I could hardly believe it. Yes, I had known it would happen, but it stung just the same. They really were going to press Giles Corey, an eighty-one-year old man to death! I read it again. Tomorrow!

"What does this mean, Zebulon?" Sarah's soft voice broke the silence.

Zebulon took her hands in his. "It means we are going to pack a few things and go away for a while."

"Why?" she asked, with a blank expression of shock.

"If the powers that be in this town can do this, then we are all in danger. We will go away until this madness ends."

I wanted to tell them that it would soon be over, but I'd really sound like a witch then, especially when after a few weeks they realized I was right. Anyway, going away might be good for Sarah's frail constitution right now. She needed to rest, not agonize over her faltering community.

"We'll be taking the horses, but you are welcome to stay here, Elizabeth," Zebulon offered. He led his wife to their room where they promptly packed a couple of bags. As they left, he leaned toward me. "If I were you, I wouldn't leave the house until Hezekiah returns."

I nodded and closed the door behind them. All alone, I paced the room. There wouldn't be any more trials, at least not recorded in the annuls of time, and with the peine forte et dure tomorrow, the hangings would happen only two days later, one day after Giles's pressing to death finally ends, after two days of inhumane torture.

Each time I walked past the notice, I shivered. Finally, I picked it up to throw in the fire on the hearth. I held it over the flames. It was singularly the most horrid of papers I'd ever held in my hands, and yet a significant, historical artifact, too. I refolded it and slipped it into my pocket.

I knew I should listen to Zebulon's warning, but I couldn't sit around all day. I opened the front door and peeked outside. Pulling my shawl tighter around my shoulders, I walked swiftly toward the main street. The courthouse had a few people milling around, probably in shock from the peine forte et dure announcement. I slowed my pace down and searched each face and then went into the shop across the street.

Strolling through the shop, I admired things that were both pretty and practical for that era. Keeping in mind that I couldn't take much back to the future with me, and not quite acclimated to spending someone else's money, I settled on small gifts for Hezekiah's mother and my hopefully, future sister-in-law. I grinned when I thought about what they had done—married to just get it over with and start their lives. I found that very romantic. I didn't forget Gabriella either and found a lovely brooch for her. I left the shop carrying a small bag.

This was a new thing for me, almost enjoying shopping, but deep down, I knew it was just a diversion. I wondered if it was a common distraction, a way to set aside for a brief moment, the challenges that beset you. I realized I was taking a risk being out and about, but with nothing to do but wait, maybe I could do a little more looking around.

"Lady Alby!" a voice called nearby. Surely, that wasn't me. I turned to see Dr. Crosby, and a woman, coming toward me.

"How lovely to see you again," he said, and then turning to the woman, he said, "This is Mathius Alby's wife, the one I told you about, Millicent."

"Good day to you," she said, her eyes stern and unrelenting. "Humph. You don't look like an Alby. I know the Albys in the next town, and you do not resemble them in the least."

Well, hopefully your family didn't inherit your sour face and pug nose. Fortunately, I had only thought that and not said it aloud. "I married Mathius later in life. I was not blessed with children." A sad look followed that pronouncement, and it was enough to melt her severe expression.

"Oh, my dear, there is no shame in that." She placed her pudgy arm around my shoulder and led me aside. "In truth, you might be more lucky than not. My two sons have been nothing but trouble for me."

"Perhaps they will grow out of it?"

She rolled her eyes. "We can only hope."

From that time on, I knew we would be the best of friends. She shooed her husband on, and we spent the rest of the afternoon shopping. Now heavily laden, I wondered what I would do with everything. I purposely avoided mentioning where I was staying. There really was only one thing that I could do. Rent a room at the inn.

I explained that Mathius might or might not return from Boston that day, and that I needed to procure a room at the inn.

"Pity you do not know for sure, because you could come back to Boston with us."

"Yes, that it true." Not. Pity, I don't have a cell phone. Life in the seventeenth century was so difficult. If only I didn't know what I was missing.

"Well, come along. Let's get a room for you. I personally know the proprietor."

I paid for a room on the first floor, using my fictitious name, in case Hezekiah checked for me at the inn. Lady Millicent insisted I get a bigger room, but I talked her out of it. "I may not need to stay the night," I reminded her. We unloaded our purchases and went back out again. All the while, I kept my eyes open for Hezekiah, Liza, and any sign of the circle girls.

Toward late afternoon, we met up with Dr. Crosby. "Ah, there you are! Millicent, my dear, it is time for us to head back to Boston."

"So soon?"

"Yes, dear." He glanced around. "We will not want to be anywhere around here tomorrow."

"No, of course not." She frowned and turned to me. "Are you sure you do not want to come with us? We could take you home."

The Hanson mansion was in Dorchester, part of Boston, really. But, I was sure Hezekiah was on his way back, if not already here. "Thank you, but I would be afraid of passing by Hez—er, Mathius."

204

"Of course, dear." She adjusted her bonnet. "Well, I hope to see you again. Perhaps at one of the charity balls?"

"Yes, of course." I fought back a sudden rush of sadness. Once I left Salem, there could be no coming back. I gave her a warm hug, sure I'd never see her again.

I went back to my room at the inn and lingered for a while, going through my various purchases. One of the gifts was for Sarah. As night was coming on, I decided I'd take it to her house first before I hunkered down for the rest of the evening in that small room.

I picked up the small package for Sarah and turned it around in my hand. She would love it. Slipping it into my pocket, I left for her house.

I was almost there, when I spied two girls coming down the street. My heart froze in my chest. It was Mercy Lewis and Betty Hubbard. Laughing, they didn't appear to notice me, but nonetheless, I still dashed behind a fence when they weren't looking.

Of all the places to stop for a chat, they stopped right in front of the fence. I could see their clothing through the spaces between the slats of wood and hear their voices clearly.

"It's horrible, simply deplorable," Mercy said.

"Yes, it is."

"If only the old man would admit to it. Hanging would be much easier on him."

"He is a dreadful wizard, Mercy, but I wonder," Betty's voice dropped low, although there appeared to be no one else around who could hear. "If he be a dreadful wizard, why then is he not using his dark arts to escape?"

"We don't know that he will," Mercy said, her voice rising to a squeak. "He could be watching us right now!"

I bit down on my tongue—a well-timed BOO, might get me in serious trouble.

"Come along Betty," Mercy said urgently. "The sun is setting. Let's go to the meeting at Reverend Parris's house. Abby will be there."

"Yes, and Ann, too. Although, I'm frightened of his house, Mercy. Remember what we saw there last February?"

I trembled as the memories of that night returned. I had been there with them and had witnessed the frightful event as well.

"With that awful Elizabeth—the witch that killed Hezekiah?"

So much for fear. My lips twisted to the side. They were accusing me of killing Hezekiah? How rude. I looked around on the ground and found a long, thin stick then stuck it through the fence, really close to their ankles.

"Yes, poor, poor Hezekiah."

"It's all that nasty Elizabeth's fault."

I could hardly see. The sun was almost down and it was quite dark. Using my fingers, I deftly felt around the fence for a small hole about the height of their faces. I put my lips on the hole, and in a hoarse whisper, cackled, "It was youuu that did it. I am coming for youuuuu." Seriously, high school acting classes were the bomb.

The girls screamed and took off at a run, but the thin stick tangled in their feet, and they fell to the cold ground. I nearly blew my cover by laughing, but decided the quicker I got out of there, the better. Following the dark fence down, I found the end of it, and slipped back on the road. I took a quick look behind me and saw the shadowy form of the two girls turning the corner down the street.

Once inside Zebulon's house, I burst into laughter. After a while, I lit one of the candles, and took my gift out for Sarah. Finding the quill and ink, and a piece of parchment paper, I wrote her a brief message.

"Sarah, Thank you for believing in me. That means a lot. I have this special gift for you, so you can always see how beautiful you are. Love, Elizabeth."

I opened the package and took out a small, handheld mirror. They were rare in this time period, only because they were so expensive. The reflective part was silver, I think. It had a dull reflection when compared to modern mirrors, but it was a lot better than pressed copper. She would love the delicate carvings on the frame and the embedded jewels. I had spent almost everything I had to buy it for her. I wished I could be around when she found it.

It would be dark outside soon, and with no street lights, I knew I'd better head out. I blew out the candle and closed the door behind me. The cool air tingled my face, and the black, starless night propelled me forward in quick strides toward the inn. I hoped my Hezekiah—my *very much alive* Hezekiah—was already there. I pushed the door open.

The room was as empty as my heart. I closed the curtains, lit a small lantern, and then ate an apple and a piece of bread. He could still come, right? Of course, he could. I had to think positive.

I had bought a small clock watch for Victoria, tiny flowers and intricate scrollwork, adorned with gilded brass with a steel hand. In my grandfather's time, it was called a pocket watch, but this was slightly bigger than the antique one my mother had inherited. I had them set it to the right time and planned to use it right up until we went back to the future. As ancient as it was, it was a lot better than being without any way to tell the time, except for the rising and setting of the sun, or a dash into the meeting house where a large tower clock stood. I took it out of its box and placed it on the table beside my bed.

I wished I had my phone with all my apps and movies. More than once I thought about how cool it would be to have downloaded every file I could about Salem for late night reading. Like I hadn't already done that. I imagined how quick they'd hang me if I was caught watching a downloaded YouTube video on a thin, rectangular box.

I shuffled through my packages, until I found a book I had purchased for Arabella. She told me she had wished she'd bought it in England, so when I saw it, I bought it for her. *La Vida Es Sueño* or, in English, *Life Is a Dream,* written by Pedro Calderón de la Barca. I turned it around in my hands. I remembered what Arabella had said about it—"It is a philosophical allegory about the mystery of life." Too bad it was written in Spanish. My Spanish was a bit rusty. I laid the book down, blew out the lantern, and crawled into bed.

But sleep did not easily befall me. My mind kept turning to Giles Corey and his last night in a cold jail and to the eight others who would soon hang by the noose.

Another thought plagued me. Betty and Mercy were probably even now recounting their latest paranormal experience, which was nothing more than a hateful prank on my part. A funny, well deserved, but nonetheless hateful, prank. I had fanned the fires of fallacy and superstition and now wondered if others had, at times, done the same. Regretting my earlier actions, I drifted off to sleep.

Twenty-One
Hezekiah

I had to get to Boston and back quickly. Leaving Bess in Salem Town to fend for herself wasn't my idea, but the idea of the most tenacious woman I'd ever met. And the most lovely.

Taking long strides through the crowd, I heard her voice, "I love you, Hezekiah," filter through the crowd. I'm sure it was her, and yet, when I turned, she was far away, her face turned in the direction of her fate.

I watched her until she rounded a corner and was gone, my heart heavy with anguish. Why did she have to be so stubborn? I should have demanded that she go with me. But she would not have listened.

Arriving at the stables, I passed by the carriage and went straight to the horse we'd borrowed from the Fieldstones. Explaining my need to get to Boston and back in haste, and leaving the carriage there as collateral, the stableman let me borrow a saddle, and soon I was galloping down the road toward Boston, formulating a plan in my mind.

A few hours later, after having stopped briefly at my parents' estate, I arrived at the jail, tied the tired horse to the hitching post, and hurried up the steps. I was surprised at what met my eyes. A stout man with a long mustache and a pleasant expression extended his hand in greeting. "What can I do fer ye this fine day, sir?"

"I am looking for the prison keeper—John Arnold."

"Aye, that would be m'brother. He be 'ome sick today." He grinned, revealing badly formed teeth. "M'name's James Arnold."

"Oh." I put my chin in my hand. "I was hoping to discuss some business with him, but maybe you could help?"

"I can try." His smile faded. "Depends on what ye need."

This was going to be more difficult that I thought. "You have a prisoner named Alden?"

The smile was gone. "Yes."

"I'd like to speak with him."

"Now, I can't be lettin' jus' anyone in ta speak with the prisoners."

Reaching into my pocket, I placed a few coins on the counter. In doing so, I noticed a curled paper laying there and could read the last few sentences—*pressed to death for standing mute.* "What is that?" I asked, pointing to it.

He frowned. "It was delivered a short while ago. I'm ta post it."

"May I?" I asked, gesturing toward the paper.

He nodded and pushed it my way.

"Unbelievable," I muttered under my breath. "This will go down in history as one of the greatest tragedies of mankind." I hadn't meant it for his ears, but was simply stating a fact I knew would come to pass.

"'Tis a true enough statement," he said sadly. "We be tired of the 'ol thing. Our jails be over filled, too many ta tend, I say." He looked down at the coins. "Ye need to speak to the capt'n?"

"Yes."

He left the coins on the counter. "Follow me."

Outside his cell, the prison keeper's brother stopped. "Ye understand I have ta lock yer in wif 'im, eh?" He cocked his head. "'Tis the rules."

"Yes." I swallowed hard. "Of course."

"He's been here nigh on fifteen weeks now, poor fellow," he said, approaching an archway to a long corridor. We came to cell number five, and he struggled with the key. I found myself peering into number four while waiting. "Who's that?" I asked, already knowing the answer.

"She be an Irish Catholic woman—O'Brien be 'er name."

"Oh." She didn't see me, but was busy rubbing the shoulders of an older woman.

"They say she be a witch, but she don' act like one."

The lock clicked, and he pushed the heavy gate open. "Good day to ye, John, do yer feel up ta a visitor?"

"That would be fine, James. How's your brother?"

"He be feverish and got the chills at the same time. Thank ye fer askin'." He turned to me. "I be back in an hour."

I was happy to hear that. "Captain Alden," I said, extending my hand. "Do you remember me?" My parents and he were in the same social circles in Boston.

"No," he said, studying my face.

"Oh, the hair," I said, remembering its color, "and, I'm wearing a mask." I pinched at the corner of the prosthetic, peeling away one of the corners, then pulled it completely off.

Alden's eyes widened in expected fright. I patted him on the arm, though he tried to pull away. "It's me, Abner Hanson's son. I'm in hiding," I whispered, careful to not let the others in the cell overhear my words. "I don't need this here, though. Folding the mask, I pushed it into my bag.

"Oh." His eyes squinted and then he nodded. "Yes, I see it now." He spoke low. "Your masquerade is safe with me, Hezekiah." He leaned toward me. "I get all the news in here, and when I heard about the Hanson child, I was most shocked." The wrinkles on his face deepened, his face resonating deep concern. "I don't understand it. Why the judges can believe those girls. The whole town has gone mad!"

I nodded in agreement.

"Wenches! They'd be unresponsive and then fall into wild fits when I looked at them," he shook his head. "But I asked the judges, why *they,* meaning the judges, didn't fall into fits when I looked at *them?"*

Good point, indeed.

"I appealed to my friend Bartholomew Gedney, one of the judges, to clear my name. And do you know what he said?" Alden clenched his fists. "He said, he had always looked on me as an honest man, but now he must alter his opinion."

Alden frowned. "I'll eventually get him to see the err of his ways. Soon as this is over, we'll have ourselves a good talk."

It was silent, with only a random cough or a few quiet words from the others in the room. John's face became grim. "They took my sword, because the girls said *my specter* used it to torture them." He raised his hands in the air. "I'm a captain, dedicated to my work, and they took my sword." He stood and paced the cell, occasionally stopping to say a word or two to his fellow inmates.

Returning to me, he sat back down. "Rumor has it I was selling weapons to the Indians." He rolled his eyes. "My son John is captive up north—do they think they'd take my son if I was selling them weapons?"

I shook my head, but I wondered about something else. "The girl that accused you, Mercy . . ."

"Mercy Lewis, yes."

"Did you know she was orphaned a few years back during a raid on her village? In late September, if I remember right."

"What did you say?"

"In Casco Bay, Maine, John—a couple hundred Indians attacked her settlement."

He drew back in surprise. "So, you think she might be accusing me for revenge?" he barely whispered. "She blames me for failing to protect her family?"

"It is altogether possible."

The lock clicked, and James stuck his head in. "It's time—" But before he could finish his sentence, a fight broke out down the long corridor, and he took off at a run, forgetting to take the key from the lock or even to close the gate.

I looked at John, then at the open gate, and then at the protruding key. With a tip of my head, I bid him goodbye, left the door open, removed the key, and slipped it into the lock right beside Alden's cell.

After opening the gate, I pushed the key back into the lock for cell number five, right where James had left it. I didn't close the gate. I knew John's fortune would be to escape the Boston jail, and had I not come, it would still have happened. I didn't want to jinx anything and left things just the way I found them.

"Martha O'Brien!" I called, disguising my voice. "The prison keeper desires to speak with thee." I gestured for her to hurry. "Come along, come along," I said firmly. I closed the gate and guided her to the front room. My coins were still there, right where James had left them. I took a few more out of my pocket and then covered the whole lot with the horrid paper, thinking that eventually—even soon, he would find the money owed him.

My horse was some rested now, and I hoisted Martha up on it. "Come along now," I said, leading the horse and my refugee away from the jail. In haste, I took swift strides toward the road. The carriage was there, just as I requested. I had no time to linger at my parents' house and only enough time to make arrangements for Martha's escape. I wanted no one near, should we be pursued.

No sooner had I got her safely inside the carriage, when a voice cried out, "I am flying! The devil is after me!" I turned to see John Alden sitting atop a fine horse, waving his hat at me, and smiling wide. He turned and galloped away, going south, in the opposite direction I was headed.

There were none in pursuit. Maybe because those that loved John, made sure of it. I did recollect a small group of men and women lingering at the jail when I had arrived earlier. Perhaps it was them that orchestrated his escape.

For some reason, that comforted me, until I remembered where I was going, and the horrific acts that would beset Salem Town in the next few days. It wasn't over yet.

Sigmund had been instructed to ride ahead. We would meet him, switch horses, and then he would take Martha to a location far away from Salem Town, with strict instructions to remove her back to the mansion, once the fervor had died down in Salem. Died down . . . an interesting choice of words. The madness would stop soon, but the memories would last forever.

I road on, stopping at the designated spot to meet Sigmund. We hadn't gone far from Boston, just to the outskirts. "Whoa!" I pulled the horse to a stop. Jumping down, I went to check on Martha, while Sigmund, who had been waiting for us, dismounted his horse.

Martha looked at me timidly, the first time she had really had the chance to study my face, and then without a sound, she said. "Ye be Hezekiah, but where be me wane?"

She spoke of Bess, of course. "She is safe." I hoped.

I promised Martha that if we could, we would meet her back at the mansion in a few months. Sigmund was taking her to a home my parents owned in the colony of Connecticut. We kept a small household of servants on hand, and occasionally would visit there. My mother loved it best. The gardens there were among her favorite. Martha

217

would be safe and Sigmund was to inform the servants that Martha would be the "lady of the house" and should be treated thus, until we came to get her.

I found it hardly a fitting reward, given the sacrifice that Martha had rendered us. She was willing to give her life to protect my Bess, and therefore, she deserved to be treated like royalty.

I mounted the Fieldstone's horse and watched the carriage go down the long road to freedom. With my heart turned toward Bess, and my horse turned toward Salem Town, I took off at a steady gait to preserve my horse's energy for the long ride ahead.

It was contagious, this excitement to see history unfold that I had only had the chance to read about in the future, and I understood Bess's addiction to time travel. *No I don't, really.* In fact, it was the one thing I worried about the most. Bess was changing, I could see it. Where once a little nudge from her my way was enough to appease her disappointments in my seventeenth-century habits, had now become a long, drawn out debate and almost a defiance on her part.

I knew it wasn't she who acted so, but the influence of those dastardly stones. I glanced down at the stone bulging in my pocket. I could throw it into the river and be done with it—keep Bess right here with me and my family.

I stopped beside the river, the noonday sun sparkling against its rushing waters. *Do it, Hezekiah! End this madness now!*

Twenty-Two
The Reunion

Liza looked out the window as the sun began to crest the horizon. Strange that a day that began so beautifully would bring such pain and suffering to an innocent man. The wooden platform constructed for Giles lay foreboding, dark against the rising sun, with tiny flecks of frost reflecting off the early rays, in vast contrast to the dreadful monstrosity they adorned.

Yet, as Liza mused upon it, an allusion of peace came upon her, for there were very few things in life that did not have a silver lining. Giles death was only mortal, his spirit would live on and return to that God Who gave him life. He would be at peace and find love unfathomable. She never did think like a Puritan, that if one didn't conform to their beliefs, one would burn in a fiery hell, regardless of what type of person they were. As she wasn't Puritan, and never would be, it was fine for her to think that way. Still, how could anyone think God so evil?

A groan from the other room roused her, and she went to check on her aunt. They had spent the better part of yesterday looking for Hezekiah's friend, but hadn't seen anyone who resembled her. A heavy sigh left her lips, knowing that the clever woman could be right in front of her, masquerading as a different person. She shivered.

Last evening, Miranda had started to feel a bit ill. They both thought it better for her to rest, so they ended their search early. Liza looked in on her and found her splayed out and breathing heavily.

"Oh, my! How are you, Miranda?"

"Horrible," she mumbled, eyes pressed tight. She waved at the water pitcher on the table. "Thirsty . . ."

"Yes, of course." Liza went right to work, getting her a drink, and wiping the sweat off her hot forehead. "I am going downstairs to speak to the proprietor. Perhaps he can tell me where to find a doctor."

"Yes," Miranda said, with a nod.

She dressed and then bounded down the stairs, realizing that it was not ladylike, and frankly not caring. Partway down the stairs, she froze in place. "Mother?" She barely breathed, staring at the woman at the front desk.

Elizabeth Senior barked, "I have looked everywhere. You must tell me if they are here!"

The proprietor looked up at Liza, his eyes wide, and then back at Elizabeth. "I, ah . . ."

"Mother?" Liza took a cautious step down, and then a wave of relief washed over her. "Mother!"

Elizabeth turned, a look of astonishment on her face. "Liza!" The proprietor coughed and took a step back.

Liza rushed down the rest of the stairs and threw her arms around her mother's neck, surprised at her sudden outburst of pent-up emotions. "I'm so sorry!" Her mother patted her head and stroked her hair. "We looked everywhere for you yesterday," Liza said, between sobs.

Elizabeth pulled her head back. "You did?" Doubt registered on her stern face.

"Yes, Mother." She wiped her fingers across the tears forming in the corners of her eyes. "It was foolhardy for me to leave with Miranda without talking to you first."

Her mother's face hardened at the mention of her sister's name. "Yes, it was."

"Mother, you mustn't be so harsh. Miranda needs you right now." Turning toward the stairs, she tugged on her mother's sleeve, but was met with resistance.

Elizabeth stood firm, jaw locked in place, eyes as cold as the frost outside. "How dare you insist that I follow you? I came for you, not her." She pointed toward the door. "Let us go, my child."

Liza dropped her hands to her sides. "No."

Elizabeth's eyes widened. "What?" She looped her arm through Liza's and pulled her toward the door. "Yes, you will."

"No, I will not, Mother." She yanked her arm away.

Elizabeth's surprised expression hardened to indignation. "If you do not return with me this instant, then do not bother returning at all." She held her head high and glared at Liza.

"Mother, you do not mean that." There was cold silence between them. "You do not understand, Mother." Her voice trembled. "Miranda is very ill. I fear for her."

"What?" Elizabeth's countenance softened, but then she tilted her head, as doubt clouded her face. "How ill?"

"Oh, Mother, is it not enough that she is sick?"

"Yes," she said, an obvious struggle raging within. "Take me to her."

Liza took her hand and they rushed up the steps. Swinging the door open, they went straight to the sickbed.

"Miranda?" Liza gently shook her, and Miranda opened her eyes in a thin slit. "Look who I found downstairs," Liza said, her voice in a quiver.

Miranda's eyes widened, and she turned away. "I need a doctor."

"Nonsense," said Elizabeth, removing her gloves and placing her hand on Miranda's forehead. "You are very warm, Sister." Turning to Liza, she barked, "Fetch me a pot of hot water." From her purse, she took a small box.

Liza hurried back down the stairs and returned with a jug of water from the proprietor, who had a bemused look on his face that was beginning to annoy Liza. Still, he had faithfully kept their secret, not knowing her intentions had changed. She wondered how to talk to her mother about everything, as she carefully set the jug on the small desk beside the bed.

Elizabeth slipped some leaves into the hot water. "We will let that steep," she said. "It will help her fever go down and her head stop hurting."

Liza had seen her do that back in Maine, too. She had often admired her mother's propensity to grow herbs and other helpful plants, but she did not know she carried them with her. "Where did you learn that?"

Elizabeth looked up at her, while dabbing her sister's forehead with a damp cloth. "Why, Goodwife Corey," she said quietly, as if afraid everyone in Salem Village was listening.

At the mention of the Coreys, Liza's hands flew to her mouth. "Oh, Mother, did you see those dreadful placards?"

"Yes, my child, I saw them." Her countenance saddened. "I did not want to be here for his execution. I thought it a hanging, but this is far worse." She gazed down at her sister and after a moment spoke again. "When Miranda pulled away in the carriage, I thought my heart tore from my chest, but when I found you gone . . ." her voice broke.

"Oh, Mother." Liza knelt beside her and held her hand. She wanted so desperately to have her questions answered, especially the truth about her father and if he was alive, why she had kept that knowledge from her.

Elizabeth put her hand back on Miranda's head. "She is so hot." Stirring the tea, she dipped a mug into it, and brought it to Miranda's lips. "Drink," she cooed. Wetting the cloth, she wrung it out again, and then placed it back on Miranda's forehead.

Liza went out into the sitting room. She sat in the chair by the window facing the jail. A few people were up and beginning to mill around the execution spot.

"Wait!" she whispered. "Is that her?" She could not be sure, but the woman standing beside the platform looked a lot like the older woman who had approached her the last time she was in Salem Town. Glancing at her mother and Miranda in the other room, she thought it best not to mention the real reason she was stepping out for a bit. "I'll be right back," she said. "Shall I bring you something to eat?"

"Yes, that would be wonderful."

She nodded, and pulled the door closed behind her.

Twenty-Three
John Hadlock

Leaving my bag in the room, I ventured outside. I looked around, hoping to see Hezekiah. Surely he was back from Boston now. I had the clock watch in my pocket and pulled it out. It was early, not quite six-thirty. Even though the sun had not yet risen, I was surprised that not many people had arrived to witness the execution yet. Salem Town was notorious for its active spectators. I closed my eyes in shame. Isn't that what I had become?

Fingering the stones in my pocket, I knelt down on the cool ground beside the platform and ran my hand over the wood. This is where it would happen. Around noon, this is where Giles Corey's life would be snuffed out. I stood up, brushed off my dress, and headed in the direction of the smell of freshly-baking bread wafting through the air.

Though there hadn't been many people walking about outside, the bakery was in full swing. As small as it was, the counter was lined with fresh tarts, pies, and bread. I stood in line to pay for a meat pie. The door opened and I glanced back, nearly dropping my pie. Betty Hubbard came in with a few coins in her hand. I got out of line and went back to the display, pretending to look for something else.

"Ah, good day, Betty," the baker said. "I'll have ye regular order ready shortly." He went back to the oven.

A woman behind the counter wiped her hands on the apron about her waist. "How be ye today, wane?"

"Not well, Goody Fletcher," Betty said.

"More of ye fits?"

Betty sighed. "Yes, I'm afraid so."

"Oh, m'dear. What 'appened now?"

She sighed. "Mercy and I had the most frightful thing happen to us last night."

"Oh? Tell me more."

The door opened again, but I was not going to turn around to see who it was.

Betty continued. "We were on the way to the reverend's house—Reverend Parris," she explained. "When the dead appeared to us."

"It was most horrible," squealed Mercy, as the door closed behind her.

Now they were both in the same room with me. I stole a quick glance. Mercy was blocking the door.

"It was the specter of that girl, Elizabeth—the one who beguiled Hezekiah Hanson."

Right. Hezekiah, *beguiled*. I rolled my eyes.

"Yes, we recognized her voice!"

The woman behind the counter's eyes widened in fright. "Ye don't say." Without skipping a beat, she stepped over to me. "Are ye ready to pay?"

I nodded and handed her a coin.

"Thank ye," she said, and then added. "I've not seen ye in these parts."

I heard Mercy and Betty chatting away, oblivious to my dilemma. "No, ma'am," I whispered. "I'm from quite far away." I took my pie, kept my head down, and slipped past them unnoticed. I thought.

"It's her, that woman that hurt me!" Mercy screamed as the door closed. Luckily for me, a young couple was about to enter the bakery, blocking me scuttling to the side of the building. From there, I took the long way around, careful to make sure I wasn't being followed. A new disguise was in order. I needed a new cover. In my haste, I tripped over the hem of my long dress. The meat pie flew up in the air, and I tumbled to the ground. In seconds, someone grabbed my hand and helped me to a nearby rock, stepping around the upside down pie.

"Shouldn't be a hurrying that fast, like you're running from a ghost," he scolded.

Not happy about my lost breakfast, I grunted, and then looked up into the blues eyes of a young man a few years younger than me. I gasped. "Seth?" He looked like an older version of my little brother, the resemblance was uncanny.

"Were you?" he asked, his eyes narrowing. "Running from a ghost?"

"Of course not." I threw my hands to my sides. I couldn't stop staring at him and forced my eyes away. "I am just in a hurry, that's all." Rubbing my sore leg, I brushed off some dirt and pieces of dead leaves.

He shuffled his feet. "You look like an old woman, but your voice does not sound old." He cocked his head to the side. "And you do not run like one either."

"I, uh . . . what?" Great. I did it again. I didn't have much of a chance in this disguise, not unless I kept my mouth closed, and didn't attempt to run away from the likes of Betty or Mercy. Like that would ever happen. I glanced down the road toward Zebulon's house. "Thank you for your help." I tried to pull myself up.

"Do you believe in witches?"

His question caught me off guard. "What? Witches, er, maybe."

"Huh," he said, a stern expression on his face. "I have heard stories, but they all seem so foolish and made up to me."

Well, I had seen things that were foolish for sure, but staged? I doubted it, some of it at least. "I guess you're right." I shrugged and started to stand again.

"They hanged my grandmother last month."

"What?" I sat back down, shocked by his words.

Tears gathered at the rims of his blue eyes. "Yes ma'am, Grandma Martin."

I brought my hands to my mouth. "Oh, my," I said, feeling woozy. "Oh, my."

"Are you all right?" he said, kneeling down beside me. "Did you know my grandmother?"

"Um, yes . . . er, no, not really." She was my eleventh-great grandmother, and I had met her, but only briefly. A rush of emotions overtook me. I hadn't meant to cry, but it was too much. Seth and Grandma Martin all at once—the one I had all but forgotten, and the other I was trying to get out of my mind. What kind of a person was I? Wretched.

I raced through my near-perfect memory. Mom was a genealogy nut, and I knew my lineage. "Susannah Martin was your grandmother?"

"Yes." He wiped his nose on his sleeve.

"What's your name?"

"John Hadlock."

I began to tremble. I came from Susannah Martin through the Hadlock line. "Your mother is Abigail?"

"Yes," he said, his eyebrows raising. "Do you know her?"

"Oh, no," I said with a laugh, "but then you must be Hannah's brother."

"What?" He made a face. "There is not anyone named Hannah in my family. There is just me, Sarah, Abigail, Samuel and Damaris—no Hannah."

I smirked. Not yet. The line I descended from was through his yet to be born sister, Hannah. She was born three years after their grandmother was hanged. Still, he was family—a tenth-great uncle, I think.

"John." I grinned. It was almost like seeing my brother again. Still the pang in my heart was shattering. I hadn't realized how much I missed my little brother. I tried to stand again, and fell back. "Ouch!"

"Sit for a while," he said. "I will get my mother."

I reached for him. "No."

He studied my face. "Why not?"

"I, um . . . ." I had no answer. Actually, I would love to meet my tenth-great grandmother, but not like this. I glanced down at my dress and ran my fingers through my gray hair.

"Oh," he said, and then he stepped back and really studied me. I felt uncomfortable at his deliberate scrutiny. "Ohh," he said slowly. "Now I know who you are."

I forced myself to remain calm. "Um, what?"

Pointing his finger at me, he said, "You are that girl who spoke up for my grandmother at her hanging." His countenance brightened. "I watched you ride up that hill and face Judge Corwin and Reverend Noyes. You told them to *leave her alone*."

New respect swept over his young face. "You said, 'One day, you will pay for this, for it is you who have committed a grievous crime in the eyes of God, and not them.'" He nodded. "I have looked everywhere for you, especially after Betty Hubbard called you a witch. I figured you were no more a witch than my grandmother."

Our grandmother.

His head bobbed, and he grinned wide. "Well, that explains your ridiculous disguise."

Yeah, I know. My lips drew up in a smirk.

He chuckled. "And then, when you told Betty 'she was lucky you were not a witch, because if you were, she would be getting more than bites and pinches from you', well, everyone laughed." His smile faded. He looked up at me through a rim of tears. "You are trying to hide from them, are you not?"

"Yes," I said in a quiet voice. "Yes, I am."

"Well, not dressed like that," he said.

Right then, a horse and rider pulled up beside us. "Mama wants you to come home. The cows got out again."

"Sarah," he said pursing his lips. "This is the girl that called out at Grandmother Martin's hanging."

I grabbed his hand to stop him, but it was too late.

"She is hiding from those wicked girls."

The horse sidestepped skittishly. Sarah petted its mane. "Shoo," she cooed and slipped off its back.

I chewed the side of my mouth and tried not to grimace, while she checked me from head to toe.

"It's not a very convincing disguise, is it?"

I put my chin in my hand and shook my head. "Evidently not."

She smiled. "First off, let me thank you." Her countenance saddened. "Not many would be so brave." She sighed. "Least of all me . . . I wish I had said those words." She reached down for me. "Well, come along, we will see what we can do."

I tried to stand, but fell back, rubbing my leg.

"Oh," she said, glancing at the ground-in dirt and tear in my dress. "Stay here, and I will fetch a carriage." Mounting the horse, she reached down for John. "Mama is waiting."

He gave me a quick glance. "Will you be all right?"

I nodded, and he swung up on the horse.

I was off the beaten path, but even so, an occasional person walked by. Checking my clock watch, I pretended that all was well. Shortly, Sarah returned with a carriage and helped me in. She was silent, but kept glancing sideways at me as we rolled along. Finally, she spoke. "You are so brave. I wish to be like you."

"Thank you," I said.

"Mama says to stay away from things in Salem Village. She is afraid. We all are."

I didn't have to imagine—I was, too. She drove the carriage up to a small farm. John was pulling a gate closed on several cows milling inside. He met us at the carriage.

"Mama has gone to town. She has the little ones with her." He helped me out of the carriage. "Let us come up with something more convincing for . . ." He looked at me surprised. "What is your name?"

"Bess," I said, resigned to at least give them my real first name, but not my last for obvious reasons.

I was both disappointed and relieved that their mother wasn't home. Glancing around at the humble surroundings, I did wonder how they would help me with a new disguise. I couldn't fathom how they could possibly change my appearance.

"She looks so much like you, John," Sarah said stepping back and comparing the two of us. "She has your blue eyes."

"Yeah, except I do not have gray hair." He smirked, and it was like I was looking at my brother again.

She held my hair in her hands. "How did you do this? It is quite bewitching."

Good choice of words. "It's hair dye."

"Hair dye? I have never heard of it."

And you won't for several years, unless you travel abroad. Gabriela had purchased the ingredients for hair dye in England, but I knew I could make it from natural ingredients right here in Salem Town. "It's just vegetable dyes made from bark and leaves," I said, guessing the source.

"Well, it has to go." Her lips pursed. "I am guessing you are not much younger than me.

"How old are you?" I asked.

"Twenty-two."

I nodded. "I'm a little younger than that."

She sighed. "That is why your disguise will never work. Your face is too young and beautiful."

"Um, thanks."

Her tongue clicked. "It was not a compliment, Bess."

"Oh."

She sighed. "Will you let me?" She went to a desk and took out a pair of shears.

"Um, why?"

Rolling her eyes, she put her hands on her hips. "To change how you look, Bess."

Okay, but how exactly? "How?"

She looked from me to John and then back to me, and then she cocked her head, and her eyes squinted. She tapped the blades of the shears against her hand seeming deep in thought. "Hmm. It could work," she said, bringing her thumb and finger to her chin. Then she laid the shears down and with arms spread wide, she compared the distance between our waists and our ankles. She picked up the shears again and stared at me.

My hands flew to my hair. "Oh, no, no, no." I was not going to masquerade as a boy!

She shrugged. "Well, I guess you can just stay hidden."

I couldn't stay hidden. I had to find Liza and Hezekiah. And then, there was also . . . Giles Corey. I needed to be there, almost as much as I needed to breathe. It would be soon—later that afternoon. "Okay, all right." I sighed. "Just do it."

She grinned. She touched my shoulder, looking at my dress, and then she turned to her brother. "John, would you get me a pair of your breeches and a shirt?" In minutes, he returned with the clothing. She thanked him then shooed him away.

"First, let me take care of your leg," she said, carefully helping me remove the cumbersome dress. Before laying the dress down on a nearby table, I slipped my hand inside the pocket for the clock watch. As I pulled it out, the bag with the stones caught on it and tumbled to the floor, spilling its contents.

Sarah reached for the stone skidding across the wooden floor at her feet. "How pretty it is!"

I grabbed it first, while scrambling for the other one. "Thank you." Ignoring her confused look, I stared at my leg.

She looked at me and then at my red leg. "It's just bruised," she said. Applying some paste from a jar, she wrapped it, and then had me slip the breeches over it. I pushed the stones into my new pocket.

Sarah pointed to the table where a bulge could be seen under the folds of my dress. "May I?" she asked, and then moving the layers of material aside, she reached into another pocket and pulled something out. "What is this?"

She held out the small ledger Victoria had given me. I had forgotten all about it. "It belongs to a friend of mine." The pockets of the breeches were deeper than the dress and it fit there perfectly. The shirt came next and was much easier than the dress to get over my head.

There was a knock on the door. "May I come back in now?"

"Yes, by all means John, you may come back into the room." She ruffled his hair as he passed.

234

John grinned at me. Apparently he'd never seen a girl wearing his clothes before. I guess it did look a little funny to him, but for me, it was total freedom. What a relief to be out of that dress. I was really getting into it and grinned back at him, until Sarah picked up the shears.

She made a face. "It will grow back, Bess."

I slumped down in the chair. She was right. It would grow back, but what if Hezekiah didn't like it?

I groaned when she lopped off the first chunk of my hair and it fell to the floor. But looking down at it, I was glad to be rid of the gray mess. "Wait. What about the color of my hair?"

She grinned. "You will see. John, fetch Mama's looking glass—the broken piece."

Shortly he returned and thrust the fragment toward me. Oh. The beginning of roots were just barely visible at my hairline. Sarah continued to shape my hair, getting as much of the gray off as possible, which left me with very short hair, about a quarter inch to my head.

I was a bit shocked. "What will people think about a boy with such short hair?" I'd never seen any man or boy with short hair like mine in this time period.

Sarah pursed her lips. "Your mother never shaved your head because of lice?"

Oh, yeah. I guess that's what they would have done in this era. Still, what an obvious way to pass judgment on someone. I imagined people with shaved heads being somehow shunned. Well, at least, they'd leave me alone now. "Lice, huh."

"Yes, but thankfully your hair has started to grow back out."

John laughed. "Since your unfortunate outbreak of lice."

"Erm, thanks." I huffed. I stood again. The swelling in my leg had lessened, though it was still a little sore.

Sarah looked from me to John, and John looked from me to Sarah. "Ah, this isn't quite ready." She pressed her lips together and motioned for John to leave again.

"What?"

"Boys don't usually have that shape," she said, pointing to my chest.

Oh. Okay, I really wasn't that well-endowed, and now I was being noticed? "Seriously? Okay, how are we going to fix that . . . exactly?"

She tilted her head. "You speak so oddly sometimes, Bess. Almost like you are from another time."

"Hmm." I pursed my lips tight.

A puff of air escaped her throat. "We shall bind you."

Oh, yeah, that sounded comfortable. Off with the shirt, she studied my modern underclothes—something I hadn't thought anyone here would ever see. "Um, can we just get this over with?"

"Yes, of course," she said, winding a long piece of thin fabric tightly round my chest. The loose shirt covered the slight bulge from the fabric perfectly, and John was welcomed back into the room to inspect. Yeah. Like that was a highlight in my life.

John walked a circle around me. "You still look like a girl in boy's clothing."

"Really?"

"You just have a girl's face," he said.

"Not much I can do about that."

"You can wear this." John handed me a hat, typical to the era, tall and black, fanned out at the sides.

I had seen men wear similar hats. I was to be disguised more as a young man than a boy. "Okay." When Sarah gave me another funny look due to my strange vernacular, I added, "I mean, all right."

Okay wasn't a common word back then, and maybe not even used at all, but it probably would be now. I was such a trend-setter, though dismayed at the idea. Introducing "okay" was someone else's brainchild.

John pushed the broken mirror to my face again, and I had to admit, with the hat on, I could pass as a boy just fine. Hopefully.

I slapped my hands against my knees and burst out, "Hey, this is great!" Their bewildered faces reminded me of my word choice. "I, um . . . ah, sorry."

"You do speak strangely, Bess, but your words are not the biggest problem."

"No?"

"You still sound like a girl," Sarah said.

Yikes. Again with the no speaking thing. Dang. I was in trouble.

"No, no," said John. "My friend Samuel sounds like a girl."

Sarah nodded. "That is true."

Okay, so maybe I could do this after all. Still, I was only going to speak when I absolutely had to open my mouth—my big, often unchecked, mouth.

I was doomed.

Twenty-Four
Recognition

Liza stood across from the jail. "Where did she go?" She had searched the entire area, but the woman she had seen earlier was gone. Some of the shops were opening, and an older man was placing an array of brooms and shovels outside his door. A few people bustled about, most of them coming and going from the local bakery. Upon entering that shop, she at once recognized two of the circle girls who were near hysteria.

"It was her—the witch!"

The man and woman behind the desk seemed concerned about the uneasiness of the customers who looked like they might change their mind and shop elsewhere.

"Now, now, me wane," the baker cooed, handing her a package. "Here be ye bread, jus' like always. Give Goodman Putnam me best."

"She didn't hurt *me*," the girl said, her lips drawn down in a pronounced pout, "she hurt Mercy."

"Sorry, Betty," the baker said, a touch of nervousness in his voice. He turned to the other girl. "Now, Mercy, how can ye be sure t'was her?"

Mercy's eyes narrowed, as if offended that he'd even questioned her.

"Pardon me," Liza said. "But my aunt has come down with a fever. I do not see any here, but might you have some chicken stew I could purchase?" She held out a few coins.

The woman's face relaxed. "Ya, we had it las' nigh'. I go and fetch ye some."

Liza tried not to make eye contact with the girls, not because she feared them, but because she was afraid of what she might say to them.

"Ye from these parts?" the baker asked, obviously relieved to move on from Mercy's glare.

"No. We are from the province of Maine." She could not help it and added. "The Coreys are good friends of ours." She frowned at the girls.

Betty's eyes narrowed to a devious glare. "Oh, I remember you now. You are the one who spoke up at his trial."

"Yes, and I remember you, too." Liza took the stew from the woman and handed her a coin. "Two of those meat pies as well," she said, pointing to the pies.

Turning back to the girls, she clicked her tongue. "I do not doubt that your fits are real. Aye, I believe most of them to be so, and not *just* the foolish, overactive imaginations of youth."

She paid the woman another coin and took the pies. "But I do doubt their source."

Liza stepped closer to the door. "Your fits come from a more diabolical source than you think." Her face saddened. She did not question the girls' sincerity. "'And no marvel; for Satan himself is transformed into an angel of light,'" she said, quoting a passage from the Bible. "Giles and Martha Corey are innocent. With your accusations, you stand as their murderers before the eyes of God."

She did not wait for their retort, but swung the door open and closed it behind her, and then scurried across the street and down the road.

At a safe distance, she stopped and looked around. A few people walked about, but she knew that was going to change. The peine forte et dure was set for midday, and she imagined by then, the town would be busy with annoying spectators. Hopefully, she would be able to see that strange woman among them. Not wanting the stew to cool down, she made her way back to the inn.

With her purchases in hand, she turned the doorknob and pushed the door open with her hip. It was quiet—not a tranquil quiet, but like the quiet one hears before thunder. The air hung heavy with tension. She did not move, but waited, not wanting to know, and fearing the worst.

Finally, Miranda's crackly voice broke the silence. "You lied to me."

"It was for the child's good."

Her voice was nearly a scream. "Good for her? *I* was good for her!"

"Yes, of course you were," Elizabeth said coldly. "Need I remind you that you've always been a part of her life?"

Miranda's voice broke. "But what about Charles? Charles . . ." she broke down in sobs, "*Charles* . . . you let me believe he was dead, for all these years." Her voice escalated to a high pitch. "You lied to me!"

Liza pushed the door closed with her foot, hard enough for them to hear. It went quiet again. "I've brought back meat pies and chicken stew," she called through the room. Biting down on her lip, she fought back the tears.

"Here they are." She set them on the table and scurried back out the door. Breathing heavily, she fell in a heap against it. She had already known about the lie, but her mother confirming it, ripped open the painful wound into a gaping abyss. She had wanted to speak with her about for so long, but this was too much. The pain was too acute, too raw—she needed time. She took off down the steps and rushed out into the midday sun.

"Liza?" a voice called behind her. "Liza Fieldstone?"

She turned and saw Deliverance Corey, now a Crosby, walking toward her. She hadn't seen her for years, but easily recognized her. "Deliverance . . ." She sobbed between breaths.

"Oh, my dear child," Deliverance cried, drawing her into an embrace. She stepped back and studied Liza. "You are here for my father." Her voice broke, and she glanced sideways at the wooden platform where he would soon be executed. A small group of people had gathered, among who was Deliverance's sister, Elizabeth, and she gave them a slight wave.

Tears rolled down Deliverance's cheek, and she dabbed at them with her handkerchief. "My family," she said, "We are handling it in our own way. I, for one, refuse to accept it."

Liza was puzzled.

Deliverance placed her hand over Liza's. "While I see it right before my eyes, my father's cruel death does not seem real to me." She wistfully added, "Maybe he will yet confess."

Before Liza could respond, Deliverance continued, "I know how insane that sounds." She sighed. "I suppose I have always been this way. I was six years old when my mother died, twenty-eight years ago. I remember thinking she was not really gone. I sat on the porch waiting for her to come back for days."

Liza knew Martha Corey was Giles's third wife. He had only been married to her for two years. Liza's mother was twelve-years old when she helped out at the Corey's after Deliverance's real mother died. They had been good friends ever since.

Another glance at the platform brought a horrified look to Deliverance's face, which she quickly shook away.

Liza pulled herself together. Her worries were nothing compared to what the Corey family was suffering. "I'm so sorry, Deliverance."

"Yes, we all are." Deliverance seemed to force herself to look at the platform longer this time. A sudden breeze swept a lock of hair in front of her face, and she pushed it away. "I'm glad to see you, Liza. I've wanted to thank you."

"Thank me?"

"Yes. I saw you at Papa's trial." A fleeting grin played about her lips, quickly replaced by anguish. "You are a brave child." She shook her head. "No, not a child anymore, you are a young woman now."

Deliverance took her hands. "Not many would speak so boldly in a court of law, especially around those wicked girls. Your words will stay with me forever." She met her eyes. "Words hold power, Liza." She seemed lost in her thoughts. "They can lift one's spirit to unparalleled heights, or they can drop them to the depths of despair."

The implication was clear to Liza. Many lives in Salem were destroyed because of the spurious words of a few.

Deliverance glanced behind Liza. "Where is your mother?"

Liza's countenance fell. She swallowed. "She is, uh, back at the inn." Apparently, her dismay at the mention of her mother registered on her face.

Deliverance tilted her head and studied Liza. "You seem unduly agitated, my dear. There is a problem?"

Liza was unsure of what to say. Giles's unjust and eminent death was far more serious than her dilemma, but Deliverance would not let it go.

"What is the matter, child?"

"There is a problem, but . . ." How could Liza discuss her situation with someone who was facing the horrific death of her father? "I cannot . . . I cannot talk about it right now." She gave a nervous wave toward the platform.

"Oh, yes, of course," Deliverance said. "But, if it will make you feel any better, perhaps listening to your woes will take my mind off mine." She shuddered. After what appeared to be a silent struggle, she added, "I think I know what troubles you, anyway."

Liza looked up at her, confused.

"And it is about time that you know, too."

Liza was taken aback. "What are you talking about?"

244

She patted her hand. "Your mother is a friend of mine. I know of her, um, eccentricities." She pursed her lips. "She is an odd one, that is true, but I do love her."

Liza nodded. She felt the same way, but this was a bit more than odd, this was downright mean spirited. Her temper flared. "How could she keep him away from me?" She had not meant to bark at Deliverance—especially with the platform looming in the background. "I'm sorry." She placed a shaky hand on Deliverance's arm.

But Deliverance was only half listening, her attention more on the platform across the street. With a quick breath, she came back into the conversation. "You see," she paused, pulling her gaze away from the platform, "this is just what I warned her of." Looping her arm through Liza's, she led her across the street.

They were greeted by other members of the Corey family and a few friends as well. Liza felt a little uncomfortable standing next to them. "I will leave you to your family," she said, giving Deliverance a hug.

"Oh, no, I will not hear of it." Deliverance took her aside. "Tell me everything," she said, sitting down on the platform.

Liza just stared. She couldn't bring herself to sit where Giles would take his last breath.

The crowd grew larger and some of the spectators gawked at Deliverance. She did not seem to notice, or if she did, she did not appear to care. A few of the other family members took her lead and sat on the platform, too.

Taking a deep breath, Deliverance patted the wood then ran her fingers over its edge. "It is but wood, my dear." She grimaced and then looked up at Liza. "I've known your mother my whole life. She used to watch me when I was a child, but you already know that."

She took Liza's hand, pulling her down beside her. "I have no qualms against Elizabeth, but I have always known this secret of hers would eventually come to light."

"Yes, that my father had not died all those years ago," Liza muttered bitterly. "Why would she keep that from me and from her sister too?"

Deliverance drew in a quick breath. She seemed reluctant to continue. "But, your mother—"

Before she could finish, a voice cried out in the crowd, "There he is!" Everyone turned toward the jail.

Giles Corey stood in the doorway, his bound hands to his face, blocking the bright sunlight. Deliverance stretched out her hand toward him. "Father!" The jailer nudged him forward and the aged man nearly tumbled out the door.

The stunned crowd parted, making a path for Giles as he took his last walk in mortality across the green tufted grass to the wooden platform.

Deliverance sank to her knees. In an instant, hands reached out for her. A sobbing woman, Deliverance's sister, Elizabeth, helped her up. Several other people milled around the grieving woman, and Liza stepped back into the crowd.

Putting her head down, Liza took quick strides through the throng of people. She could not take any more. The lies from her own mother were intolerable and worse than that, the heartless execution of a family friend was beyond comprehension. She needed to go somewhere to think.

It seemed as though the whole town was at the execution, but she would not be. Making her way to the barn where they had secured the carriage and horses, she prepared the carriage to leave. She would be back, but for right now, she needed to get away. She knew of a secluded spot by the river that she had been to as a child and guided the horses toward it.

Twenty-Five
Peine Forte et Dure

I looked down at the breeches John had let me wear. It was a fairly good cover. I was pretty sure that not many Puritan women dressed like boys. Maybe this would work. Running my fingers through my super short hair, I felt tremendous relief. The hair dye had really frizzed my hair, and I was relieved that it was gone. Actually, I kind of liked it short, well maybe not this short. Now for the hard part. I swallowed. "Um, I need to get back to town."

John stared at me, then nodded. "Me, too." He glanced at his sister who frowned. I think Sarah understood both of our reasons, which were probably the same—Giles Corey.

"I cannot go with you," she said. "I told Mama I would start the stew." She gestured toward the piece of raw beef lying on the table.

John looked out the window. "Mama's home."

"Go! Take my horse, too, John." Turning to me, her voice broke. "Honestly, Bess, I will never forget what you said to those men at my grandmother's hanging. It is one of the few things that brings me comfort when I think of that horrible ordeal." She hugged me. "I hope I get to see you again."

"Me too," I said, suppressing a sob.

I wasn't supposed to go back in time, meet my relatives, and then become endeared to them, but I had done just that.

They were no longer a name recorded in time, but real people with all the hopes and dreams I had. I think that was why I was so upset with modern-day writers who made up lies about real people just to sell a book. If I ever were to become a writer, I would try to use every last word about that person, recorded in history, and somehow make a good story from it. It just seemed right to honor them in that way.

John opened the side door, and we slipped out. In seconds, we were headed back to the center of town.

"What shall I call you?" John yelled, as we trotted down the road.

I hadn't thought about that, but right away knew the name I wanted. "Seth," I said, a lump in my throat.

Nearing the main part of town, we tethered the horses to a post and walked the rest of the way in. Much more crowded than earlier, a throng of restless people milled around the empty platform.

We worked our way to the front and found a spot to sit on. Obvious things aside, it was a peaceful, fall afternoon. The sun was shining, and the sky was a turquoise blue as far as you could see. The leafy trees were still green, awaiting the full effects of fall, which wouldn't happen for a couple more weeks.

I just wanted to forget everything—the upcoming execution, the approaching hangings, and getting Liza to her dad. A heavy weight settled upon me, until I remembered. No matter what, I had control over how I would react. It would be my choice to be happy or miserable regardless of the outcome. Yeah, keep thinking that, Bess. It's easy to think, but hard to do, and I wondered if I would crumple under the intense pressure I felt.

A side door opened on the jail. No one made a sound—not a gasp, not a cry, not a whimper—until a man called out, "There he is!"

Giles Corey, his hands bound in front of him, walked slowly to the platform, escorted by two men on either side. So cruel. So beastly cruel! I clenched my fists tight and noticed that John had done the same.

The door opened again and out stepped Judge Corwin. To think I had often admired his house, dubbed "The Witches House" in the future—the only remaining structure in Salem from 1692.

After Giles's death, Corwin would go to the Coreys and attempt to seize his estate, or at the least, collect the money the Coreys owed for his and Martha's prison bills. Fortunately, one of his sons-in-law sold some of the livestock to pay the bill and saved the farm from being seized, only because Giles had had the foresight to deed it to him.

Corwin stepped to the platform. Giles's old, limp body hung from the arms of the two men. Corwin seemed uncomfortable. Perhaps he thought it would never have gone this far. "Goodman Corey," he said. "Wilt thou reconsider? Save thyself!"

"Just say the word, *please* Goodman Corey," John breathed out quietly beside me.

I glanced around and saw the same expression of hopelessness on each person's face, as if they were all inwardly pleading for Giles to speak. I found myself praying for the same. Silly, huh? I knew how history would unfold, and yet, I still longed for a different ending to this poor man's life.

When Corey uttered not a word, Corwin swept his hand in a half-circle, indicating for them to continue. The men untied Giles wrists and laid him down, face up, on the platform. Then they tied his wrists and ankles to stakes sticking out of the ground on its sides.

One of the men leaned forward and whispered in Giles's ear and then patted him on the shoulder. I half expected Corwin, or Hathorne, who had just arrived, to bark at the man, but they did not.

"Goodman Henderson." Hathorne pointed to the man who had whispered in Giles's ear. "Thomas," he said, using his first name, "please continue."

I hadn't noticed the long planks of wood and large rocks lying to the side of the platform until now. Maybe my mind blocked them out, or maybe they had brought them while I was at the Hadlock home. They now lay ominous before me, like an immovable mountain of stone and wood, cold and unrelenting.

Thomas picked up one of the planks, and laid it carefully on Giles's chest, and then he laid another. Giles's groan was the most pitiful thing that I had ever heard—that any of us had ever heard, I was sure, for we all knew what was coming next.

Hathorne gestured toward the rocks. Thomas stood still. He stared down at them, apparently unable to pick one up. He looked back to Hathorne with pleading eyes. I found myself cheering him on—hoping for his sake, he would not do the deed before him. I couldn't imagine what it would be like to have been the one who placed the rocks on Giles Corey's chest.

Hathorne waved him away with a grunt and gestured for the other man to take his place. It was obvious that this man had been drinking—how else could he have done it so easily, without compassion? Or perhaps, in his condition, he merely fumbled. He dropped a rock on the plank by Giles's thigh. A loud moan came from Giles's lips and a gasp came from the crowd.

In long, wide steps, Thomas swiftly returned to the platform, ignoring the judge's dismissal. He pushed the drunkard out of the way. With tears, he picked up the next stone and carefully laid it on Giles's chest.

"Another," Hathorne said.

Thomas balked at the command, but cautiously placed the next stone beside the other.

The pain on Giles's face was excruciating to watch. His eyes pressed tight and tears trickled down the sides of his face. Still, he remained mute.

Hathorne raised his hand. "That is enough for now." Turning to Corwin, he said, "He won't last long."

I bit down on my tongue. History had recorded that for two days Giles would suffer—*two days!*

The crowd stared at Giles. Some openly prayed. Others, like myself, cried. John elbowed me.

"Men don't cry," he whispered, his voice strained. "Leastwise not in public."

I looked at him through my tears, knowing that where I came from, that ill-bred notion would linger for years, but would eventually ease somewhat. I sucked it in and wiped my eyes, feeling like I would explode from pent-up anguish and sorrow.

I counted three good-sized rocks on top of the heavy planks and watched as the crowd thinned, probably thinking he would expire before too long.

Two women lingered close to the platform, at times, taking the dying man's hand in theirs.

John spoke in hushed tones. "That's his family." He stuck his chin out toward them. "The taller one is Elizabeth Moulton, and that's her sister, Deliverance Crosby."

"Oh."

John shifted his weight from one foot to the other "Do you want to come to my house for some stew?"

I shook my head. He wouldn't understand that I knew I could go away and come back the next day and Giles would still be fighting to live. "That's okay, er, all right, I mean. I'll stay here for a while."

"Well, I'll bring you back something to eat then, ah, *okay?*" he asked, deliberately using the word foreign to his speech.

"Okay," I said, rolling my eyes. I watched him walk away.

There were only a handful of us left. I surmised the two men standing near Elizabeth and Deliverance to be their husbands—the ones Giles had deeded his estate to. I stayed back while the sisters prayed beside their dying father. The prison guard, Thomas, stood nearby.

Elizabeth knelt over Giles. "Won't you reconsider, Father?" she pled.

"I cannot. I will not," Giles said, between labored breaths.

"But, Papa," Deliverance sobbed. "You hurt so!" She looked up at Thomas. "Make it stop! Please, make it stop!"

"Hush, Deliverance," Elizabeth cooed. "He will make us leave."

"I will not make you leave," Thomas said. "Giles is a good man."

"Then why, why?" Deliverance sobbed. She turned back to her sister. "Why, Elizabeth?"

Elizabeth stroked her sister's arm. "Thomas is merely a puppet, Deliverance. One forced to comply."

"Yes, you are right." She looked up at him. "Poor man."

I agreed and wondered how he would handle his part in Giles's death throughout the years.

John returned with one gourd filled with warm stew and another with dirty water from the river. You'd think I'd be used to drinking brown water, but the clean water from my mother's reverse osmosis in the future made it impossible to forget what water could taste like. Ugh.

I was famished and ate quickly, taking sips from the river water as needed. As dusk arrived, John said his goodbyes, and told me he'd be back in the morning after he milked the cows and fed the chickens.

"Are you sure you don't want to come home with my sister and me? Mama wouldn't mind."

Aw. That's sweet. I shook my head. "Don't worry about me. I've a room at the inn." I pointed across the street.

"*Okay,*" he said, with a grin.

I clicked my tongue against the roof of my mouth. I had created a vernacular monster. He picked up the stew gourd and slung it over his shoulder. There was still some water in the other gourd, so he left that one behind. I watched him leave then removed myself to a far corner, where in the shadows, I was hidden from view.

Late into the night, his daughters finally left, and only the guard remained. I wondered what Thomas would do if I approached Giles. I mean, what was the worst thing he would do, shoo me away? With the kindness I had seen in him earlier, I doubted that. Anyhow, Thomas had fallen asleep, sitting against the pile of rocks.

"Mr. Corey, er, Goodman Corey?"

Giles turned his eyes toward me, his labored breaths slow and rhythmic. I didn't want to excite him. For the moment, he seemed to be withstanding the weight.

"I, um, I want you to know that you are my hero. I will forever look up to you, sir."

His eyes seemed to brighten for a second.

"In fact, many will remember your bravery in the face of injustice."

He was still listening, so I continued. "I believe this cruel peine forte et dure will end what is happening here in Salem."

"I hope so," Thomas said, sitting up straight.

He startled me, and I dropped the water gourd, quickly picking it back up.

"Is that for him?" Thomas gestured to the gourd.

I was surprised. "May I?" He nodded. With shaky hands, I raised the gourd to Giles's mouth and let the water touch his lips. Instinctively, I knew that putting too much water into his belly would cause him more pain, so I only allowed a few drops to moisten his mouth. The calmness that settled over him was unlike anything I had witnessed before—like I was giving him the very dews from heaven.

"Thank . . . you, sweet . . . child," he said hoarsely. Out of breath, he looked away.

"God be with you," I whispered. I had heard or read those words somewhere before, but never uttered them. But I meant it. "God, be with you, Giles Corey."

A tear trickled down the corner of his eye. He had heard my plea to God in his behalf, and he had accepted it.

I knew he wouldn't die this evening, and I knew the kind guard was nearby, but I still stayed in my secluded spot, hidden in the trees, until the morning sun crested the horizon.

"What?" I looked down at myself. Someone had placed a blanket around my shoulders. I glanced over at Thomas. It had to have been him.

Shivering, I walked across the frosty ground. "Thank you, sir," I said, handing the blanket to Thomas. I looked over at Giles. A wool blanket draped about his shoulders, too, the only part of his body exposed from under the planks of wood. "Thank you," I repeated, a sob catching in my throat.

Thomas nodded. "The good Lord says, 'do unto others as you would have them do unto you.'" He went silent, and

I wondered if he was thinking of justice for the judges like I was right now.

People started to arrive, and finding Giles still alive, began a prayer vigil in his behalf. Others walked straight by him, as if he had already died and left their memories.

I saw John coming from a distance and went up to meet him. He handed me a chunk of warm bread and a small crock with buttery honey. Oh, my, I was in heaven. "Thank you."

"How is he?"

"Very much alive."

He seemed surprised by my words.

"Cruel, huh? It's a slow death, John."

"Should we bring him . . ." He gestured toward the food. "You know . . ."

I wished I could tell him what I knew about human digestion and things. "I'm afraid he'd have no room in his pressed belly, and it would be even more painful than it is right now."

"Aye," he said nodding. "For a girl, you know a lot about things," he said, bobbing his head.

"Thanks," I said, with a touch of sarcasm. Seriously. That was so narrow-minded.

"Hello, John."

Startled by her sudden appearance, I turned to see Betty Hubbard strolling toward us, and shoved a larger piece of the bread into my mouth. If I chewed slowly, I wouldn't have to talk.

"Who is your friend?" she asked, eyeing my hat, which had somehow fallen partway over my eyes.

"Oh, him?" John said, calmly. "He's my cousin, Seth."

"Hello, Seth."

I gave her a quick nod and turned away, pretending to be looking at something in the distance. Unfortunately, my gaze fell on Giles and the small crowd that had gathered.

"I know," Betty said, with a heavy sigh. "I wish he would hurry up and die."

I gagged on the bread, and John slapped my back. "Excuse us, Betty," he said, leading me away.

We got to a safe distance, and John threw his hat to the ground. "I never did like that Betty Hubbard."

"Yeah," I said, fuming. "The nerve of some people."

"The nerve of some people?" he repeated, processing what I had said. "Yeah, the nerve of some people."

My shoulders dropped. I had introduced another new phrase to an era that probably wasn't ready for it yet.

John bent down and picked up his hat, brushing off the loose dirt. "I brought you more water." He patted the gourd slung over his shoulder. He handing it to me and then took the empty one I'd been carrying. "I have to get back to the farm. Papa and I are putting up stronger fence posts to keep the cows in."

We waved at me farther down the road and then turned a corner. I returned to the field by the jailhouse where a dozen or so other people had already arrived. Giles's daughters sat near him, speaking soft words into his ears. Every once in a while they looked over at me. With curiosity on her face, Deliverance came near.

"Are you the young man who sat with my father during the night?"

I was afraid to speak, girl voice and all, so I just nodded.

"Thank you," she whispered. She fingered a small, wooden cross in her hands. Glancing back at her father, she handed it to me. "My father wants you to have this."

I drew back, astounded. A gift from Giles Corey? Tears were building fast. Act like a man. Act like a man, Bess. Another quick nod was all I could manage, as she pressed the cross into my hands.

"He made one for each of his children and grandchildren."

My eyes widened. This was too precious of a gift for a stranger. I thrust it back toward her, but she waved it away.

"You comforted him, when no one else would."

Not true, I pointed toward the guard and pushed the cross toward him.

"Oh, yes, Thomas. He was so kind yesterday." She stared at him. "Was it he who put the blanket about his shoulders?"

I nodded vigorously.

Her voice softened. "Really?" She looked from me to him and then back at me. "May I?" She took the cross from my outstretched hands.

She patted my arm. "You are a very thoughtful, young man." In light steps, she was at his side. He seemed quite moved by her gesture, and readily accepted the gift.

Noon fast approached on this, the second day of Giles's cruel punishment. His parched, bleeding lips and pasty skin sickened me. It was almost too much to witness, and yet, how selfish of me. I would live to see another day and someday forget the scene before me. But for Giles, this was the bitter end. A larger crowd had arrived, but the two daughters refused to let me slip away into the crowd, and bade me stay.

Corwin came to the platform. Stunned to see Giles still breathing, his audible gasp grated on me. I imagined him in his nice home sipping tea and talking politics, expecting to find Corey dead when he arrived.

"Now, Giles?" Corey asked. "Wilt thou confess to being a witch?"

Giles's red-rimmed eyes met his. His parched lips shuddered as he parted them to speak. The crowd hushed. Everyone waited. Giles drew in a shallow breath, and with a crackly voice cried, "More weight!"

It was like everything stopped right then, so quiet was the world. You read about things like this in history. Film makers dare to imitate their meaning with props and actors, but nothing can touch the real event. My heart hung heavy for the poor man and his family.

"No!" Deliverance broke down into tears. "No, Papa, no!"

"Stay back!" Corwin barked. "And give that man more weight." Corwin gestured toward the pile of rocks near the platform. He walked away toward the bakery.

With each rock added to the heap, the small crowd groaned along with Giles. I could hardly stand it. The tears wouldn't stop. I didn't care what anyone thought about my manhood. Seriously. Why should I care?

Evening approached, and Giles still held on. It had been a hot day, and under Corwin's command, no one had been allowed to come near and offer him even a few drops of water. His tongue lopped out of his mouth, dangling to the side, and his breaths were short and forced. Deliverance put her face in her hands and wept, and Elizabeth prayed silently.

I wanted to defy Corwin. Oh, I wanted to so badly. But I knew that one of the most revolting acts in history was about to take place. One that had been seen by a young spectator in this crowd, and passed down from generation to generation, no doubt spoken of in hushed tones around family tables, and in front of stone hearths. I had read about it in junior high.

Corwin walked over to the dying man. He stared down at him for some time and then using the tip of his walking stick, he poked Giles's tongue back into his mouth.

I wished his daughters hadn't seen that. I wished I hadn't either. But I was done. Come what may. I could take no more. I stood and boldly walked toward Giles and then bent down and let slip a few drops of water from my gourd onto his arched lips.

"Remove that man!" cried Corwin, in a rage.

Thomas looked at me and then at Corwin. "Remove him yourself, sir." He threw his keys down and stepped into the cheering crowd.

Deliverance ran up to Corwin. "Kind sir," she pled. "It is almost finished." With trembling fingers, she pointed toward her father.

Corwin nodded and walked away, allowing Giles's daughters to gather around the platform for their father's last breath.

Giles's eyes searched theirs, and then he grinned. I'd never imagined, that a man in so much pain could smile— his last gift to his daughters. So peaceful was his passing, it was as if angels surrounded him, and maybe they did. I'd like to believe that happens to one whose life was taken away so wrongfully. And who knows, maybe that's what awaits all of us. One can hope.

I looked toward the inn. I would rest tonight and with any luck, the morning would bring me news of Hezekiah and contact with Charles's daughter, Liza.

Deliverance came up to me and threw her arms around my neck. "Thank you, thank you," she said between sobs.

When she finally released me, I nodded and crossed the street.

Twenty-Six
The Struggle

I should have ended it. Thrown that dastardly stone into the river and been done with it! The stones had been the bane of my beloved Bess's mental deterioration. I was sure of it. If I had interpreted the pages of de Nostredame's book correctly, the more she used the stones, the deeper the stones entwined their mystical powers into her soul— like threaded, invasive fibers threading themselves through every neural pathway of her brain. Still, one mistranslated word could change the entire meaning. I had to study more. I had to get back to the future and delve deeper into those ancient pages. I stood there at the edge of the river then sat down, rolling the blue stone around in my fingers.

If I threw it away, it would end this madness. I would have Bess here in 1692 forever. We would be insanely happy—get married, have children. I could give her a good life here, nay, an excellent one. The stone felt heavy in my hands, as I struggled to release it to a watery grave.

An approaching carriage broke my thoughts. Though partially hidden by a shrub, I could see through the woody branches. A woman drove the carriage, and she was alone. I had tethered my horse to a tree beside me. Having already drunk from the edge of the river bank, he stood as still as the clouds in the sky, with an occasional paw of his hoof in the loose dirt.

The woman had but to look our way, and she would have seen my horse. Facing away from us, she stared at the rushing water passing by, wiping at what seemed to be tears streaming down her face.

It seemed like I was not the only one who needed some private time to themselves. Embarrassed that I witnessed a moment of apparent anguish, I turned away. I did not wish to startle her by leaving, so I sat still. I looked down at the blue stone, and, with great reluctance, slipped it back into my pocket. Close enough to hear her words, I listened, feeling uncomfortable with my involuntary espionage.

"Lies! Lies!"

I looked back at her. She sat down on a large boulder and put her face in her hands, and I wondered where I had heard that voice before. I grimaced. It used to be easy to know such things, but when one time travels, names, faces, and voices become a blur.

"I am so mad!" the woman yelled, angrily slapping the boulder. "Ouch." She drew her hand up quickly, no doubt regretting that move. "How could she keep this secret from me?" Then she banged her hands against her sides, a short growl leaving her lips.

I tried not to stare. I was hearing too much, and yet, it was quite interesting. She was quiet for some time after that short outburst. *Good.* She must have worked it out, and rid whatever distressed her out of her system.

I needed to get going. I really could not wait any longer. Looking down at my pocket watch, I determined that I must go. It was time for the peine forte et dure to begin, and I knew I would find Bess there.

The woman jumped up, before I had a chance to stand. "You robbed me of my father!" she screamed into the nothingness. "Charles Fieldstone never died!"

I scrambled to my feet. "Liza?" I shouted toward her. "Liza Fieldstone?"

I should have been more discreet. She turned suddenly and her feet tangled in her long dress. It sent her backward tumbling into the cold river. With a loud splash, streams of water flew in all directions. Within seconds, the rushing current spit her out, and she bobbed downriver toward me, gasping for air.

There was no time to take my boots off or even my shirt. Dropping my clock watch to the ground, I jumped into the cold water and swam toward her. "I've got you!" I grabbed her shoulders. The strong current swept us farther down, but took us to a bend in the meandering river where it slowed down considerably.

"Stop fighting me!" She thrashed about so, making it nearly impossible for me to pull her to safety. "We're almost there!" I pulled her toward the curve of the river bend and then up to its muddy bank. Safely out of the raging waters, we fell into the sludge and looked up at the sky. I remained quiet, unsure of what to say next. "I am sorry I startled you."

She turned sideways to me, her wet hair stuck to the sides of her face. "As well you should be, sir."

"Ah," I said slightly offended. "I just rescued you."

She glared at me and raised up on her elbows. "You frightened me." She scowled. "Otherwise, I would not have fallen into the river."

267

I had to concede to that. "Yes, that is the part I am sorry for."

"Oh." Laying back down, she looked up at the treetops. After some time, she pulled herself up into a sitting position. "You called me by name. Do I know you, sir?"

I got up and helped her to stand. "I met you at your house, remember?"

She stared at me for some time and then pointed at my hair. "Oh, my."

I had no idea what she was talking about, until I remembered my hair was black the last time she saw me. "It is a disguise, Liza. The girls accusing the witches turned their unwarranted fury on us and . . ."

"Oh. You need say no more." She sat forward seeming to be more interested. "You are Hezekiah Hanson."

I nodded.

"You have word of my father?" She wrapped her arms around her quavering shoulders.

"Yes." I wanted to tell her everything, but of course, I could not. It was most important to get her back to town where she could change into dry clothing.

I looked down at my dripping clothes. I could change at Zebulon's house. "Are you staying in Salem Village?" I assumed she was there for the Coreys. I gestured toward her carriage farther upstream.

Her face hardened. "I cannot go back there."

"You cannot remain like this." I pointed to her muddy, wet clothes.

Her lips pressed tight. Taking long strides toward her carriage, she called over her shoulder. "I will walk about until they dry, sir."

I followed her, stopping at my horse to untether him and to pick up my clock watch. At her carriage, she took out a small blanket and wrapped it about her shoulders. She walked about, just as she said she would do. I watched her silently. Every time she passed by me, she threw a few words my way.

"Where is he, my father?" She made the next loop around the carriage. "And why did he leave me?" She paused and gave me an angry glare. Next time around, she asked, "Did you know him well?"

I sighed. "I know you have questions." She walked right past me so I followed. "And I have answers."

At that, she stopped walking and turned toward me. "I . . . I am afraid to know them, Hezekiah. What kind of man forgets about his daughter?"

I did not know the answer to that. "Why don't you ask him yourself?"

She stared at me for some time. "Yes." She nodded. "Take me to him."

That was the hard part. I wasn't sure how that would pan out. Liza Fieldstone would have to go 323 years into the future to see her dad. "We need Bess."

"The one masquerading as an old woman?"

I grinned. "That'd be her."

She sneezed. "Salem Village?" Her voice shook, and I hoped it was only from being cold. She sneezed again.

Theresa Sneed

"My cousin lives in Salem Village. I am sure his wife will let you borrow some dry clothes."

"No, thank you, sir. I will purchase my own." She threw her foot up on the running board of the carriage, then pushed my hands away as I tried to assist her.

She didn't wait for me, but pulled the carriage back onto the dirt road and took off toward Salem Village. I mounted my horse and followed, a little bewildered with her actions. *I was just trying to help. Women.*

I was glad my courting days were over, and my mind turned back to Bess. I guess they really weren't over at all. Bess had captured my heart, but I was not completely sure I had captured hers. She could be so distant at times.

The stones. Those dastardly stones. They were to blame. I glanced at the carriage rolling along ahead of me. I could not destroy the stone just yet, but as God was my witness, I would.

I was not surprised to see the large crowds in Salem Town. Many people had gathered for the sensational event. It would at least help to divert attention away from me, now that my prosthetic mask was in my bag instead of on my face.

I pulled up beside the carriage. Liza was already getting out. "Shall we meet somewhere?" I was going to Zebulon's to change and reapply the mask.

She blinked. "I thought I was going with you. I certainly cannot change in the street. I will buy a new dress here." She strutted off toward the dressmaker's shop.

I waited, staying in the shadows and observing things from a distance, hoping that Bess would pass me by. It was

270

a bit cool, as it would be for late September. Chilled, I needed to get out of my wet clothing, too. Shortly, Liza returned with a large package.

After a series of sneezes, she said, "How far away is Zebulon's?"

I pointed down the road. "May I?" I reached for her package. She pulled it tighter to her chest. "Do you at least want to take the carriage?"

She frowned. "No. It belongs to Miranda." She sneezed again.

"Then let us move along," I said. Putting my hand to the small of her back, I guided her toward the road. The blanket about her shoulders slipped down, so I fixed it. She let me, which was a surprise, and she even gave me a tiny grin. She sneezed again and shivered, so I did what any gentleman would do. I put my arm around her quivering shoulders and walked her swiftly toward my cousin's house. That lasted about a minute, and she pushed my arm down.

"Kind, sir, I appreciate what you are doing." She stopped walking. "But I am fine. Thank you."

We were silent the rest of the way to the house. Once there, I knocked on the front door then opened it. I peered inside. "Zebulon? Sarah?" Turning to Liza who stood nearby, shivering from head to toe, I said, "They must not be home." I opened the door wider and gestured for her to come inside.

"I will not, sir," she said firmly. Her arms about her shoulders, she trembled.

"What?" I said bewildered.

271

"There is no one home." Her teeth chattered, and she bit her lip. "It is not proper."

"Oh." I sighed. "Then you go into the house first, and I will wait here." She gave me a quick nod and slipped past me, closing the door behind her. I sat down on the steps on the front porch.

The door flew open. "It is impossible!" she called out. "They are too slippery, and I cannot undo the buttons!" Tears streamed down her face.

I jumped up. "Do you want me to . . . um," I stammered, pointing at her dress.

"No," she whimpered. A quick puff of air escaped her throat. "Yes," she said, angrily. Turning her back to me, she reached behind herself and pointed to the long row of buttons.

How in the world did women ever put up with tiny buttons trailing down their backs? My fingers were too big for them, and I fumbled with the irksome things, then stepped back. The door slammed, with not even a thank you. I supposed she was embarrassed. I know I was.

Still, it took some time before the door opened again. She stood before me. The new dress looked fine, but her hair lay against her head in a most unfashionable way. Her eyes were wet with tears, as she ran her fingers through her muddy tresses.

"Let me help," I said, this time not approaching her. "There is soap on the shelf and water in the basin." I pointed toward the kitchen area.

She sneezed. "Yes, please." Stepping aside, she let me pass.

Washing the mud out of her hair was an interesting experience. I knew instinctively that it should have been Bess's hair that I lathered and wondered what Bess would think.

Retrieving a towel from a cupboard, I handed it to Liza, and then took broad steps away. "I, um, I'll be right back." I patted my wet clothes.

"No," she said. "Wait." Rubbing her hair in the towel, she then thrust the wet towel toward me. "Ah, thank you, Hezekiah." She scuttled to the front door. "I'll be out here while you change."

The door closed. I looked down at the muddied water in the basin. Running my hand across my dirty hair, I combed out the dried mud with my fingers, then hurried to Zebulon's wardrobe and picked the first thing I found.

After replacing the water in the basin, I went outside to where Liza sat quietly on the porch steps. I looked down at my pocket clock and couldn't believe how late it was, before pushing it into a pocket. "Are you ready?"

She sneezed and looked at me strange. "Ready? Giles Corey is even now being pressed to death." Rubbing at her red nose, she mumbled, "I will never be ready to see the likes of that."

I nodded in agreement. I would not either, but I knew, without a doubt, that that was where we would find Bess. I reached out for Liza's hand, but she once again refused it. Standing threw her off balance, and she sank back down on the steps. "I, ah . . ."

"Are you all right?" I moved toward her, but she waved me away.

Her complexion waned, and she looked piqued and weary. All at once I remembered that I had not eaten a thing that day, and she might not have either. "Are you hungry?"

"Ugh, no." She made a face and turned into the railing running up the porch steps.

Without a word, and because I knew she would not allow it, I came near and put my hand on her forehead. She was burning hot. "Liza!"

Slumping into the railing, she did not respond. I had no idea where she was staying. Not knowing all the details of their departure from one another, I wasn't sure a reunion would even be smart.

I raced back into Zebulon's house and grabbed a blanket, the one Liza had used was considerably soiled and damp. Then leaping down the steps beside her, I placed it about her shoulders. "I'll be right back."

I had never run so fast as I headed back toward the stables in the barn. Zebulon had four good horses, but they were all gone. I wondered on that, but not for long, as I hurried down the dirt road toward where we had left Miranda's carriage and horses. I was keenly aware of the obnoxious crowd that slowed me down in my flight, and flustered that I had not seen a trace of Bess.

Still, I made good time and within the hour was back beside Liza. She looked quite a bit worse and was breathing heavily. "Let me take you to your mother, Liza."

She looked up at me bewildered. "My mother? Is she here?" She looked around and groaned.

"Where is she, Liza?"

274

"What?" she said between labored breaths.

I struggled with the idea of searching for a doctor. The town was crawling with people, and finding a doctor in that rambunctious crowd would be everlastingly difficult.

Liza groaned. It was clear that she needed assistance, even if she refused it from me. I swept her up in my arms. She thrashed about, trying to get me to drop her, I assumed. But, I did not, and with some effort was able to get her into the carriage. I made her as comfortable as I could and then headed off toward Dorchester, to the one woman I knew could help—my own mother.

It was with great reluctance that I left Salem Town without my Bess. As soon as I had Liza safe at my parents' home, I would return for her.

Every opportunity I got, I stopped to check on Liza, but finding her distressed assured the urgency to get to Dorchester and hurried me along all the faster. "Dastardly slow horses."

Knowing what the future held in technology and travel annoyed me in the past. I knew how quickly I could get to my parents by car or helicopter and bemoaned the fact that it would take me much longer by horse and carriage. Alone, I could have easily made it to Dorchester in a couple hours, but by carriage, no less than four. It was nearing dark, and I was most concerned with the colder air affecting Liza's condition.

I drove the horses hard, the evening stars lighting the way, only slowing down when absolutely necessary. Feeling guilty with my plan, I tried to focus on other things. I could leave Liza with my mother and would not have to stay at her side. It seemed selfish and cold to me, but I needed to find my Bess.

By late evening, we pulled down the long drive. As it happened, Sigmund was walking from the barn to the house. Upon seeing me, he came near.

"Master Hanson! Yer mother will be happy to see ye!"

"Yes, Sigmund," I jumped off the carriage. "I have an ill passenger." I gestured toward Liza laying in the back. "Help me get her into the house."

Without another word, Sigmund went right to work. Getting Liza into the carriage was easier than getting her out, though the long rest had seemed to help her recover a bit. "Don't touch me!" She slapped his hands away. "Get away!"

I stepped back. "Liza?"

Peering out at me, she grimaced. "What are you doing?" she demanded. Raising up on her elbows, her eyes widened. "Where am I?" She sneezed and then moaned.

My mother, along with Gabriella, rushed out of the house. "Hezekiah!" She scurried to my side, but when she saw Liza, she stopped. "What is going on here?"

"Who is she?" asked Gabriella, wagging her finger at Liza.

"This is Liza," I said, extending my hand to Liza. With reluctance, she took it and let me help her from the carriage. "Liza, this is my mother, Victoria Hanson."

"Oh, my," Victoria said. "You are ill." She had quickly appraised the situation in the way only a mother could. Liza's puffy eyes and red nose helped, too.

Liza sneezed loudly.

276

"Come along, child," my mother cooed. She wrapped her arm around Liza's shoulders and led her up the steps into the house.

"Bring me my horse, Sigmund." With a nod, Sigmund took off toward the stables. I could be back in Salem Town a few hours past midnight if I hurried.

Gabriella grabbed my arm. "Your mother is waving to you from the door."

I strode toward my mother and followed her into the house. "I need to get back to Salem Town," I said.

"Of course you do, dear. But you must not run off so fast. You do not need to be there until morning. At least stay the night."

That was true. If I got there at two-thirty in the morning, it would not do me any good. Bess would be sound asleep in the inn. But knowing Bess that was a big maybe.

My mother seemed troubled. "Mother?"

Wringing her hands, she burst out, "I thought I could be strong, but when is your father coming home?"

I drew her near. "It will be over soon." I hoped. My heart fell. To keep Bess here with me forever, also meant to keep my father in the future. I would not allow that to happen. There had to be another way.

"But then, you will go away again?"

When I did not answer right away, she threw her arms around me.

"Just come back to us, Hezekiah." She wiped her face. "But, if not, I will pretend you are across the waters, and I

277

will know that all is well—that just an ocean separates us." She turned into my shoulder stifling a sob.

When the time came, saying goodbye to my family would be the hardest thing I would ever do. In the back of my mind, I hoped I could convince Bess to make our final time travel destination here. I was in such anguish. One of us would have to give up family and would suffer keen loss, worse than death. Death, at least, is a certainty, but knowing time overlaps was torturous. I wasn't sure I could be chivalrous and give up everything I knew and loved here in this time. I hoped that Bess's love for me would be enough for her to see it my way.

I was exhausted. My mother was right about staying the night. "Where did you put Liza?"

"In Bess's room. I hope that is all right." Her nose wrinkled, as it often did when she was curious. "Hezekiah, who is she?"

"Mother," I said, slowly releasing air from my lips. "Liza is Charles's daughter."

She drew her head back. "His daughter? Why, Charles never spoke of a daughter."

"Not even once?" Liza's weak voice trailed down the hall. She leaned against the door trim.

Victoria walked toward her. "You ought to be in bed, child."

"Yes, I know," Liza said, rubbing her nose. "I heard you talking, and I have so many questions."

"Of course you do, Liza," she said softly.

"Your son was kind enough to bring me here." She glanced around. "Did my father work here long?"

"Yes, for many years."

Liza shook her head. "I was raised in the province of Maine by his sister, whom I have called mother all of my life. I don't understand." Her face hardened. "I have visited his grave on our land!"

"Charles has a gravesite?" I couldn't believe it.

Liza nodded and wiped at her nose. "Why would my mother go to all this trouble to hide him from me?"

"I do not know, Liza," Victoria said. "But I do know the Charles that we know would have at least talked to us about you."

Her eyes opened wide in a quizzical look. "So you think . . . he may not have even known about me?"

Victoria frowned. "What did your mother tell you about Charles?"

"That he died in an Indian raid before I was born. Shortly thereafter, my birth mother died from small-pox."

"You do not remember your mother?"

"No, not at all. I was very young, an infant."

"And you were raised by your aunt," Victoria said, seeming deep in thought.

"My two aunts." Liza coughed and then sneezed.

"Oh, dear," Victoria said. "You need your rest. There will be plenty of time to talk in the morning." She put her hand on Liza's arm and guided her back inside the bed chamber. "Hezekiah, will you wait for me?" she called over her shoulder.

Shortly, she came out of the room. Pointing down the hall to Bess's room, she whispered. "So, Liza is there, and

Charles," she threw her arms wide into the air, "is *far* from here, and you and Bess want to . . . ?"

"Reunite them, Mother."

Her shoulders fell forward. "Of course, reunite them. And bring Abner back." She frowned. "Exactly, how are you going to do this?"

I had no idea. "I'm working on it." I hugged her. "Good night, Mother."

Exhausted, I dragged myself to my room. I thought about going to my underground chamber, but compared to its future counterpart, it would only disappoint.

Nestled in my bed, I stared up at the ceiling. I had placed the blue stone on the small table beside me. It glimmered in the moonlight that filtered through the parted curtains. Once things settled and everyone was where they needed to be, that stone was history. I grimaced at my choice of words. Everything here was history where Bess came from, and I did not want to become part of that history.

Twenty-Seven
Diversion

The morning came quicker than I needed. Although I was anxious to get to Bess, I found myself dragging my feet as we neared the end of our adventure. I scoffed. *Adventure?* It was more like a nightmare. And that it was the end of the nightmare would take nothing short of a miracle. The servants had already filled my bath in the next room and the steam from it wreathed up to the ceiling in the cool, morning air. I soaked just long enough to plan my day ahead. I wondered how my father was enjoying the showers of the future. Still, nothing beat a hot soaking in a private setting.

Staring at my reflection in the mirror, I decided to keep the beard that was forming. Bess wouldn't care much for it, but that was an easy fix. And with my gray hair, the beard, and a hat pulled over my eyes, it would be harder for anyone to recognize me.

My mother met me in the hall. "Did you sleep well?"

I nodded. "And Liza?"

"She's in the bath. She asked me to tell you thank you, and would you please wait, so she can speak to you. Breakfast will be ready shortly."

I hadn't planned on eating a formal breakfast, but I guess, I was now. If Liza was up, she must be feeling better. "She's not planning on coming with me, is she?"

"Why not?" Liza called from behind me.

Surprised to hear her voice, I turned toward her. "Because you haven't fully recovered yet."

"How would you know that?" Her eyes narrowed.

I turned to my mother for support, but she turned away. I pressed my lips tight before saying. "Liza, why would you want to go back to Salem Town?"

"I've been thinking a lot about it. My mother has some explaining to do." She got quiet. "She must be miserable worrying about me." She glanced at my mother. "I guess I miss her." Sighing, she continued, "Your mother explained a few things to me."

Victoria broke in, "Yes, about how a mother might act out of sorts if it meant protecting her child." She placed her hand on Liza's arm. "And how a child might act out of sorts because she might not have all the facts."

Brilliant. My mother was simply brilliant. Except now I had to wonder where her thinking came from. What had happened in her life that brought her such deep understanding? I guess I really did not know her very well. I knew her as "mother", but, she was far more than that. My heart was heavy, as I realized I might not get that chance.

Liza was a big hit with Gabriella and Arabella. She fit in so well with my family, that it was as if she had always been a part of it. I almost wanted to leave her there and take off to Salem Town by myself, but knew the right thing was to wait patiently while she finished her goodbyes.

Gabriella was finishing the touches on Liza's hair. I thought it all nonsense, but understood that for women, hair appeared to be all important. In truth, she did look better with her tresses piled on top of her head and all the tangles completely brushed out.

I stood by the carriage anxious to leave. Finally, I could take it no longer. "We must go, Liza. Hurry along."

And there was that look I had become accustomed to from her. I ignored it and glanced down at my pocket clock. Swinging up into the seat, I patted the spot beside me. I suppose I should have helped her in, and that might explain the look of dismay on my mother's face. Surely she must have thought she had taught me better. I jumped back down and offered my hand.

"No, thank you," Liza said curtly. "I can get in on my own."

I grunted and climbed back on the seat beside her. With a tip of my hat toward my family and a deep pang in my heart at what lay ahead, I took off with a start. "Yah!"

The horses galloped down the drive and out onto the dirt road toward Salem Town, my Bess, and the hardest decision I would ever have to make.

Liza was different today. Very quiet yesterday, today she was quite chatty. I learned things about her I was not sure I wanted to know, and yet, knowing things about her brought a whole new perspective on who she was.

We spoke mostly about Charles. I told her every little thing I could think of about him. It seemed to comfort her and at times, her nose would wrinkle and the corners of her lips would turn up in a half grin. Of course, I kept my eyes mostly on the road, but driving horses down a dirt road, even in a gallop, was not as intense as speeding down a road in an automobile. I could steal a glance her way quite often, if I chose.

I chose not to.

It was early evening when we arrived. She stared at the field beside the jailhouse. An empty platform, with planks and rocks thrown to the side, met our gaze.

"It is over," she said, breaking into a sob. "We have missed it all." Her last words were not a lament, but a relief. I could tell that she, like myself, had not wanted to witness the event.

"They have already buried him," she said, her voice heavy with sadness. "Tomorrow, they will hang his wife."

Tomorrow would be the last of the hangings. I wished I could tell her that. Knowing the future had its good points and its bad points. While I was grateful to know that Salem Town would soon begin its long and hard road to healing, I also knew she not only had the anguish of the next day's hangings, but also the fear of many more to come.

It was like how one feels when watching an intense movie in the future. The first time viewed is always the hardest. Any time thereafter, knowing the ending eases the difficulty of watching it. Grimacing, I berated myself for thinking so—this was not a movie. The empty platform and strewn rocks were not props, and Giles Corey would never go back to the farm and the life that he loved.

I walked her over to the inn. Her reluctance to enter was evident. We stood at the entrance, while she fidgeted with her hands. "I'll see you in the morning," I said, opening the door for her. "I'll be at my cousin's."

She gave me a quick nod, but then turned to me, her eyes moist. "Thank you, Hezekiah. I had an enjoyable time, er, except for falling into the river."

I wished I could say the same, but other than seeing my family again, this had been an unwanted diversion. I could have been back in Salem Town yesterday afternoon, if I had not happened upon Liza Fieldstone. Of course, I realized with a frown, she was exactly who we were looking for.

"I will see you tomorrow. I'll be off now." I turned on my heels and walked away.

It was rude, I know, but her flirtatious look was disconcerting. Had we not spoken of my Bess? Oh, that must be it. She must not realize that Bess and I are nearly engaged. It did seem strange to me that my family must not have spoken of my relationship with Bess either. I would fix that immediately.

Only steps away, I heard hurried footsteps behind me. I turned to see a woman strutting toward Liza.

"Liza?" Elizabeth Senior rushed toward her. "Oh, Liza, I've been looking for you everywhere." Her voice was thick with anguish. "You cannot know my suffering!"

Not wanting to be seen, I slunk into the shadows. But what I saw surprised me. Without hesitation, Liza threw her arms around her mother's neck, seeming to readily forgive her.

The morning brought me to my feet. I rummaged through my cousin's pantry and found something to eat and then took off toward the inn. We had agreed to meet at the baker house early and begin our search for Bess. I glanced down at my pocket clock, wondering if she was up, and remembering how long it had taken her yesterday to be ready.

"Hezekiah!" Liza's voice rang through the air. I was surprised and pleased she was there, but dismayed that she had used my name out loud. Glancing quickly around, I saw we were alone. "Don't use my name, Liza."

Her eyes widened. "Oh, oh, of course—the girls, those wicked girls." She pouted. "What shall I call you?"

I had not applied the prosthetic mask, as it was everlastingly hard to do so, and I had little adhesive left to hold it in place. Still, with the gray hair and beard, it would be harder to identify me, unless spoken to directly face-to-face.

"Try not to call me by name at all, but if you must, call me, Seth." Bess's younger brother's name seemed perfect.

"Seth," she said, my name rolling of her tongue. "Then Seth, it is, or not at all."

She looped her arm through mine, which made me feel most uncomfortable. I patted her hand and pulled my arm away. Facing her, I said, "How did it go last night?" Where that came from, I did not know. I had meant to say, "'I'm in a relationship'"—coining future dialect, she probably would not get at first.

Her face saddened. "Last night was most disappointing," she said. "Right away, I asked about my father, but my mother said it was not the time to talk." Liza frowned. "Apparently, she had had a rough day." She rolled her eyes and then sighed. "I suppose, she had. It was rather selfish of me to take off like that."

286

"She had to expect it, Liza."

She looked up at me, her eyes once again moist.

"Your mother had to expect that at some point you were going to find out and would react just the way you did. She ought to be grateful you returned at all."

"Yes, you are right," she said, studying my eyes with that blasted look again. "You are so intuitive—for a man," she said softly. She placed a trembling hand on my arm.

This was going to be a lot harder than I had imagined. I had been able to pull away as a gentleman would before, but now, it was clear, I needed to be more firm.

Right at that moment, two girls walked toward us. My heart sunk as Betty Hubbard and Mercy Lewis came near. Beard or no, they would recognize me immediately. There was no time to think of any other diversion. "Forgive me," I whispered to Liza, and then pulled her into an embrace, hiding my face in her thick tresses.

Twenty-Eight
The Last Hangings

Alone in my bed, I stared up at the ceiling. Nervous, my fingers curled up and then flexed. Crazy day. Crazy, hopeful day. Crazy, because today was the last of the hangings in 1692. Hopeful, because I might finally hook up with Hezekiah.

Hangings. I shuddered. I wished I could tell the world that it would soon be over, at least the murderous, hanging part. Still, the very fact that eight people would lose their lives to foolish superstition and erroneous judgment on this day, dulled the illusory sunrise seeping through the window.

Sitting up, I ran my fingers through my short hair, surprised at first, but then grateful for such an effective disguise. The proprietor had even stopped me when I came back to the inn last night, but I assured him, in the deepest voice that I could, that I was Felicity's nephew, Seth.

My stomach was in knots. I had laid awake for some time last evening worried about Hezekiah. I had expected to see him traipse into town yesterday. Knowing the gentleman that he was, I was sure he had taken another room, or perhaps he had stayed at Zebulon's. I would check there first, if his name wasn't on the inn's registry.

A grin played about my lips. He was in for a surprise with my latest guise. Ruffling my hair, I wondered what he would think. That was enough to hurry me along, and I quickly dressed and left the room.

"Good day to you," I said, tipping my hat to the proprietor of the inn. "I am looking for Hez, er, my *uncle,*

Mathius Alby. My aunt is concerned that he didn't show up last night. Did he perchance take another room?"

Giving me a prolonged and rather odd look, he searched the inn's registry. "No, there is not anyone here by that name." He glanced up at me inquisitively.

I wasn't about to linger for questioning, and thanking him, I rushed off. Just outside the inn, Betty and Mercy passed by me—right by me. Shocked, I mumbled under my breath, "Thanks, John," grateful for my tenth great uncle's clever ruse, and the use of his boyish clothing.

Betty and Mercy walked toward the bakery which was bad for me as that is exactly where I had intended to go on my way to Zebulon's. I watched them cross the street. Glancing down at my pocket clock, I realized the hangings would begin in about an hour. Already, the small town filled with people.

I walked swiftly across the street and hid myself in an alley where I could peer around the corner and monitor Betty and Mercy's whereabouts. I was determined to get a bite to eat, knowing that as the day progressed, I wouldn't be able to eat a thing. Just thinking about the hangings made me feel sick to my stomach.

The door opened to the bakery, and they stepped out. They moved to one side of the door and continued their lively chat. Oh, come on! Move on, girls. Move on!

Across the street and down a little ways from me, the front door to the inn opened and a young woman stepped out. I nearly gagged—it was Liza! I held myself back from running across the street, hoping that Betty and Mercy would turn and walk the other way. I certainly couldn't make a scene in front of them.

From down the street, coming the other way, a man approached. His hat was tipped over his eyes, and he had a scruffy beard, but something leaped within me. I was sure it was Hezekiah. I glanced back at the girls, still lingering in front of the bakery. Apparently, Hezekiah had not seen them, but he must have recognized Liza, because he headed straight toward her.

This was so exciting! And nerve-wracking. I glanced once again at the girls and then back at Liza, who seemed to be looking right at Hezekiah, as if she recognized him, too. I bit down on my pinky and looked from the girls, to Hezekiah, to Liza, and then back again. At least, we could finally talk to her and somehow convince her to come back to the future with us. Lame. I know. Exactly how were we going to do that? *Hello, Liza. It's me, Bess—the young girl, old woman, and now a boy? Yep, we're taking you 323 years into the future.* My lips twisted to the side, knowing the hardest part was ahead of us.

They neared each other, and she smiled sweetly. They must have hooked up before today that much was evident. I couldn't quite put my finger on it, but something was wrong.

"Hezekiah!" Liza's voice carried from across the street.

Hezekiah took quick strides to her side, dismay covering his face. He looked nervously around, but not down the street where the circle girls chatted. "Don't use my name, Liza," I heard him tell her.

Okay, so she knew somewhat of our masquerade.

Her hands flew to her mouth. She pouted.

My eyes narrowed with her pronounced pout. Seriously? I knew that look, mastered by so many women, but apparently not by me. It was so, um, *girlish.* I glanced down at my clothing and scowled.

Hezekiah said something, but I couldn't quite hear him. He had dropped his voice too low. Stepping in front of her, he blocked her words as well, but not her actions. She looped her arm through his—the nerve. My fists clenched to my sides. I was fuming mad. And I didn't care if anyone, including the girls, saw my reaction.

Calm down, Bess. He's just being a gentleman. I was right too, as I saw him remove her arm from his. A puff of air escaped my throat, and I unclenched my fists. They were talking too soft for me to hear everything, but I did hear the words, "'mother and father'" coming from Liza. They began their stroll toward the bakery.

Look up, Hezekiah! Apparently enthralled with Liza, he didn't even see the girls, who had crossed the street to their side.

His voice a little louder, I heard him say, "She had to expect it, Liza." She looked up at him with a look I didn't appreciate. I heard the words "mother," "react," and "grateful you returned at all."

Evidently, she now believed what I had been trying to tell her all along. Good. One step out of the way.

She looked up into his eyes—those gorgeous, green eyes that belonged to me! *Back off, girl.* I fumed.

She said something to him and giggled. She placed her arm on his.

My mouth dropped open. The circle girls were walking toward them, but I didn't care. I stormed out onto the street, strutting toward Hezekiah and that little *wench*, hat bouncing against my short hair. But before I could reach them, Hezekiah turned Liza into him, and wrapped his strong arms around her, in an embrace that should have only been for me.

The circle girls stopped and stared. On the other side of Hezekiah and Liza, I did the same.

"Do I know you?" Betty asked, studying Hezekiah from head to toe.

Liza pulled away. Surprised by the girls, or maybe woozy from the warm embrace, she cooed, "Come along, Seth."

"Seth?" Mercy said inquisitively.

"Seth?" I whispered, shocked.

"Yes, Seth," Hezekiah mumbled, looping his arm through Liza's. He kept his head down and walked straight past the girls and away from me. Stunned, I watched him walk away. The circle girls paid no more attention to him, but continued their animated conversation.

"It's a terrible shame," said Mercy, with a long sigh.

"No, it' is not," Betty snapped. "It is their own fault— witches ought to be hanged," she added haughtily, barely glancing at me.

Under different circumstances, I would have been livid at her words, but I was numb and too distressed about Hezekiah and Liza. I passed by the girls and followed the lovebirds from a distance. They headed back toward the jail, where a large crowd had gathered.

Pulled by two oxen, the wooden cart used for all three hangings, paused ominously in front of the jail, awaiting its next victims. Even though I had expected to see it, it still shocked me, and weighed heavy in my heart.

I glanced back at Hezekiah. He had not removed his arm from Liza. It's just a cover, Bess. Just a cover. Still, my eyes filled with tears, and I fought the urge to cry. As I glanced around, many of the crowd had teary eyes—even the men. If the hangings weren't right here, right now, I would have been spitting bullets at Hezekiah, but with the approaching, eminent horror, I was constrained to tears instead of the furious outburst that I knew was to come.

The door to the jail opened and Judge Corwin stepped out. A hush fell over the crowd. He stretched and looked up into the cloudy sky. "Aye, it started off sunny, but it's clouding over."

"Appropriate for this horrible day," I mumbled quietly. Only those who stood nearby heard me, and one man nodded in agreement.

Corwin looked out over the crowd. "I do believe there's a storm a coming."

Truer words could not have been spoken.

A small figure appeared in the doorway, her eyes pressed closed, as if she did not want to look out on the world that had betrayed her. With a deep rise of her chest, she breathed in the cool, outside air. Her eyes opened, and her breath escaped in a long, sad sigh.

Corwin stepped aside, as Thomas Henderson, kindhearted man that he was, gently led the recently widowed Martha Corey from the jail.

The entire crowd fixed their eyes on her. Dazed, she looked out over the throng of people with deep sorrow etched into her aged face, and my heart panged within me.

Here was tragedy much greater than anything real or imagined that I was going through. I couldn't fathom being in her place, knowing that she would soon hang from the gallows tree and then be unceremoniously tossed into a shallow, common grave, like she was of no worth.

A few hands reached for her and many called out her name. She craned her neck past the crowd until her gaze fell upon the platform and rocks where her beloved Giles's life had been taken. Her lips parted and a pitiful gasp came out. Not a sound was made as Thomas helped the old woman into the cart and then went back inside the jailhouse for the next of the condemned.

One by one, he led the rest of the eight victims to the cart. Some he tethered to posts sticking up on the sides of the cart. Others, like Martha, had a small, wooden plank to sit on. I swallowed hard, knowing that the wooden plank would become the stepstool each would stand on when it came their turn for the rope to be placed over their head and around their throat.

The only man to be hanged that day, Samuel Wardwell, seemed resolved to the fact that his life would soon end. He whispered soft words to the others beside him and occasionally glanced out over the crowd with a look of profound sadness, much like Martha's—much like *all* of them.

Mary Easty had several family members near her who had woven their hands through the wooden slats to touch the hem of her long dress. One held up a child for her to kiss, and a sob caught in my throat.

All prisoners crowded into the small cart, like cattle going to a slaughterhouse. The ox-driven wagon pulled forward with a start, beginning the long, eerie procession to their unfair demise. The stunned crowd walked in front, beside, and behind the cart that carried their loved ones and friends to their deaths.

I followed at the end, sometimes walking, sometimes running to catch up, careful to keep Hezekiah in my sights. He and Liza walked off to the side, arm in arm. My head was spinning, such sorrow and pain, I'd never experienced. I could run away right now, get away from the whole thing, the hangings, and the anguish I felt from watching those two together.

Deep inside, I knew she was a better match for him. She was from his era. He could stay here and be with his family! How selfish I had been! I loved this man, and yet, I was robbing him from certain happiness.

Ugh. I groaned. My stomach hurt and now my head throbbed. How I was able to keep up with the crowd was a mystery, but instinctively, I knew I needed that stone Hezekiah still had. It was my only way home—my only way back to sanity.

The weary procession crossed the causeway over the North River. The steep hill lay just ahead, the large, ominous tree silhouetted against the clouding sky. The cart came to a sudden stop. A murmur of anguish passed through the crowd.

"Step aside! Step aside!" Corwin barked as several people pressed near the cart. From where I stood, I understood the look of chaotic optimism on their faces. The ugly procession at a halt was like watching a car crash paused in time, hoping beyond hope that it wouldn't come to pass.

"What seems to be the matter?" Hathorne asked, trotting up beside the cart on his horse. "Oh, I see. The wheels are stuck in the mire."

Even with the deep anguish I suffered, I was fascinated. I remembered reading about that in a history book. Near a good-sized boulder, I sat down and waited while several men stood around the cart discussing how to free the wheels from the mud.

"We'll need to take them out," said one man, pointing to the victims tied in the cart.

"Whatever for?" barked Hathorne. Glancing out at the pressing crowd, a wave of nervousness passed over his face, perhaps sure some would snatch their loved ones away, once off the cart.

Dumbfounded, I watched as the eight bounced around like ragdolls while the men labored to remove the wheels from the mud.

But my mind was more on Hezekiah than the wheels. He had stepped aside with that woman, and they appeared to be deep in conversation. How dare they? Couldn't they see what was happening before them was greater than their little tryst? Couldn't they see they were killing me, too? Clutching my hand to my chest, I sobbed.

A scream broke through the crowd. "There! There! The devil!" Mercy yelled, pointing to the cart.

"He is there!" echoed Betty loudly. "He holds back the cart!"

Really? Right now? I moaned. Sensational to the end, the circle girls cried out in one way or another that it was the devil who hindered the cart from moving forward. I rolled my eyes. Mud. It was just mud.

The cart lurched forward, and the procession followed. The oxen pulled the cart holding the condemned up the hill to the ill-omened tree growing near its rocky ledge. Hathorne waited until everyone had made the steep climb. How nice of him. I grimaced and wiped at new tears forming in my eyes. A hand touched my shoulder.

"Hi, Seth," John said quietly, his eyes round as if in shock.

I deeply felt his pain. Strange how just his presence comforted me—knowing that family was near calmed my troubled mind. Family. A longing for my real home—where my mother and brother waited—flickered in my heart.

Corwin took his place at the highest point of the hill. Facing the cart, he bellowed, "O, ye wretched witches! Wilt thou now confess?" The sky darkened and a low rumble sounded from afar.

A cool breeze rustled Mary Easty's hair and a long strand of it flapped about her face. With hands bound behind her back, she was not able to do anything about it.

If I just had the courage to crawl up on the wagon, I could tuck it behind her ear.

Great sadness overcame me as I realized that she couldn't even wipe the stream of tears that flowed down her face. But her words were clear, and they cut through the profound silence. "I am innocent."

One by one, each of the eight professed their innocence as well. You would think that true witches would be casting spells right and left or at least spewing off very colorful language. Their words were as sweet as a tender prayer, but fell on unfeeling hearts, and ears that would not hear.

Corwin waved his hand toward Martha Corey. With the compassion of a saint, Thomas helped the old woman to climb up on the wooden plank. Tying her dress around her legs, he reluctantly stepped aside.

A pipe dangling from his mouth, the executioner came forward, a long wreath of smoke twisting up to the sky. I remembered him from Giles's peine forte et dure. He was the drunkard Thomas had shooed away. I would drink too, if I had such a job. With rope in hand, he began to slip it over her head.

Martha strained her head away from his approaching hand. "I would speak," she said, in a trembling voice, trying to move her head away from the rope.

Hathorne's eyes narrowed, but seeing the anxious crowd and probably realizing the growing animosity toward the hangings, he allowed her to continue.

"I am innocent," she repeated. She cast her eyes toward heaven. "I am innocent before God." And then defying the customs of her day, where women were frowned upon to pray aloud, she mouthed words sweeter than any prayer I had heard before, once again proclaiming her innocence and the innocence of those beside her—pleading her cause before her God, her family, and her friends.

She looked like she wanted to say more, but she paused too long. The executioner slipped the rope over her head, and then jumped over the side of the cart to the ground. Corwin gave the signal, and the executioner slapped the rump of the nearest ox. The animal jerked forward, pulling the cart away from the frightened woman.

Hanging from her neck, her bare feet desperately sought for something to stand on. Within seconds, her toes stopped wiggling, her eyes bulged, and a few sharp gurgles escaped her throat. Martha Corey's spirit left mortality only one day after the murderous death of her husband.

How cruel! How unfounded! And yet, imagining Giles's spirit standing on the hill, arms outstretched for his beloved wife, brought me peace. Crazy, huh? But what if that was true? What if the most horrendous trial we faced would one day melt away to the joy and peace of reuniting with the ones we love? I had to hope for that—I had to!

Margaret Scott was next. "I am innocent!" The executioner secured her dress about her legs and slipped the rope over her head. "Please, sir! I have done no harm!" But the oxen lurched forward, and her body hanged lifeless beside Martha's.

Ann Pudeator followed in the same manner, also declaring her innocence. With each hanging, the crowd grew more restless. No longer entertained, there was a feeling of revolt. The monthly hangings had gone on too long. There were too many left in the jails awaiting the gruesome fate.

The jailors repositioned the cart to a part of the tree where three thick limbs twisted to the sky. Mary Parker was next, amid cries of woe, but just as the others before her, she soon swayed in the cool breeze. No relation to Mary, Alice Parker stood bravely on the wooden plank. "I am innocent," she said, before her life was snapped from her, too.

Wilmot Redd, the kind woman who had saved my life those many months ago, stepped up onto the wooden plank. Her legs were tied together. My heart was heavy. She was no witch, but only a woman who knew how to use herbs for healing. Seriously? I reached toward her as the cart moved forward, slower this time—more cruel—and her legs thudded over its side, leaving her hanging in the air, dangling on a limb not far from the others.

Only two remained, and I felt more for them than any of others. They had had to witness each execution, the bodies hanging within feet of each other, swaying lifelessly in the morning breeze.

Mary Easty shook with fear, small gasps leaving her lips, as Thomas helped her to the wooden plank.

"I am not conscious of any guilt in the least degree of the crime I am to be hanged of," she said, with a short gasp. "I am innocent before God."

Searching the crowd, her eyes rested upon a man. He must have been her husband. He was the man who had held the small child up, no doubt their grandchild, for her to kiss earlier. "Goodbye, Isaac," she said to him, her voice deep in sadness. "You have brought me such happiness." Many wept at her tender words. "And to my children—I love you!"

"Mother!" Several people reached for her, their eyes streaming with tears. "Mother! Mother!"

It seemed that an awful lot were calling her mother. I turned to John with questioning eyes. "How many children does she have?"

"Fifteen," he said, his voice catching. "Goody Easty has fifteen children."

Oh, my. Fifteen children would soon lose their mother because of the heartlessness of pious judges. Oh, the injustice! The dreadfulness! I glanced around at the horror-stricken faces, realizing that the crowd was full of the children, grandchildren, and spouses of the hanged. I groaned within.

I hadn't noticed that the executioner had already put the noose about her neck. I jerked forward with the cart as it lunged. She didn't struggle, her life snatched from her brutally, in an instant. Mournful wails beset the crowd. Her children and grandchildren fell to the ground crying, and many wept with them.

Samuel Wardwell didn't need help to mount the small plank, though I am sure it was the hardest step he had ever taken. The executioner stood nearby, trails of his pipe smoke rolling past Wardwell's face.

"I am . . . *ahem, ahem* . . . I am . . . *ahem,*" Wardwell coughed, trying to state his innocence, or at least speak his last words to the crowd, but instead, he gagged on the bothersome smoke.

"The devil hinders him!" screamed Betty. "The devil directs the smoke to silence his words!"

She stood nearer to me than I had known, and heard me when I yelled, "Oh, just be quiet for once! Can't you just keep that big, ugly mouth of yours closed?"

Oops.

Everything stopped—the crying, the wailing, and the chatter in the crowd. A cool breeze blew past my face. The cart wheels creaked as it pulled forward, bringing Wardwell to a nasty and unfair end.

Um. I wished everyone would look at him, instead of me. I knew what was coming and braced myself for the worst.

"Witch!" Betty screeched. "Witch!"

But I guess the majority of the people had heard enough. A few stepped between me and her and held their hands up. "It's time to stop this, Betty," someone said. With no support from those who beforehand had been so eager to fall at her feet, Betty threw her arms to her sides and stormed off.

Grinning from ear to ear, John slapped my back. "Oh, my," he chuckled, "I have wanted to say that to her forever."

But the injustice wasn't quite over. Reverend Nicholas Noyes split through the silence with his infamous words, "What a sad thing it is to see eight firebrands of hell hanging there."

Stunned with his callous words in the presence of their loved ones, I fell back. Clenching my fists to my sides, I vowed, if I stayed behind in 1692, I would visit his parish, and I would have a thing or two to say to him. I straightened. Such foolish words for one who had to leave as quickly as I. I didn't belong here. I never did.

"Bess?" Hezekiah said quietly, coming up behind me.

His voice sent tingles all over my body. Stop Bess. He cannot be yours—you know that—323 years separate you. I pressed my eyes tight, opened them, and then turned around.

Twenty-Nine
All Things Must End

Turning to Hezekiah, I noted his brilliant green eyes full of worry with a touch of excitement, or maybe relief. I studied his strong features and perfect nose, his half-grin, no doubt at my short hair, and his own tousled, gray hair, longer than usual. I wanted to run my fingers through his scruffy beard and pull his lips to mine, but instead, I breathed in his wonderful smell.

And then, I spied Liza standing close behind him.

My countenance plummeted, and before he could pull me near, I backed away.

He glanced around, and then back at me, and there was that grin again. "Oh, I get it—boy disguise and all." Leaning close to me, he whispered. "Good call."

What? No. That wasn't very intuitive of him.

Then he grabbed Liza and drew her into our circle. "See who I found?"

I certainly did. She studied me with an odd look of amusement that annoyed me. I ignored her.

Staring at John, I guessed Hezekiah expected an introduction. "This is my, er," I couldn't say uncle, so I said, "cousin, John."

"Hi, John," Hezekiah said. He glanced from John to me and then back again.

John tipped his hat then turned his attention back to the hanged. "They will hang for a while—to make sure they are really dead," he said seeming bitter.

"John's grandmother, Susannah Martin, was hanged in July," I said, glancing at Hezekiah.

Hezekiah's eyebrows raised at the mention of my great grandmother. "Oh," he said, now understanding my real connection with John.

"Oh, that is horrible!" Liza piped in, resting her hand on John's arm. "I am sorry for your loss."

I blinked. While it was a kind thing to say, I wished she'd keep her hands off my men. Oh wait, not my men—*not my man*. I stole a sideways glance at Hezekiah, whose eyes bore into my soul, I think. At least, that's what he looked like he was doing.

"It's time to go," he said gravely.

He was right. It was time. I nodded.

A few seconds passed before anyone moved. He probably was as unsure as I as to what to do next. Well, at least, *how* to do what needed to be done.

I turned to John, "I've got to go."

"*Okay,*" he said, still amused with that word, but when I didn't return the jest, he frowned. "Where are you going?"

Oh. Hard question to answer. "Home," I said, fighting back the tears.

"Far away?"

I nodded and then looked apologetically down at my, er, *his* clothes, that I wore.

"Ah, you can have them," he said with a shrug. "They are too small for me now anyhow." He glanced up at the hat on my head and appeared not as quick to relinquish it.

I snatched it off. "Oh, here," I said, handing it to him with a smile. It had been the icing on the cake—the final touch to the best disguise I had had in my time in the past.

Turning it around in his hands, he grinned. "Naw, you keep it." He thrust it back toward me. "To remember me by."

"To remember you by," I repeated, a sob caught in my throat. He gave me a quick hug, and then I watched him saunter away. Goodbye, my dear tenth great-uncle. I shall find and visit your grave in the future. Sort of a morbid thought to some, but to me, it brought comfort.

Turning my attention to Hezekiah and Liza, I pointed toward the road where the stables were, assuming that Liza's carriage must still be there, and knowing that Hezekiah's horse was probably there as well.

It was obvious that he wanted to talk to me, but I was quick to answer what I could, and left most of the talking between them.

I could tell that it troubled Hezekiah, but also that it oddly relieved him. I fought the urge to scream—to fight for my man—but I was sure that it was already over.

The crowd hadn't dispersed, and the roads were still packed with pedestrians. We maneuvered past them in Liza's carriage to the place I had requested, the woods, where my first adventure in Salem had had its beginning. Upon arriving, we tethered the horses.

"Shall we?" I pointed toward the edge of the trees, and then took long strides toward it, fingering the stones in my pocket, expecting them to follow.

I knew they were behind me, and I knew she was probably struggling to keep up in that ridiculous petticoat, but I pushed relentlessly on, eager to have the whole thing over. I was close to the trees, before I turned around.

Down over the hill, the small town was full of people. Many walked about in small clusters, no doubt dazed from the day's horrendous events, completely oblivious to the three of us walking up the hill away from them.

A horse and female rider pranced about in the distance, the woman's long, black cloak hanging over each side of the horse, the hood hiding her face. A pall hung over the whole town. It seemed, like the many others, she was unsure of where to go, or what to do next. She rode off slowly.

My eyes turned and rested on Hezekiah and Liza.

It shouldn't have surprised me to find them so far behind, and it shouldn't have saddened me so to see her arm looped through his, while he led her through the tall grass and rough briars.

He glanced up at me with a look of bewilderment, and I quickly went into the trees and hid myself from his view. Sitting down on a fallen tree, I waited for them to catch up. The stones seemed to grow in my pocket, becoming warm, almost hot to the touch.

I'd been having headaches lately, and the one that began now felt like something pinching my brain. Pressing my fingers into my throbbing forehead, I cried out in pain. It passed quickly, leaving me somewhat dizzy.

Instinctively, my fingers wrapped around the stones, bringing me instant comfort. They were my stones. Not his. My choice, not his. My hands balled up into fists. I would do what I may with them. I was in control. My head spun, and I couldn't think clearly. Sweat gathered at my brow, and I felt woozy. My eyes narrowed as they drew near. Why did I care if she ever saw her father again? I couldn't see mine. Deal with it Liza. I've had to.

Ugh. Where did that thought come from? That wasn't me. As suddenly as the dark cloud of despair had covered me, it dissipated, like hazy fog kissed by the morning sun. I could see clearly what I must do. Tell her everything and then get her to her dad.

"Liza," I called, patting the tree beside me. "I owe you an apology." Those words surprised me, but seemed to delight her.

"Whatever for?" She twisted a loose strand of hair around her finger.

I frowned. I wasn't one to play games and wouldn't play along. I changed the subject to what I really wanted to talk about anyhow. "How much has Hezekiah told you?" She pursed her lips tight, and I figured that what they had spoken about was private. "About your father," I pressed, feeling slightly irritated.

"Oh," she said. "Really, not much."

My teeth clicked. I had expected as much.

Hezekiah came near. "Bess, what's wrong?"

Wrong? You two little lovebirds haven't even discussed Charles—you know, the reason we were looking for her in the first place. "What have you told her about Charles?"

He licked his lips. "Only that he is alive, and we want to take her to him."

"And?" I folded my arms across my chest and waited.

He tilted his head. "I'm not really sure how to tell her that, Bess."

"No?" I said snootily. Catty of me, huh? How does one explain something so out-of-the-world extraordinary to someone who probably has never imagined anything greater than the seventeenth century?

"Tell me what?" Liza asked.

I don't know what possessed me to say what I said next. Possibly insanity. "Just that he could be dead."

"What?" She jumped up from the tree.

I ignored Hezekiah's groan. "Well, the last time we saw him, which was just *a few days ago,*" I stressed, "he was in a hospital bed." Her hands flew to her mouth, but before she could ask more, I added, "in a place you have to trust us to take you to."

She studied my face and then Hezekiah's. "I trust you."

Wow. That was easier than I thought. Of course, she had no earthy idea where we were taking her.

From the shadows, a form stepped out of the trees, her long cloak settling next to her slender body. "Take me too," she said. "Take me to Charles." Miranda stood before us, her face damp with tears. "I trust you, too."

"Miranda!" Liza rushed into her arms.

Stunned, I turned to Hezekiah. He stared at me with his own shocked expression. Putting his hand to the small of my back, he led me aside. "Bess," he whispered into my ear. His warm breath sent a tremble through my body. "Hold on, sweetheart."

What the heck did he mean by that? I would've pulled away and questioned him, but being so near to him was the only thing I wanted. Once I stepped away, I might never be so close to him again. Looking up into those eyes, my voice trembled. "What do you mean?"

"The stones, Bess," his voice broke, "those dastardly stones." Holding the blue stone between his fingers, his face soured. "The very thing we need, is the very thing that is hurting you, messing with your mind."

I gasped. He knew?

"It's written in the book, Bess, the ancient book." He patted his pocket.

Oh. My skin prickled, tiny waves of electricity passing over me. I was afraid to hear more. Meda had warned me of them, too. I bit down on my lower lip. I needed those stones, and the missing one was right within my grasp. I couldn't take my eyes off it.

"This has to be the final time." His voice was solemn.

I knew that was true, but how would we get them back again, to their own time, *him* back to *his* own time? My body swayed. He seemed to know my thoughts. Looking into my eyes, he said. "Whatever you're thinking about us, know this," he grabbed my shoulders, his eyes locked onto mine, "—I am yours forever."

I wiped at my nose, my senses fogging over. Forever? Forever is a long time that no one can promise. I pressed my eyes tight. No. I didn't believe that. I *hoped* that the forever in fairy tales was real, believing that even they had their beginning in ancient, sacred writings. Forever with him would be heaven. I buried my face in his chest, breathing in his scent, memorizing how it felt to be in his arms, knowing what I had to do.

He guided me over to the other two women. "It's time, Bess."

Time. Gah. I looked from him to Liza, who was chatting softly with her aunt. Okay, so he liked me better than her, but was he really thinking clearly?

Pressing the stone into the palm of my trembling hand, he closed his fingers around it and held on, not letting go, no doubt for fear that I would leave without him. That part might have been true. Miranda and Liza were now totally focused on us. I suppose we did look a little odd— especially me with my short hair and boyish clothing. "Um," I said, a tiny smirk forming in the corner of my lips. "Just remember, you said you would trust us."

I made sure that we were all touching each other, and noted that to make that connection complete, Hezekiah had wrapped his other arm around Liza. Without a second thought, I thrust the last stone into my pocket, joining it with its brothers.

Brilliant blue lights danced around us, as our bodies morphed into thin streams of color, gyrating in perfect harmony like a finely orchestrated movement. I heard Liza gasp and maybe even scream, but suddenly, in an instant, it was over.

Hezekiah and I had returned with our guests to the very place and time we had left.

Thirty
Where to Begin

The whirlwind stopped and the four of us swayed in its aftereffects. In an instant, the bright lights in the ceiling of the waiting room replaced the darkening sky and thick trees of the forest outside of Salem Town.

Unprepared for time travel, screams came from our horror-stricken guests. Shaking violently, Miranda fell to the floor, clutching at her chest. Liza huddled near her, searching the room with wild eyes. Helping Miranda to her feet, they both backed away, keeping a safe distance from us.

Fortunately, only Abner and André were in the room when we returned from 1692. Their faces held almost as much shock as our visitors.

"Witch?" Liza said in a thin, high voice. "You really *are* a witch?" She pointed at me with a shaky finger.

Really? Again? I'm barely back in my own time, and I'm already accused of witchcraft. "No, of course not," I snapped, a little belligerently.

Hezekiah was much kinder. "Bess, this is new for her. Remember your first time?"

True. When I discovered I was in 1692, I was a bit freaked out. That was an understatement. I had a meltdown—a full-blown emotional eruption. My countenance softened. Coming from the thick woods to a modern, pristine room had to be an unexplainable and bizarre shock. Humph. Wait until they discover they aren't in the seventeenth century anymore.

Miranda grasped Liza's shoulder. "Trees . . . *then room* . . . ." she whispered, nervously glancing at the ceiling lights, modern furniture, and long windows darkened by the night sky. Her gaze looked fearful when it fell upon the television monitor hanging from the wall. Cable news was blasting a newsflash happening somewhere in the world.

A terrifying scream erupted from Miranda's throat, and she fell back against Liza, who echoed her aunt's horrified reaction with a wild, high shriek.

Abner waved his hand. "Hush," he said firmly.

Imposing in stature and voice, the women stopped almost instantly and stared at him. I thought it a bit weird, but taking in Abner's fine, seventeenth-century clothing, they probably surmised his wealth and social standing. I tried hard not to grimace at their obvious appraisal of him compared to their harsh judgment of me.

Abner's gaze settled on me. "It's not witchcraft."

Finally! I was grateful for his words.

He continued. "It's merely advanced science. Once explained, you will understand it perfectly."

Maybe not perfectly. I studied Liza's confused expression.

"They are the experts, and you must listen to them." Abner motioned to André and then to Hezekiah. I was surprised when he also swept his hand out to include me.

"André de Nostredame," André said politely, with a bow. He seemed rather amused with everything, but then again, once educated to the truths of the universe, common things can appear trivial—not as all important as they once had been. As a scientist who had spent a great deal of his young life exploring the possible, André was completely at ease with what he had found and probably expected everyone else would feel the same way.

Abner cleared his throat. "I realize this is quite a shock." He swept his hand out over the room. "It was for us, too."

"Not witches nor warlocks?" Liza said, with a nervous twinge in her voice.

I smirked. At least the men were included in her assessment now.

Hezekiah laughed. "No, Liza, not at all. We're just three men and a woman who fell upon one of the most extraordinary events in the history of mankind."

"And that would be?" Miranda asked, still shaking. She stole glances at the monitor which kept her countenance in a frenzy.

I went over to it and turned it off. Her eyes widened at that, and I shook my head, already hearing the word, "witch" forming in her head.

"Advanced science," Abner repeated, following her gaze to the now black monitor. Extending his hand, he continued. "Let me introduce myself. I'm Abner Hanson."

Liza cocked her head to the side. "Hezekiah's father?"

Hezekiah stepped beside him and grinned. I loved that grin and was saddened that he'd shared it with her. Silly me. Silly, silly, me. Abner placed his hand on Hezekiah's shoulder. "Yes. This is my son."

Liza studied the both of them. "I see the resemblance."

315

I could too, but wished she'd stop staring at them—Hezekiah mostly. Cut it out, Bess. He's going back to his own time, remember? A sudden pang gripped my heart, but I knew it was true. I wasn't sure how I was going to get them back, but I knew I must. Wait. The stones. They might need the stones.

My eyes darted from Liza to Hezekiah. An image of them taking my stones with them came to my mind and instantly, my countenance darkened, and my eyes narrowed. *They couldn't take them.* But just as suddenly, I snapped back to reality. Glancing around, I was grateful that no one had seen my fleeting moment of insanity.

I searched for a chair and sat. My mind in a daze, confusion, thick with anxiety, muddled my thoughts. What was happening to me? My hand brushed against the stones in my pocket and a wave of peace fell over me, like a warm, comforting blanket on a bitter cold night. Studying Hezekiah and Liza from afar, I realized how silly I had been. They couldn't even use the stones without me.

Me. Back in 1692? I bit down on my little finger. If I went back, I would never return here again, this much I knew.

Onida. Child of the sky.

The waiting room gone, the lush meadow took its place. I swallowed hard, reluctant to hear what she might say. "Yes?" I turned to see her standing in the meadow—Meda—prophetess of my people. Only this time, she was different. Her long, black hair drifted about her slender body, carried about by a gentle breeze. Her thoughts came to me on the breeze.

The worth of your soul, Onida, is greater than the sum of your woes.

She faded away and the room returned to normal—if you can call one modern person in a room full of seventeenth-century people normal. I thought on Meda's words. That sage advice was supposed to help me? What did it even mean? That my woes would be my fate? I groaned.

Fighting deciphering each word of that cryptic message, I leaned back against the seat and returned to the struggle raging within. There was a way they could go back to 1692 without me or my stones. Maybe I had purposely forgotten all about it until now.

The contraption.

I could put them in the rift and use it to propel them back to their time. I could access the tools in the twenty-first century to pinpoint when and where the next aurora borealis would happen to find the ideal time and conditions needed to use that box.

Reluctantly, I returned to them and overheard Liza's next words.

"You are my father's boss?" she asked.

Abner nodded, but then shook his head. Surprised at his actions, I looked at Hezekiah with questioning eyes. I feared the worst had happened, but Abner just grinned, looking more like his son now. "He never was in my employ."

What? Of course he was. He was the Hanson's butler, er, coachman, um, what exactly was he?

"Charles would not take a dime from me."

That didn't make any sense. I remembered Charles had told me he went looking for a way to pay for Liza's medical expenses.

"He was very private about his affairs, but did mention his father's will once. I believe he came into a substantial amount of land." He looked directly at Liza. "He struggled with something, but never spoke of it. Working for me without pay seemed to be some kind of self-proclaimed penitence."

"And he's here, somewhere?" Miranda glanced around, no longer shaking violently, but still quite jittery. It was clear she was very frightened of her unexplainable surroundings.

I jumped in. "How long were we, er, gone from here, um, exactly?"

"Long enough for us to notice, but back in just seconds," said André. He glanced down at the book in Hezekiah's hand and shook his head in awe. "Of course," he mumbled, taking it from him. He opened it and ran his finger down one of its yellowed pages. It was obvious he was just now understanding something written there.

I studied Miranda and Liza before continuing, unsure of how they would react. "Charles, he is, um, still is in surgery then?"

Miranda groaned and pointed to me. "Bess told me," she said, "that Charles had a nasty fall and hit his head."

She didn't know the worst of it—the whole truth. "Miranda," I said, careful to choose the right words. "Charles didn't fall out of a tree like I previously told you."

Her eyes narrowed. "What happened to him?"

"Well, he *did* have a head injury," Hezekiah added, stepping nearer to me, to support me, I guess.

I lowered my eyes. A bit condescending, yeah, but I was in the moment. "It was from something that will be difficult for you to understand."

Liza scoffed. "More difficult than this, ah, *advanced science?*" She spread her hand out over the room with its modern lights and TV.

I blinked. "No. Exactly like this." I pressed my lips together. "Only much more." She pulled back, a subdued expression hardening on her face. It was obvious that she was in for an even greater shock with what I was about to reveal.

A nurse strutted into the waiting room. Upon seeing us, she paused, staring at us with an odd look.

"Elizabeth Fieldstone?" she asked, looking around the room. "I was told she was in this room."

"That is me," said Liza. "I am Elizabeth Fieldstone."

"Oh." She tapped her tablet. "Well, Elizabeth," she said. "Your father made it through surgery."

"That's great!" I said, relieved.

"That is wonderful," Liza whispered.

"But," the nurse said firmly. "He hasn't regained consciousness yet."

"How soon can we, er, she see him?" I said, gesturing toward his real daughter.

"I'll come back to get you, but it will be in an hour or so."

"Oh." Three people entered the waiting room, chatting away about a new birth or something. "Is there a more private room?" I knew it would be important to prepare our seventeenth-century guests for what they were about to hear and see.

"Yes, right here." The nurse opened a door at the end of the room. She led us into it and then left.

It was best to get just it over with. Seeing Charles was going to be difficult enough for the both of them. Miranda hadn't seen her brother for many years, and Liza was a young child when he disappeared from her life. On top of that, he'd probably be hooked up to all kinds of monitors, the likes of which they'd never seen. Plus, the walk to the recovery room would be full of surprises. We were four stories up, the east side of the long hallway was glass, and the twinkling lights of the large city lay beyond.

Where to begin? I cleared my throat and gestured for them to sit.

"Do you need some help?" Hezekiah placed his hand on my shoulder. It sent warm tingles throughout me.

"Um, maybe," I said. Glancing from Abner to André, and then to Hezekiah, I sighed. "I think the four of us need to explain this, er, advanced science to them."

They pulled chairs around to face Liza and Miranda, but waited for me to begin. I suppose it was out of respect for me, but it could have been that they, like me, were unsure of where to start.

I shrugged and then blurted out, "We're time travelers." Hezekiah looked at me with surprise. "What? It's what we ultimately have to tell them, isn't it?"

Miranda laughed out loud. "Oh, my!" But when none of us returned her jovial outburst, her face sobered.

"Time travelers?" Liza drew her head back. "You are saying . . ." Her eyes popped open. "That is ridiculous!"

I extended my hand. "Hello, my name is Bess Martin, and I am from the twenty-first century."

A nervous laugh escaped Liza's throat. She looked at me strangely, like I was on drugs, or something. "No, you are not," she responded, rather snootily.

A great retort was on the tip of my tongue, but Miranda spoke first, "That actually makes sense," she said, seemingly awestruck.

"What?" Liza swung around to her. "You cannot be serious, Miranda."

"But, I am," she said, a newfound expression of wonderment on her face. "It *could be* advanced science."

Liza rolled her eyes. "You read too much, Miranda."

Miranda nodded and reached into a leather satchel hidden beneath her long cloak. "I know they are just words, but I often asked myself, what else was out there—other than what we already know?" She pulled out a thin book.

André reached for it. "May I?" He read the title and then chuckled. "I have this book." He tapped it. "Sir Francis Bacon is a genius."

Curious, I reached for it. "New Atlantis?"

"Yes, he is quite the visionary," André said. "I had the occasion to meet him in London."

Huh. Whatever Bacon had written on those pages had somehow enlightened Miranda—stretched her ability to see beyond the known. I loved words and what they could do for humankind. I handed him back the book.

"Ha! The twenty-first century?" Liza jumped up waving her arms wildly. "If it is true," she slammed her hands on her hips, "which I know it is not," she gave us a stern look, "then how did you get from the twenty-first century to this time? Huh?" She added, scornfully.

Now for the hard part. I opened my mouth to explain, but André beat me to it.

"Liza," he said firmly. "*This time* is not 1692." He patted his knee and leaned forward. "You are in the future."

Thirty-One
Revelations

Liza fell back and shook her head vehemently. "I would like to leave, please. Come on Miranda, let us go." Miranda stood at the window, peering outside through its partially opened slats.

"Here, let me," I said, walking over to her. Grabbing the strings, I pulled the blinds open, revealing the parking lot crammed with cars and the twinkling lights of the city below.

Miranda fell back slightly, her body trembling. "This is incredible," she said turning to us, eyes wide with obvious wonder. Looking back to the window, she dropped her hands and stared.

André stepped to Miranda's side and whispered softly. "Do not fear that which you do not understand."

She nodded.

He then approached Liza. "It is not witchcraft, Liza," he said, "but science which has advanced throughout the past 323 years."

Liza rolled her eyes. "323 years?" she asked, then scoffed, stepping to the window.

I rather enjoyed her curdling scream.

Yeah, I know, not very nice on my part. What I didn't like was how quickly Hezekiah was at her side, catching her in her abrupt faint. I watched from a distance as the men and Miranda surrounded her, helping her to a nearby chair. It wasn't that I didn't want to help her, but I somehow felt detached from the whole thing.

An orderly opened the door and stuck his head inside. "What's wrong? Everything okay in here?"

"Yes," Abner said. "She is just shocked by the news, of, er . . ."

"Her father's surgery," I said covering for her.

As the orderly left, I remembered the stones in my pocket. I could go anywhere in the world with my stones and to any time I chose.

Stop, Bess. Focus.

I hurried to Liza's side and joined in with comforting her as best I could. I understood her shock. I truly felt her fear and confusion.

"Liza, it's not as bad as you think." Except that I knew she was away from her mother and how difficult that probably felt for her. "I brought you here on purpose," I said firmly.

"What?" She sat up straight, and her eyes hardened. "You did this? You *are* a witch!"

"Okay," I said with a sigh, and then I shrugged. "If you insist. I'm a witch." Actually, I did have those incredibly magical stones that answered to my will, or maybe I answered to *their* will. Ugh.

"No, stop it Bess," Hezekiah said, pulling away from Liza and moving closer to me. "You're as much a witch as she is—she time traveled too, right?"

"I guess so. Witch," I mumbled her way.

"I am not a witch," she whimpered.

"Yes, but be careful who you tell your time travel story to when you get back to 1692."

"Get back?" Her eyes widened. "You can send me back, too?"

"That's been my intention all along—to send you back to where you're supposed to be."

"And Charles too?" Miranda asked.

"Of course. That's been our whole purpose," said Hezekiah.

"Charles told me," I began, carefully choosing my words, "that there wasn't any reason for him to go on."

"What do you mean?" Liza asked, wiping at her nose with her handkerchief.

"We accidently traveled through time with Hezekiah and Bess," Abner said. "They were trying to get away from one of the girls who accused Bess . . ." He stopped and looked apologetically at me. I noted that Liza's eyes hardened. Abner continued, "Charles's time travel sent him rolling hard against a rocky road."

More like concrete, but I knew why he hadn't used the correct word. There would be plenty of time to teach our visitors about such things. I couldn't send them back until Charles was able to travel.

My eyes rested on Hezekiah and I was heavy with sorrow. Maybe he didn't have to go back. Maybe he could stay with me. I bit my lower lip, unsure of what to do. No, Bess. You know exactly what to do. The right thing. Meda's words applied to more than just me. *The worth of a soul is greater than their woes.* I kind of got it now. Everything would turn out just right.

"That's how he got his head injury?" Miranda asked, her voice rising, breaking through my thoughts.

325

I nodded and then tried to explain myself. "I didn't know he would come, too. He was driving the carriage!" I didn't mention how even the horses had come to the future with us, as I had no idea how either of those things had happened.

"We couldn't send him back in his condition," Hezekiah added.

Sitting in front of Liza, I looked directly in her eyes and said, "And he was asking for you."

"For me?" She sniffled.

"That's why we, er, I went looking for you." I shook my head. "He didn't think he had a reason to live, Liza. I was trying to save his life."

She blinked. All at once, her arms wrapped around my neck, and she hugged me for a long while before continuing.

"I'm so sorry, Bess." Sobbing, she pulled away, leaving me quite surprised. "This is so hard," she said in a whisper, gesturing toward the window. "But, it must be true." She looked around and then stood. Walking back to the window, she stared outside at the cars coming and going in the parking lot below. "The twenty-first century?" She turned to us for confirmation.

"Yes," we said in unison.

She turned back to the window. "Amazing," she mumbled, "truly amazing." She pointed at something below. Turning to us, she gasped. "Horseless carriages?"

"Oui," André said and chuckled. "Welcome to the future!"

A knock on the door brought our attention to the returning nurse. She smiled. "He's awake, and he's asking for Elizabeth." Liza and I stared at each other.

Liza wrung her hands. "What do I say?"

"Bess should go first," Hezekiah said. "He'll at least know who she is."

Liza nodded. She seemed quite nervous. "Yes, I agree. Bess will prepare him for . . . us." She looked at Miranda.

That seemed reasonable. "Okay," I said, completely unsure of how to tell Charles that his daughter and his sister had come for a visit. "Um, does he still have the bandages, you know . . . ?" I circled my head with my finger.

"Oh, no," the nurse said, with a grin. "We took those off during surgery.

Eeks. "And he sees just fine now?" My voice raised into a squeak.

"Oh yeah, totally fine, although he was quite perplexed at first."

I'll just bet. Wait. "At first?" I exchanged curious looks with Hezekiah.

"Yeah, but then he mentioned something about some "'odd portraits'" he had seen."

"Oh, really," I said shocked. Charles must have seen the pictures Hezekiah had with him when we whisked back to the past. Wow. He could really keep a secret. He would've called them portraits, not knowing the modern term "photos." My mind worked quickly. "Oh, my portraits of the future. I like to dabble in the what-ifs of tomorrow."

"Oh, I'd love to see them!" the nurse said.

Yikes. Another ruse to continue. "Er, thanks," I said, stumbling over my words. Hezekiah's look was near to laughing, and André covered his grin with his hand.

"Um, so, when can I see him?"

She shrugged. "Right now."

With a quick glance over my shoulder, I left the room with the nurse. I spoke to her as we walked. "How long do you think he'll be in recovery?"

"We never know. A lot depends on his will to get better. I know that sounds silly," she said, "but that's what I've noticed in patients."

"That doesn't sound silly at all." I hoped that knowing that his daughter and sister were near would give him that will.

"Here we are," she said, gesturing to a partially opened door.

I hesitated outside the door and then pulled it closed. "Um," I said, turning to the nurse. "Could you do me a favor?"

"I can try."

"He hasn't seen his daughter for several years, and I'd like about fifteen minutes to prepare him for the shock first, so if you could have her and Charles's sister wait just outside this door, that'd be great."

"Wow," she said. "Really? They haven't seen each other for a while?"

"Uh-huh." More than 300 years, actually.

"Hey, do you want me to record it?" She appeared a bit too eager.

Was that even legal? Hmm. A reality show where an estranged daughter meets her father for the first time after several years. That sounded more like a soap opera. In the end, I did what was right. "No, it'll be way too private for that."

"Yes, of course you're right," she said apologetically. "I'll go get them."

I watched her walk away, took a deep breath, and opened the door. Charles was watching the television monitor. He didn't see me at first, but then jerked his head my way. He studied my clothing, my face, and my short hair, and then he grinned. "Lady Elizabeth?"

I rushed to his side, overcome with tears. "I'm so sorry, Charles!"

"Why, my dear?" He searched my teary eyes. "Oh, you mean for this?" He brought his hand up to his head which now had a wide bandage across part of it.

"Well, yeah," I said, whimpering.

"There is nothing to apologize for. I am going to be fine."

I swallowed. "Do you know where you are?"

He searched the room. "In a hospital."

"Yes, but . . . ."

"In the future," he added calmly, pointing to the date written on the medical whiteboard.

Stunned, I opened my mouth to explain, but then closed it. There would be time to talk about that later. He needed to know about his daughter. "Charles." I exhaled slowly. "Um, I have to tell you something."

"Yes?" He looked at me curiously and then gasped. "Oh, no." He jerked slightly forward. "Master Hanson?"

"What? No, he's fine, we're all fine."

"And here as well?"

"Yes, they're waiting to see you."

"Wonderful. Bring them in."

"Um . . . but first," I sighed. "I'm not sure how to say this."

He seemed genuinely concerned. "Say what?"

"So, I kind of . . . went back to 1692 again."

He stared at me. "You did what?"

"Charles, for whatever reason, I can travel through time." I could see the gears turning in his brain and wondered if he thought me a witch, too. "Weird, huh?"

He glanced at the television monitor. "Weird?" He nodded. "Maybe a little. But much more wonderful." He made an attempt to sit straighter and groaned. "I am thrilled you brought me here."

"What?" I said, surprised at his reaction. "But, I'm going to bring you back!"

"Oh, Lady Elizabeth, I hope not."

Well, well," I stammered. "Uh!" I sighed heavily.

A knock sounded on the door, and I hadn't prepared him yet. I jumped up and opened it a crack. "One more minute," I said quietly.

He looked toward the door. "Who is there? Master Hanson?"

"Um, yes, but also someone else."

"That French man, de Nostredame?"

"Ah, yeah, but someone else, too."

His eyes narrowed, no doubt searching his memory for who else was in the carriage with us on that fated day.

"Charles," I said slowly, "I went back to 1692 to get Elizabeth."

"Elizabeth?" He sucked in a slow breath. "My daughter?" His words were so soft, I could hardly hear them. "She's here?"

"Yes." I reached over and patted his hand. "I also brought your sister."

At the mention of sister, his face soured. "Elizabeth Senior?"

I shook my head. "No, not that sister. I brought Miranda here."

He looked at me oddly. "But, I do not have a sister named Miranda."

Apparently, Liza could wait no longer and the door burst open. I was too stunned at Charles's proclamation to register the gravity of the situation as the two stepped into the room. Charles barely looked at his daughter. His eyes locked onto Miranda. "Mary?" he whispered, a sudden tremble in his voice.

"Charles," she cried, rushing to his side. "Oh, Charles, Charles, Charles!"

He pulled her face to his chest and held her tight. After a long moment of broken sobs, he spoke. "She told me you had died!"

Liza and I exchanged looks of astonishment, bordering horror, as his words sunk in. I didn't need to second-guess who he was talking about. But to Liza, this pronouncement was much more. She stepped back, stunned.

"What?" her voice was breathless. "You and he—*you are* . . . my *mother?*"

"Yes! A thousand times yes!" It was as if she had wanted to say that forever. Her countenance sobered, no doubt from the shocked look on Liza's face. "I am so sorry, my dear child." She reached for her.

Liza backed farther away. "Sorry for not telling me that you were my *mother?* You took me to her grave every birthday and at each holiday!" She blinked, as apparent realization swept over her face. "Mary M. Fieldstone's grave."

"Yes," Miranda said softly. "Mary *Miranda* Fieldstone."

With a groan, Charles pulled himself up straighter. "I do not know what to say." His expression was one of shock and joy at the same time, and his voice was so soft I could barely hear him. "Mary . . . *alive* . . . *and* with my daughter, Liza." His chest heaved and he broke out in sobs. "I have dreamed of this, but is it true?" He looked from Miranda to Mary. "You stand before me, in this . . . strange and wonderful place." His shoulders fell as he looked around. "Perhaps it is a dream," he whispered, seeming deep in thought.

"This is *not* a dream, sir," Liza snapped. She turned and glared at Miranda. "And you could have *at least* told me you were my mother!"

"I wanted to, so many times . . ."

Liza flitted around, throwing her hands in the air. "Then why did you not?"

Exasperated, Miranda blurted out, "What could I possibly give you? Your father's sister was wealthy, and I had nothing."

"Wrong," Liza said, stamping her foot. "I never needed money. I only needed you."

"But you *did* have me." Miranda stumbled over her words. "And you have never needed money, because you have always had it. Liza, we would have been paupers, living on the streets."

Liza wiped at tears rolling down her face. "No. We would have had each other. We could have survived anything."

A puff of air escaped Miranda's lips. "But we did survive," she said, her voice catching. "We have always had each other." Her face went blank, and she turned to Charles. "No . . . we did not have you."

"Yes, and why exactly was that?" Liza said, turning an angry glare his way. It was clear she was more mad than excited about these revelations.

Charles reached for her. She didn't move. He sighed. "You were ill and needed expensive medicine. I left to track down Edward Small and sell him some of my land he had wanted earlier. When I returned, my sister told me you both had died of small pox." Charles turned to Miranda. His voice broke. "She told me she had buried you together in the same grave."

Stunned, Liza sat on a nearby chair.

"I secretly came to your grave every year, and just a year ago, I saw . . . my daughter kneeling beside the grave." He swallowed hard.

"I knew it was you, Liza, because you look so much like Mary. I knew then my sister had lied to me. So, I waited inside the trees by the barn and confronted her when she came near."

He took Miranda's hand. "I never saw you, Mary, otherwise, I would have barreled in there to get you two, but she convinced me that telling my daughter would be most unwise. She told me of Liza's weak constitution and that a shock like that would kill her."

"My weak constitution?" Liza jumped in, clearly agitated. "Do I look weak to you?"

The corner of Charles's mouth turned up in a half-grin. "No, not at all." He shook his head slowly and groaned from the movement. "But I believed her. You were ill the last time I had seen you as an infant."

Miranda's face went blank. "I do not remember Liza being ill, Charles."

"Do you not?" He searched her eyes. "It was why I left."

"You left to deliver a package to Pemaquid."

"No, I—"

"Yes! To deliver supplies to the people in Pemaquid!"

He shook his head. "No, Mary. My sister told me our daughter was quite ill and that I had better get the funds needed for her care." Shock registered on his face. "I ran to her room and looked down at her. She seemed to be restless. You were quite sick yourself." He took her hand. "Do you not remember me telling you I would return as soon as I could?"

"Yes, I was ill, and I remember you leaving, but—" Miranda drew her hands to her face. Her voice dropped to a whisper, "She told me you died at Pemaquid in an Indian raid."

"I never was at Pemaquid, Mary," he said, dumfounded. "I sold some of my land to get the funds, and when I returned . . . Elizabeth told me you both had died. She showed me your grave." His head fell forward and he sobbed. Mary was quick at his side.

Charles pointed at Liza. "Just a year ago, when I discovered her deceit, she gave me a portrait miniature of you, but I never imagined she had lied about your mother, too." He wrung his hands. "I have been such a fool."

"You are not a fool, dear," Mary cooed, taking his hands in hers. "She duped us all."

He sighed long and heavy and then faced Liza again. "I always intended on waiting for your twentieth birthday, or whenever you married, to present myself to you."

Liza pressed her lips together. She stepped toward the door. "I need to be alone."

"Liza," Miranda said, stretching out her hand toward her.

"No!" Liza said forcefully. "I need to think."

I followed her to the door. "I'm not going to go with you," I said, waving my hands when she gave me an odd look, "but I can take you to a secluded garden they have at this hospital where you can be alone."

"Actually," she said. "I want you to come along."

"Oh, okay," I said surprised.

"I am fairly sure I will get lost out there."

That was an understatement. Hospitals had the worst kind of mazes, but I had a feeling she'd get more than just lost. She hadn't seen much of this time period, and having a tour guide along was not only helpful, but necessary. Any wild outbursts, dressed as she was, would surely send her straight to the mental health center, and that could be disastrous for us all.

Thirty-Two
A Better Life

I looked down at my clothes and glanced over at Liza's. We looked like we were part of a cult. Ugh. We passed by the hospital's boutique, and I glanced inside. "Liza," I said, stopping her. "I'm going to buy a new outfit." I glanced down at John's boyish clothing and dug deep into my pocket for the small change purse I always kept with me. No use to me in 1692, my debit card was like gold to me here.

She followed me inside, her eyes round with wonder. "Oh, my," she mumbled, looking at the brightly colored shirts. She had been watching each person we passed by, and they had been watching her, too. Her outfit, along with mine, had turned nearly every head.

Grabbing a pair of jeans in my size, I snatched the first T-shirt I saw—black, with '"Attitude"' scrawled across its front. After paying for it, I read its smaller words, '"I'm a Witch. Deal With It."' Ugh. Even though we were in Boston, anything to do with Salem was a big racket here.

Liza fingered a white blouse—a little too frilly for me, but I figured it was perfect for her. I showed her a pair of stylish pants, and her mouth fell open. "I cannot wear this."

I pointed at her long dress. "No one wears that anymore." I handed the pants and the blouse to her. "Anyhow, once you try them, you'll never want to wear a dress again."

"I doubt that," she said stiffly.

I shrugged. "Trust me on this, Liza."

She looked at the bag with my new clothes. "Then, I think I would rather have clothes like yours." She pointed at my bag.

"Seriously?" I had misjudged the girl. "Okay." I gestured to the rack with the T-shirts, but her gaze had fallen on something else.

"Oh my," she gasped, pointing to a nearly naked mannequin showcasing underclothes.

Oh well, it was a good way to explain modern day underwear, though her obvious shock at such indecent exposure caused me to reflect on how desensitized we had become to modesty. When had such things become the norm for us?

Within minutes, we had left the shop and found a bathroom to change in. "You go first." The small room was only for one person.

She stood still, staring through the door. "What is this place?"

I smirked. "A twenty-first century outhouse."

She went inside and touched the sink. "And this?"

"Running water," I said, swiping my hand under the facet. Water spewed out, and she backed away.

"Witchcraft!"

"Uh!" I rolled my eyes and put my fingers under it again, letting the clear water run through my fingers. "No, it's not witchcraft, Liza."

"Advanced science," she said, in a shaky voice.

"Um, yeah." I nodded.

"And that?" Her finger trembled as she pointed to the toilet. Before I could stop her, she stuck her hand in the clean water. "What on earth is that for?"

"Don't touch that!" I gave her a strange look and pulled her hand out.

She seemed offended. "It's just water."

"It's a *toilet*. It's where we, um, yeah . . . you know— the *outhouse*." I squatted and then stood back up.

"Ew!" She flipped her wet hand around.

"Stop, Liza, stop!" I ran my hand under the automatic paper towel dispenser and pulled a few off for her to use. Her mouth dropped open, and she took them from me and dried her hand. I pointed to the toilet. "It's automatic, too. It, ah, flushes by itself."

"Flushes?" Her nose wrinkled.

Annoyed with having to teach her every little thing, I pulled a long strand of toilet paper, wadded it up, plopped it into the toilet, and then stepped back away from it.

I really wished she hadn't screamed like that. "Liza, it's nothing." I pointed to the sensor on the back of the toilet. "This gadget reads when you are finished and stand up."

She frowned and tilted her head. "It is looking at your backside?"

Hmm. I hadn't thought of it that way. "I guess so."

"Well," she huffed. "That is most improper. I do not like it."

When you look at it that way, neither did I. Ugh. New perspectives could be so disconcerting. "Pfft. You're just going to have to get used to it."

"I will not." She looked around the room and crossed her hands in front of her chest.

"Whatever. But at some point, you're going to have to use it."

"I do not want anyone watching me," she whimpered.

"What?" I looked down at the toilet. "No one's watching you, Liza."

"Then how do they know to, er, what did you call it—flushes?"

I bit down on both lips, suppressing a laugh. "No, no, Liza. It's just a *machine*." Her eyebrows crinkled in confusion. "A very tiny machine," I repeated, holding my fingers up to the size of the sensor, "that runs all by itself."

"Advanced science . . ." she muttered.

"Exactly." I stepped out of the room and let the door close behind me.

A few minutes passed, and she called through the door. "Bess, how do you do this?" Opening the door a crack, she let me in. Her dress was laying across the baby changing table. She had pulled the T-shirt over her shoulders and put the jeans on, but struggled with the zipper.

"Just pull straight up," I said, amused.

"Oh."

It was my turn to change. I handed her the big dress. "Don't go anywhere, okay?"

She smirked. "Of that, you need not worry."

I slipped out of John's breeches and into the blue jeans, careful to push the stones into separate pockets. I had forgotten all about Charles's ledger. Turning it around in my hands, I dropped it inside the shopping bag along with John's antiquated clothing.

A small bump inside the breeches caught my fingers as I pushed them deeper into the bag. "What's that?" I mumbled, pulling it out of the pocket.

I fell back and stared down at the wooden cross Giles Corey had given to me. Deliverance must have slipped it into my pocket when she hugged me goodbye.

A sob caught in my throat—he must have really wanted me to have it. Tears welled up in my eyes, and I pressed the old relic to my trembling lips. I would cherish it forever.

I joined Liza outside the bathroom door, me in my witch T-shirt, and her with one that read, "'Not Every Witch Lives in Salem.'" I was no longer worried about Liza. She'd fit right in here.

I was concerned about her relationship with her parents though. "Quite a shock, huh?"

She looked over at me and pressed her lips tight. I guess being bathroom buddies hadn't given me the right to be so personal.

"Sorry," I said, apologetically.

"Oh, no," she said, patting my arm. "It is just more than I can bear at the moment."

"I guess so," I said, with a shrug.

She looked at me strangely. "What do you mean?"

"Well, you just found out that someone you've loved all of your life is your mother, a mother you'd thought was gone from you forever." When she grumbled, I forged ahead, "and that your father is . . . well, alive. I'd give

341

anything to find out that my father was still alive, no matter what he'd done to me." She seemed to ignore me. You'd think she'd at least acknowledge the fact that I was fatherless and be grateful that she wasn't.

She didn't.

"But she lied!"

"Uh!" I looked over at her. "To give you a better life." Seriously, this girl didn't know anything about poverty.

We were at the door to the gardens now and entered the small courtyard outside. She barely glanced at the rich foliage. Seeming bitter, she muttered, "A *better* life."

"Yes!" I might have said that too aggressively.

Her lips twisted off to the side. What was probably an angry reply formed in her narrowing eyes, but then she relaxed. "I am sorry about your father, Bess."

That surprised me. "Er, thanks."

An awkward silence followed, as if she was waiting for me to talk about my dad. Frankly, I didn't feel like it. Oh. Wait. My shoulders fell forward as I realized my hypocrisy. Why was it that the thing we expected of others we were not willing to give ourselves?

There was silence between us for some time. Until, I thought about something that had been nagging at me. "What I don't get," I blurted out, "is the whole money thing. How is it that Elizabeth Senior had all the family money and not your father?"

She looked over at me. "Because it never was Fieldstone money to begin with. My mother—er, Elizabeth Senior—got her money from her late husband."

"She went back to her maiden name?"

342

Liza nodded. "She told me once what her married name had been. I do not remember why she went back to the Fieldstone name." She wrung her hands. "My mind hurts, Bess." Pressing fingers to her forehead, her eyes closed tight. "It is full of memories—all of them lies."

I dug into my bag and then thrust a small pad of paper on her lap. "Here." I handed her a pen. "Write it down, all of it." I had done that. After my dad died, I wrote for days, angry with the world for taking him from me. Later, I buried the pages in our backyard. I didn't protect them in anyway . . . wanting them to decay back into the earth, just like my dad had.

She stared at the pen for a long time. "How do you use this contraption?"

Oh. The pen. I pushed the button that released the ballpoint and then handed it to her. This new technology didn't frighten her in the least. She rather enjoyed pushing the clicker up and down. I took it from her and showed her how to press it against the paper to write.

"Oh. Much cleaner than liquid ink," she said.

"Yeah." She stared at the blank paper for several minutes. I was about to prompt her with what she might say, when she began writing. Quietly at first, but then she became one with her writing, seeming to totally forget I was there. She spoke some of her words a loud.

"It was cruel! Reckless! You had no right!" The pen flew over the page. "Robbed me! I trusted you!" At that, she jumped up, pad in hand, and strolled the area in front of us, pausing to add more words. "Heartless!

Unimaginable!" Finding another seat, she sat and wrote furiously amidst exasperated breaths fueled by her anger.

Several minutes passed. Much quieter now, I wondered what she was writing, but then got caught up in my own thoughts. What would, or should, I write to Hezekiah before he leaves? I inwardly groaned.

"There," she said, tapping the pad against her lap. "It is finished." A sad look came over her. "You are right, Bess. I do still love her."

Huh. It worked. I swallowed hard. Now my turn. I would steal a moment soon and pen my own words.

On the way back to Charles's hospital room, we were quiet. Once there, I let her go in alone, and closed the door after her. Leaning against the door trim, I sighed. Two major things were solved, well, *almost* solved. Charles's family was reunited, and soon I would send them all back to 1692, where they belonged. I looked up to see Hezekiah, Abner, and André approaching.

"So, how did it go?" Hezekiah grinned, when he read my T-shirt.

"As expected," I mumbled. "She threw a fit but then seemed to be okay."

He nodded, studying my short hair. "I really do like your hair, Bess." He ran his fingers across the top of my head.

"Thanks." His touch sent tingles through me, followed by a sudden wave of sadness.

"What is wrong, Bess?" Abner asked, picking up on my sullen mood.

"It's just . . . it's time for you to go now."

"Back to my life," he said soberly. "I do miss Victoria."

"Excusez-moi, but if it is all the same to you," André said, taking my hand in his, "I'd rather stay here, Bess."

"What? You too?"

Hezekiah pulled his head back. "Liza wants to stay?"

I grimaced. "No. Charles."

"Charles?" Abner said shocked.

"Yes, he, um . . . has totally embraced this century."

André chuckled. "Oui, I get that." He nodded, his head bobbing.

I rolled my eyes. Of course a scientist would get it, but I was amazed that a common person would, too. I guess the pictures Charles had accidently seen in 1692 must have prepared him for this time.

Hezekiah pointed to the door. "Shall we?"

"Sure, why not?" I opened the door and stuck my head around it. Miranda was sitting on a chair close to the narrow bed, and Liza was standing on the other side of it, staring at the monitor and tubes. They both held one of Charles's hands. I sighed a breath of relief and pushed the door open. He looked up at us and smiled wide.

"Master Hanson!" Charles said.

"So good to see you are well," Abner said, joining them. "We were worried." He leaned forward. "I see you have reunited with your daughter," he said, and then added, "And your sister."

"Ha!" Liza called out, apparently still holding onto some traces of anger. Correcting her sudden outburst, she continued. "This is Mary—his wife—and my, um, *mother*."

"Oh, my," exclaimed Abner, in an astonished tone.

Hezekiah's face registered shock as well, but André just grinned.

Remembering the ledger, I pulled it from my bag. "Victoria gave this to me, in hopes it might help us find you, but I forgot all about it. Anyhow, here it is." I handed it to Charles.

Charles leafed through it. "Well, it will not do me any good now, will it?"

I made a face. He could take whatever it was back with him. I was glad I had remembered to give it to him.

Dr. Sava came into the room. Studying Miranda's odd clothing, he sighed. I imagined he was getting used to us, but still surprised.

Charles was quick to speak. "How long will I have to stay here?" He laid his ledger down, and Abner picked it up. I thought it a bit rude, but didn't say anything.

"You're looking great, Mr. Fieldstone. Just want to run a few tests on you," Dr. Sava said.

"Yes, and?" Charles pressed.

Dr. Sava shrugged. "Maybe today, but that's a *maybe*." Patting Charles on the foot, he turned and left the room.

Abner spoke softly to Charles, probably telling him not to rush his healing. At least, that's what I would tell him. Dr. Sava's appraisal was really good news. I could move my plan forward soon. How was I going to get them all to agree with it?

I had messed with time, and I had to fix it. Everything had to be put back in its rightful place. The stones felt heavy in my pockets, pulling toward each other, with a need stronger than desire—like mega magnets held too close.

The room got still, or perhaps it was just me. Strange lights appeared that were both calming and frightening. And then, Meda's voice came to me, as if she was standing beside me, whispering in my ear.

Onida—the one chosen. Somethings are meant to be. Do not tempt fate.

I groaned, completely unsure at what that had meant. Fate? I didn't believe in fate. At any rate, I wasn't sure whose destiny she spoke of, too many lives were involved. The one chosen, yes, that was me!—not Hezekiah, not André, not Charles, nor Abner. Me! I came out of my trancelike state and found them surrounding me now.

"Are you okay, Bess?"

I shook it off. "Yes," I said, my body unsteady. "I have come to a decision." Avoiding Hezekiah's eyes, the words tumbled from my mouth. "I'm sending all of you back when Charles is ready." I pulled one of the stones out of my pocket.

André laughed. "Non tu ne l'es pas," he said, shaking his head firmly. "No, you are not."

"Yes, I am."

I didn't see him lunge forward, but felt Hezekiah's hand brush against mine. "No, you are not, Bess," he said softly, taking the stone from my hand.

He had stolen another stone! My eyes glazed over. "Give it back to me, Hezekiah—*both* of them."

"I will not," he said soberly. "Not now, not like this."

I studied his fantastically green eyes, getting caught up in them. I shook it off. "Um, but you *have* to go back, Hezekiah." I stammered, tripping over my words. "It's fate, and there's nothing we can do about it."

"Fate?" André's face sobered. "Trois sœurs, ah, *three sisters*," he continued, "Clotho, Lachesis, and Atropos. Hmm." He bit his lip, seeming deep in thought. "The daughters of Erebus and Nyx—darkness and night. Very old works, written by Hesiod in 906, I believe." He circled the room.

"They were three goddesses," André continued, "who presided over the birth and life of mortals—each person's destiny given by the three fates." His gaze seemed to rest on the three women in the room.

"What? Er, no, not fate like *that*," I said.

"Then fate like what?" Hezekiah said, rolling the stone around in his fingers.

"Like things that were meant to be," I said, exasperated.

"Like us?"

Dang. He had to say that.

He stepped close. I could feel his breath against my face. "Meant to be . . . means things that are meant to remain the way they are—*to be*."

"The way they are?" My voice seemed small compared to the call of the universe.

"Oui, Bess," André piped in. "Fate doesn't come from gods," he said softly, "but from each of us." He swept his hand out over Hezekiah, Abner, Charles, Miranda, Liza, and then back to himself. "We determine our own destiny." A tiny grin played at his lips. "And I choose to stay in the twenty-first century."

"Me too," said Charles.

"We, as well," Miranda added, taking Liza's willing hand in hers.

My eyes narrowed. "But . . . but," I stuttered.

"Bess, would you send Honovi and Magena back, too?"

I glanced up at him. Low blow, Hezekiah. He knew I couldn't do that—Magena was already dead and buried in an Indian mound in the past, and I could never rip Honovi from her arms. I searched their eager faces. They all wanted to stay? Looking from person to person, my gaze fell upon Abner.

"I cannot stay," he said sadly. "My place is with Victoria."

Meda's voice filled my mind.

Onida, the one chosen. You understand, child of the sky? This must be their choice and not yours. No one holds destiny in the palm of their hands, save the true barer of fate—each person of their own accord.

I nodded, and that seemed to appease the masses. The good news—no, the *best* news was that Hezekiah could stay, if he chose!

The bad news was that so could Liza, who couldn't seem to keep her eyes off him.

Maybe, I could send *her* back. Catty, huh? Stop it, Bess. When was I going to trust Hezekiah? Maybe, just maybe, I would give him a chance to choose for himself.

I moved aside and let everyone talk, watching them laugh and exchange hugs. Something reflected in the lights overhead, and when I got closer, I saw the portrait miniature, its chain dangling from the table. It lay on top of Liza's folded letter, with Elizabeth Fieldstone Senior scribbled across its back.

It was wrong, I know, but I picked up the portrait miniature with one hand, and the letter with the other, and turned them over in my fingers. For whatever ill-fated reason, Hezekiah had laid one of the stolen stones under the letter—or perhaps, the stone had found its way there on its own. Without a sound, I reunited it with the others in my pocket.

Hezekiah and André spoke quietly. They seemed troubled. I inched my way over and got as close as I could.

"I worry about her," Hezekiah said. "Each time she time travels, the headaches, and, ah, brief moments of confusion, get worse. And why her? Why not me?"

Confusion? The headaches were obvious, but he knew about the confusion, too?

"Oui," André said, nodding. "It is because she is a Keeper." His voice dropped low, but I could still hear him. "The stones seek to purify . . . to cleanse."

Yikes. Like I needed to hear that.

"To prepare her for greater things."

I trembled and sank down in the chair behind them. So that explained the headaches and subsequent confusion. The stones were giving me the once-over.

"So, the contraption?" Hezekiah asked.

"Oui, it is the only way."

"But, just the two of us—and my father."

"Oui."

I closed my eyes as if asleep. If they were to look behind them, at least they would think I had not heard their dangerous plan.

I stayed that way for a while. Everyone left me alone and it was kind of nice to pretend none of this was real. Of course, that would mean Hezekiah wasn't either. I opened my eyes. He was chatting with his dad. I watched them for several minutes. Meda had told me that everyone chose their own fate—Abner's choice was to be with his wife. His *right* was to be back in his own time.

Waiting for whatever Hezekiah and his father were talking about to be over, I joined them, stepping in between father and son. Stuffing my hands in my pockets, I reached up and kissed Hezekiah on the cheek, and then whispered, "I love you," into his ear. He grinned wide.

We were now inches apart, and I made sure we were not touching, before I looped my arm through his father's. The remaining stone still danced in Hezekiah's fingers, when I grabbed it away, and willed myself to the Hanson mansion back in 1692, not knowing if I'd ever get the chance to return again to my time, my family, and my Hezekiah

Thirty-Three
It is Time

We landed in the parlor, just as Victoria walked by the entrance. Upon seeing us, the tray she carried fell to the floor and tea splattered everywhere. "Abner!" she screamed, running to him. Their reunion was too private, and I went past them into the hallway.

The headaches came on stronger than ever before—with each time travel, the headaches had worsened. I wondered if I could physically *and* mentally take the return journey back to my own time. Pressing my fingers to my forehead, I massaged my temples.

"Lady Elizabeth!" Gyles called, but then appraising my short hair and odd outfit, he burst into laughter.

"Oh, oh yeah," I said glancing down at the words on my T-shirt. I rather liked my short hair, and fluffed it with my fingers.

He grinned.

"I can't stay long." At least, I hoped that was the case. My head hurt—the throbbing was incessant.

"Of course," he said, a sadness falling over him. "Of course."

"But there is something I need you to do for me."

"Anything, Lady Elizabeth. You have but to ask."

Pulling the letter and portrait miniature from my pocket, I handed it to him. "Liza's mother has a room in the inn across from the jail in Salem Town. She's looking for her daughter, and this might bring her comfort." Pulling one stone from my pocket, I stared down at it.

"Leaving so soon?" Abner asked, walking into the room arm-in-arm with Victoria. He held Charles's ledger in his hand. Seeing my curiosity, he added. "I've been instructed to pull his Amsterdam Stock Exchange certificates from his drawer and place them in a, ah, *safe place* for future use." He tilted his head toward the gardens outside.

"What?" I wrinkled my nose. "Amsterdam Stock Exchange?"

He grinned. "They may or may not be worth a penny in the future, but just in case." He patted the ledger.

"Oh." I hadn't realized that stocks existed then, and hoped that would pan out for Charles and his family, though I realized that with Hezekiah's wealth, they would be well taken care of anyhow.

I tried to hold my head steady, to keep the pain from overcoming me. I took one last look at them, fairly certain I would never see them again. I wiped a tear from my eye and pulled out the other stones. "Goodbye," I said, a sob caught in my throat.

"Thank you, Lady Elizabeth," were the last words I heard, as blue lights shimmered and blazed in my face, hotter and more intense than ever before, and then my body twisted, gyrating away from 1692. But as I left, I saw a distinct vision of Liza's letter and the portrait miniature lying on a table, chain glistening, caught by the morning sun seeping through the window of the room in the inn, and Elizabeth Senior's swift feet approaching them.

The swirling stopped, and horror struck me. I had not returned to the twenty-first century. Abner, Victoria, and

Gyles rushed to my side. I gasped and looked down at the stones disintegrating into fine, blue powder in my hands.

My knees went weak and I fell to the floor, great sobs of anguish overtaking me. I had misused time and now was destined to remain 323 years in the past.

Onida, have you not been listening? The worth of your soul is greater than your woes. You must believe!

"What?" Get out of my head, Meda! I *did* listen to you! Now I'm stuck back here, in a time and place I loathe—*without* Hezekiah. I groaned, the blue sand seeping through my fingers and onto the floor, the crippling headache leaving me almost at once.

Ha! Meda whispered. *You listened, and yet, you did not.*

"What?" I said, barely feeling the comforting arms of the Hanson's around me.

I no longer need the stones, and neither do you.

Still on the floor, I sat straighter. Meda, the prophetess, was a *Keeper and* had the stones at one time, too? "I do not . . . I do not need the stones?"

No.

The headache gone, my mind cleared. I didn't know how much time passed, but ideas, and thoughts, and feelings came to me, like a river pouring into my brain. Was this the purification André spoke of? I understood things I'd never understood before. With that knowledge, for the first time, in a long time, I was at peace.

A gentle breeze caught a wisp of my hair and pulled it in front of my face. I pushed it aside. Meda stood before me in that lush, green meadow, white daisies blowing in the breeze, filling the green void that spread out forever behind her. Her arms outstretched, she welcomed me into them.

It is time.

Time? I laughed at the irony and pulled away, but she only smiled.

You have done well, Onida. But one such as you must always be cautious. Do not trifle with gifts given, but use them wisely.

"What?" I asked. And then it came to me. Some say we use a small percentage of our brain, others say almost all of it is active at any given time. It was the *almost all of it,* that intrigued me. I say *that unused part,* once discovered, would change the world. *That* was what I had tapped into—*that* was why I could time travel. The stones had prepared me, opened a locked part of my brain. And now, I no longer needed them.

"Do you mean?" Tripping over my next words, I stuttered, "That . . . that I can . . . ?"

Yes, Onida—child of the sky. You are ready.

In an instant, suddenly, I was back, to the great astonishment of Hezekiah, the others, and myself. As they gathered around, hugging and kissing me, I held the secret deep within my heart, one that I intended to keep hidden forever. I could time travel without the aurora borealis or the blue stones. I could time travel at will.

Imagine where I could go and who I could see. My mother had recently told me we were related to Lady Godiva . . . hmm. I wonder what she was like.

Stop it, Bess. Stop it right now.

Sighing, I turned into Hezekiah's warm embrace, meeting his lips with mine—a tingle of excitement swirling through me, like a thousand prickles of radiant energy.

Maybe I *was* a witch . . . or at the very least, bewitched. Ha! I laughed, knowing without a doubt, that in reality, I had stumbled upon the most incredible, the most stupendous, and the *best* advanced science ever.

One has just to believe.

Meanings of Native American Names

Awenita - fawn
Nashota - twin
Magena - moon
Ayiana – eternal blossom
Honovi - strong
Anevay - superior
Elan - friendly
Igasho – wanders
Meda - prophetess
Onida – the one searched for

Author Theresa Sneed's Ancestral Line

Susannah North **Martin**, b. 1621 (71 years old when hanged on July 19, 1692 in Salem, MA, USA)

Abigail Martin **Hadlock**, b. 1659 (33 years old when her mother was hanged)

Hannah Hadlock **Bowley**, b. 1695 (born three years after her grandmother was hanged)

Oliver **Bowley**, b. 1726

Gideon **Bowley**, b. 1748

Oliver **Bowley** II, b. 1780 (a 17-year-old father to John)

John **Bowley**, b. 1797

Hiram **Bowley**, b. 1838

Clarence Lester **Bowley**, b. 1864

Lucy Mabel Bowley **Harris**, b. 1894

Judith Harris **Small**, b. 1930

Theresa Small **Sneed**, b. 1957

Author Bio

Author Theresa Sneed graduated cum laude with a BA in education, and loves teaching her 2nd grade students, especially about writing!

Her books are unique; each story taking you places you've never imagined before. She writes across five genres: mystery and suspense, fantasy, historical fiction/time travel, realistic paranormal, and nonfiction motivational. All of Theresa's fiction books have elements of sweet romance, and while none of her books have profanity or sexually explicit scenes, each book is intriguing and white-knuckle intense—the kind you can't put down.

Her nonfiction books are *So You Want to Write: A Guide to Writing Your First Book* where Theresa has pulled together her fifteen steps to writing success; *Fantastic Covers and How to Make Them,* and *Facing Mortality: Dreams & Other Significant Things* a compilation of Theresa's paranormal experiences that drove her to write her *No Angel* series and many scenes in her other works.

The *No Angel* series is the story about a guardian angel with an attitude, and the ever present, but misunderstood spirit world. There are four published books in the series with many more to come. Book one, formerly called *No Angel*, is now called *Angel with an Attitude;* book two, formerly called Earthbound, is now called *Earthbound Angel;* book three is called *Destiny's Angel;* and book four is called *Earth Angel*.

The *Sons of Elderberry* series has two books out called *Elias of Elderberry* and *The Wood Fairies of Estraelia*. Harry-Potterish—with wizards, fairies, elves, pixies, yōkai shapeshifters, and dragons, this story has it all! Theresa anticipates another three to five books to finish that series.

Escape is the story of a fifteen-year-old girl abducted by a corrupt sheriff in the 70's. He keeps her captive in his cellar for five years until she escapes with his truck and his young daughter. *Escape* is book one in a two book series.

Salem Witch Haunt was intended to be a standalone book, until the shocking ending made it apparent that the characters were not finished telling their story. Hence, *Return to Salem*, where the second set of trials and hangings in Salem, 1692, are masterfully woven into the story. *Salem Bewitched* completes this series with the last of the trials and hangings and the peine forte et dure of Giles Corey.

As the ninth great-granddaughter of one of the women hanged as a witch in Salem, Theresa has a vested interest in this epic time travel. Thoroughly researched, all interactions with real people from that era are based on primary sources. In book one, the trial scene with Theresa's great-grandmother, Susannah Martin, is taken from Reverend Samuel Parris's handwritten transcript verbatim. An additional book, *Stranger than Fiction*, is being compiled on the primary sources Theresa used in her Salem Witch Haunt series.

All of Theresa Sneed's books may be purchased through Amazon or from links on her website at www.theresasneed.com. She loves hearing from her readers and may be contacted through her website or through her email at tmsneed.author@yahoo.com.

Stay connected with new releases and free e book offers by signing up at her website or from her Facebook author page at www.facebook.com/TheresaMSneed/